THE

WOMAN WHO

RAN AWAY

JOANNE HOMER

Visit my website and subscribe –

there is a giveaways page where you can

always get a free book

www.joannehomer.com

Facebook – joannehomerauthor

Instagram – joanne.homerbooks

For my wonderful children, who are a source

of constant joy. Thank you for your enduring

patience.

And for my mother Dorothy.

Chapter 1 Meeting

Juliet stood at the bus stop in the dark shivering from the cold, her breath forming clouds in the freezing air. She hoped that the bus would come soon, her nerves were on edge. She listened out for footsteps in the darkness. It was still early just a little before 6.30am, the street was deserted and there was no one else at the bus stop. She would hear if someone was approaching. A milk float came passed as she waited, the whir of its electric engine breaking the silence. She nervously looked over her shoulder.

He could come around the corner at any minute and her plan would be thwarted. She could feel her heart pounding in her chest at the thought. She was just being stupid she told herself but it seemed like the longest seven minutes of her life before the X90 came trundling into view along the London Road. She stepped out of the bus stop to make herself visible in the darkness and the bus driver indicated to pull in. She would be safe once she was on the bus and that was all she could think of right now.

The bus came to a stop, the doors opened and Juliet stepped in. She heard the swish of the doors closing behind her, paid her fare and exhaled. Ticket in hand she walked to the back of the bus and found a lone seat. Putting her bag in the overhead rack she sat down, relieved for now that she was on her way and safe if only for a while.

It took some time for the fear to subside and her breathing to return to something resembling normality. Part of her wished she hadn't said yes to this and then part of her knew that she had no choice but to go through with her plan. She had known for a long time that if this opportunity ever presented itself, she would have no hesitation in grasping it firmly with both hands.

The bus trundled on into the darkness and Juliet could just see the outline of the Chilterns against the faint glow of dawn behind the hills. It would be well over an hour before it got truly light. The winter landscape looked bleak. The bare skeletons of trees dotting the landscape eerily silhouetted in the half light. There had been a frost during the night and it had left behind its sparkling mantle covering the countryside. Juliet wriggled her toes inside her boots, despite wearing a thick pair of socks they were still recovering from waiting outside in the cold.

The mobile phone stayed silent in her bag. He had her number but he wouldn't text or phone, he knew better than to do that not knowing if she was alone yet. She checked it to make sure and was relieved in a way that she hadn't had a text from him or from someone else. She wondered if he was awake and whether he was feeling excited and nervous like she was. You never knew with him what was going on in his heart. Just why had he contacted her and after all this time?

She hadn't seen Alex for twelve years. She had honestly thought that she would never see him again. Not as though he had ever been completely out of her heart or her mind. Very often he would enter her head, usually when she was at a low ebb and she would let her mind wander over what had been and what could have been. Often musing on what was he doing now? Where he was in the world. Had he married? Did he have children? In her moments of reverie and boredom at work she had Googled his name but found out very little. Often outdated news articles from when he was working as a solicitor, or a defunct website page detailing the training courses he had offered years ago

The dawn was beginning to break over the frozen landscape and it would be another cold January day. There had been heavy snow over Christmas and the weeks that followed and there were still stubborn patches in places where the sun didn't reach.

She would walk from the bus stop to St Pancras rather than take a taxi. Money was something that Juliet didn't have a lot of despite working full time and she saved her pennies where she could. It would be about a mile from the bus stop in Baker Street but that was no distance for Juliet, she had plenty of time on her hands and it allowed her to be alone with her thoughts.

The bus was nearing London and the nervousness had kicked in again but for a different reason this time. She had looked forward to this day with trepidation for a couple of months and now finally she and Alex were going to meet again after twelve years. Throughout the years that had passed and the thoughts of Alex she had played a little fantasy game wondering how her life might have been different if she had been with him. It helped her escape from the darkness she found herself lost in at times but in reality she never ever thought she would see him again. She wondered if there would still be a spark.

It had been three months earlier that he had made contact with her. She had sat at work one day and his name had magically appeared in her in box. Her heart had leapt into her mouth when she had read his name, still not quite certain that she could believe her eyes.

6

After all the years and all the fantasies he had emailed her through her work address. Her picture, her name and her email address were on the work website. As she sat staring at her screen a million thoughts raced through her mind but she hesitated before opening it. It was like Pandora's box and once she had clicked on it there would be no going back. But her fate had already been decided. She knew she had no choice but to open it.

"Hi Juliet

Is that really you? I found your work profile when I Googled your name. I wanted to know how you are. I hope you reply.

Alex"

She waited for a full two hours before replying. She just had to reply whatever the consequences and there would be consequences, of that she was certain. There always was with him but the lure was too strong.

She emailed him tentatively but it wasn't long before their correspondence became a regular occurrence. It was slow and steady once a day to begin with but it gathered momentum and some days they would have a conversation by email. She looked forward to seeing his name in her in box, although it was through her private email that they now corresponded. It was like talking to an old friend and the years fell away. It brightened her day at work and gave her something to look forward to in the sad little life that she led.

They had a lot of time to make up for, so much to catch up on. He hadn't married and he didn't have any children. He had long ago given up his professional career as a Senior Prosecutor and now he was working in a temporary job in a youth hostel in Wales to earn a bit of cash. And then one day he had sent these words,

"Would you like to go to Paris for a few days after Christmas?" Juliet jumped at the chance and replied swiftly to say yes.

They hadn't spoken on the telephone as he had no mobile signal where he was but that didn't matter because his voice   came drifting off the screen as she read his emails. And now after twelve years, Juliet was on her way to meet him.

The bus pulled into Baker Street and Juliet collected her bag from the overhead rack and left the bus. A sharp wind was blowing as she stepped out onto the pavement and she pulled the collar of her faux fur coat up around her neck to keep her warm. It was 7.30am and she was meeting Alex at 9am at St Pancras.

She walked along the pavement, weaving her way through throngs of commuters heading to work. The butterflies in her stomach were still there and she was suddenly filled with dread. Would he show? Don't be stupid Juliet, she thought to herself. Of course he would, why on earth would anyone arrange to meet and then not show? It was not like him to pull a stunt like that. She put that stupid irrational thought out of her mind.   The adrenalin was coursing through her veins as the time slipped by, getting nearer and nearer to the time of the rendezvous.

She arrived at St Pancras and it was nearly 8am. Inside it was crowded with people and she wondered if Alex was already there, sitting drinking a coffee somewhere. The thought was tantalising, but she needed to find a ladies to touch up her makeup and do her hair first, she had to look her best to meet him. It had been early when she had left home and she had applied her makeup in the bathroom with very poor light, goodness what she looked like in broad daylight. She had been planning this day with precision for weeks, going over the details again and again.

In the ladies she put her gas curling tongs to heat and touched up her makeup. She took off her walking boots and slipped them into a plastic bag and then into her tapestry overnight bag, and replaced them with little black ankle boots with a small heel. She looked at herself in the mirror as she curled her hair. She had tried to take care over her outfit as much as she could given the weather. She was wearing a white shirt and a pair of jeans. Over the shirt she wore a navy blue cardigan, with the shirt cuffs turned back over the cardigan. She looked okay but it had been twelve years and she was no longer thirty one, she was forty three and older than him. She just hoped that he would still find her attractive.

It was twenty past eight when Juliet stepped out of the ladies. The time was dragging and it seemed ages until 9 o'clock, the time they had arranged to meet. She decided to slip outside for a cigarette. She knew from their emails that Alex had given up smoking and she would try and limit her smoking as much as possible in his company but her nerves were so bad that she felt she needed a cigarette now. She stepped out onto the pavement and soon found other travellers lighting up. The sun made an appearance as she lit her cigarette and inhaled deeply the rays of sun warming her face. She didn't know how she would manage to pass the next forty minutes, the suspense was killing her now as it was and then she had an idea.

I have his number, she thought. He must be here now. I could phone him. So she stubbed her cigarette out on the pavement, took her phone out of her bag and dialled his number and listened to the ringing tone. Her heart was pounding in her chest as she waited and then he answered;

"Hello Juliet," he said. Juliet went weak at the knees and her heart was filled with joy. It had been twelve years since she had heard that deep sexy voice and it hadn't changed at all.

"Hello Alex," she replied, "I am at St Pancras now and I was wondering if you were too?"

"Yes, I'm here. Where are you?" he said.

"I am up by The Circle," replied Juliet.

"Stay there and I will come to you. See you in a minute," and with that the line went dead.

Chapter 2– St Pancras

Juliet pushed her phone into her handbag, picked up her overnight bag and marched inside. The Circle was very busy and full of people. Alex was tall and Juliet knew that she would be able to see him easily in the crowd. There was only one way into the circle from the inside of St Pancras and Alex would come that way. Juliet stood scanning the throngs of people coming from that direction. She was as excited as a small child on Christmas morning and then he appeared.

Juliet smiled to herself, he hadn't changed at all. She saw his blonde hair shining like a halo above the crowd and immediately recognised him. She waved frantically but he wasn't wearing his glasses and Juliet knew he wouldn't be able to see her, not at that distance. He was looking for her as Juliet pushed her way forward to meet him. Finally she forced her way through the crowd and ran over to him flinging her arm up around his neck and kissing him on the cheek. "Hello, it's so good to see you," she said. The relief of this morning's nerves and worries melted away in his presence, giving way to happiness and joy.

Alex stood and looked at Juliet and smiled, "it is good to see you too, I was worried about you, I didn't know whether you would manage to get away," he said.

"Wild horses wouldn't stop me going to Paris with you," said Juliet and laughed.

They stood still for a while, just looking at each other in their own little bubble while commuters pushed past them, eager to complete their journeys. "Would you like to get a coffee?" said Alex.

"Yes thanks, that would be great," Juliet replied, and Alex bent down and took Juliet's overnight bag out of her hand and went towards a nearby Costa Coffee. She still couldn't believe she was here with him as they walked into the cafe.

They managed to find a seat and Alex went to the counter. Juliet watched him as he stood there. He was as handsome as she had remembered. She was so glad she had come, so glad she had opened his email. Whatever came of this she would have no regrets. She had toyed with this over the past few months. She knew what is would be. Nothing more than a brief fling, a few short days of happiness. Given how her life had been over the last ten years she was happy to take what little joy she could get.

He had told her that he was going out to Yemen to work in February and Juliet had known then that this would just be short and sweet. But she had thought so often about him over the years that she knew she had to see him again No man had ever made her feel like Alex did and she doubted that anyone else ever would. She would have given almost anything to spend time with him again that was the depth of her feelings and now she had the chance.

Alex brought their coffees over to the table and sat down opposite Juliet. Time had not ravaged him, there were no lines on his face and Juliet sat admiring the angular masculine structure of his features and remembered the startling blue colour of his eyes. She had never had a photo of him, only her memory and it had served her well. She knew immediately that she wanted him.

It hadn't gone away or faded over time, the attraction she felt towards him was like no other she had experienced.

"You haven't changed at all Juliet."

"You neither Alex but I think you are too kind to me. I am not thirty anymore."

"Neither am I," he laughed and Juliet joined in.

"But it is really good to see you," said Juliet, "how was your journey here? The snow was so bad over Christmas, I just hoped it would clear up in time for our trip. And you have come from Wales, is it bad there?"

"Well it was over Christmas, but it is not so bad now. I came to London by train yesterday and stayed in a Youth Hostel, although I have to say I am getting too old to stay in a dorm with a bunch of twenty something's who want to party all night."

Juliet laughed, Alex old? That will never happen, she thought to herself. They sipped their coffees and sat looking at each other. "I have been really excited about this trip," said Juliet.

"Have you been to Paris before Juliet?" said Alex.

Juliet's heart lurched, "Well, yes I have," Juliet said hesitantly.

"You should have said, we could have gone somewhere else," replied Alex.

He didn't realise that this wasn't just a little holiday for Juliet, it was Alex she wanted to see. It wouldn't have mattered where they had gone as long as it had been with him, but the fact it had been Paris he had chosen made it all the more special

"I want to go to Paris with you Alex. It is a long story. I didn't enjoy my previous trip to Paris very much for many reasons mainly the company, but I fell in love with the City and that was why I was so excited when you suggested it. I knew that Paris with you would be fantastic."

"Well, I am flattered you think that Juliet, I just hope I live up to your expectations."

I am sure you will, thought Juliet to herself and smiled, relieved for now that he hadn't pried anymore about her previous visit to Paris.

They finished their coffees and left. "Shall we get a sandwich for lunch on the train?" Juliet said. Neither of them were wealthy and this trip was definitely on a budget. Alex agreed and they made their way to Marks and Spencer. "Shall we get a bottle of wine?" said Juliet.

Alex laughed, "We are going to Paris, why would we want a bottle of wine from Marks and Spencer?"

To calm my nerves thought Juliet silently but said nothing. The air between them was crackling with sexual tension. The spark was definitely still there and a glass of wine would have helped her tremendously.

They stood in the queue for security and the guard called Alex over. He only had a small rucksack. Juliet hoped and prayed that he didn't want to look in her bag. Although they had skirted around the issue in emails about whether or not they would be lovers again, Juliet knew that they would probably end up sleeping together. Alex had even gone so far to say that they could just go to Paris as friends, and although he couldn't afford separate rooms, they could have separate beds. Juliet had laughed when she had read this and in her usual brutally honest way had wasted no time in replying the following,

"Alex, given the fact that we could never keep our hands off each other, I think you should arrange a room with a double bed. You are under no obligation to sleep with me if you don't want to, but it would be a disaster to have single beds."

He had replied saying *"You might not want to sleep with me"*. Which had made Juliet wonder what on earth had happened to him, for him to make a statement such as this. Juliet had not taken any chances and had come prepared with sexy lingerie. This was the chance of a

14

lifetime that she thought she would never have and she wasn't going to waste it.

Thankfully the guard made a cursory check of the contents of Alex's rucksack and declared everything was in order. "It is a good job I left the anal intruder with the rotating fist attachment at home" laughed Alex. Juliet blushed. It was an outrageous thing to say but it was hilarious and Juliet was left in no doubt that Alex had sex on his mind too.

They boarded the train and found their seats. Alex put their luggage in the overhead rack and they sat down together. He was very close, almost touching and electricity shot through Juliet. There had always been something very primeval about the chemistry between the two of them; Juliet had been bowled over by it the first time she had gone to bed with Alex all those years ago. She had never experienced anything like it before or since then, she doubted she ever would. It was as good as it gets. She had been quite taken with Alex when she had first met him but it was as she grew to know him as a person that she had fallen head over heels in love with him and it was quite some time before their friendship had moved into a sexual relationship. She had been surprised at how gentle he was given his large physical size and he made her feel so small and feminine in his arms.

They sat eating their sandwiches talking about their respective lives. They had so much to catch up on, twelve years of life. Twelve years where they had had no contact with each other and there was a lot to tell. He was warm to be with and caring and he was a natural listener. "Would you like me to peel your orange for you," he said to Juliet. It was such a simple act of kindness yet Juliet was quite taken aback by it.

"Thank you Alex," she said.

The time was slipping by like sand in an hour glass and then there was an announcement that the Eurostar would shortly be arriving in Paris.

Chapter 3– Paris – Gare du Nord

They got off the train and walked into the art nouveau beauty of the Gare du Nord with its sweeping wrought iron arches and glass roof. Alex carried his rucksack slung over his left shoulder and thankfully had given up on vanity and was wearing his glasses.

It was only the second time that Juliet had been to Paris but she still marvelled at the beauty of it all. She was reminded how on her last trip she had been in a taxi making the final journey to the Gare du Nord to get her homebound train. That Sunday morning in the height of Summer she had sat and watched her last glimpses of Paris slip by and told herself how much she loved Paris and vowed to return. She had thought what a beautiful city it was and how different the weekend would have been with Alex and what fun they would have had. It was rather odd that less than two years later she was here again and this time with Alex.

"Do you know where you are going?" asked Juliet.

"The hotel is near the Eiffel Tower," replied Alex. He had sent her the details of the hotel before Christmas and she knew exactly where the hotel was. In fact she was shocked that in a city as large as Paris the hotel was just around the corner from the hotel where she had stayed before but she had told Alex nothing of this.

Alex stepped up to the ticket counter and in French asked for two metro tickets. Given that Juliet's French was non-existent she was seriously impressed but then he had intended her to be.

It was early afternoon as they made their way down the steps and through the tunnels to the platform in the metro station. They were headed for Trocadero and Juliet had left it to Alex to determine the route. For the first time in a long time she was letting someone else take control. It was a relief not to have to do it herself.

It wasn't busy and they boarded the next train that came along and found a seat. Alex made her laugh but then he had always been able to do that easily. He told her about how he had been celibate for the past five years but had not explained why and she didn't ask. How he had burnt himself out with the stress of prosecuting and had turned his back on lecturing.

He had spent the past few years teaching English as a foreign language abroad before doing a stint at the YHA in Wales before Christmas for a bit of pocket money.

"I thought it would give me a little humility" he said.

. Juliet laughed at this. "Why on earth do you need to get some humility? You won't do that cleaning toilets and deep cleaning ovens," He laughed with her and the years were falling away. It was so good to be with him again.

As they stepped out of the Trocadero metro station, they turned to see the Eiffel Tower looming high behind them in the early afternoon light. It was a spectacular sight even though it was a grey day. They headed straight up the Avenue Georges Mandel and took a left into Rue Decamps where twenty metres along the street was their hotel.

This will be interesting,thought Juliet. He would have booked it under his name and they had different surnames and given their age they weren't exactly young lovers. Juliet was wearing a wedding ring, she hadn't taken it off. Alex handed over the printout with his reservation on it and the man on reception asked for their passports. They handed them over and as he inspected them Alex couldn't help whispering "he thinks we are married and playing away."

"Obviously" giggled Juliet, "it is Paris after all." Of course, the very act of Alex whispering and Juliet giggling made it look as though they were guilty of the crime and the receptionist eyed them suspiciously as he gave Alex the key to their room.

They squeezed into the tiny lift with barely enough room for their two small bags and immediately let out peals of laughter. They were very close, so close she could smell him. He didn't wear aftershave but he smelled good. It was a manly scent and intoxicating in its sexiness.

The room was clean and functional but not what you would describe as glamorous, however it was warm and it had a double bed and a shower. "We have got a shit room as he thought we were up to no good and wouldn't be bothered with the surroundings," said Alex.

"Oh it's not bad," replied Juliet as she started to unpack her tapestry bag and took out the travel kettle.

Alex laughed when he saw it, "What else have you got in there?"

"Wouldn't you like to know?" she said, "The girls call me Mary Poppins when they see this bag."

He laughed, "Well that is true, fancy bringing a travel kettle with you. I would have thought that they would have had tea making facilities in the room."

Juliet knew from her previous trip that they didn't. "You will thank me for that, when you see the price of a coffee," and laughed. She felt tingly with anticipation now that they were alone together.

"What would you like to do this afternoon?" said Alex. He was sitting on the bed with his legs outstretched in front of him.

She knew exactly what she wanted to do but she couldn't very well say it. "I don't mind," said Juliet, "but I am enjoying being with you and in any case the weather is cold and I have been up since the crack of dawn. I would actually just like to relax, that is if you don't have any objection?"

She could see him studying her out of the corner of her eye. "No, I don't if you don't. Look, why don't we go and get a bottle of wine and just chill in the warmth for a couple of hours?" he said.

"Sounds good to me," she replied.

Out on the street the weather had turned cold and wintry as they set off in search of a supermarket. They hadn't taken many steps when Alex turned to her and said, "Can I hold your hand?"

A thrill shot through her coupled with a tinge of remorse and sadness. How long had it been since someone had held her hand? Too long she thought, she really couldn't remember when it had been. "I would like that very much," said Juliet and as his hand was un-gloved, she slipped her glove off and put her hand in his. It was warm and strong and clasped her tiny hand firmly. She felt happiness spread through her as they walked up the street. It was a good sign. She had been right about meeting him again.

They quickly found a supermarket a couple of streets away. One of her favourite things was foreign supermarkets with their variety of different products and even better, a French supermarket with its vast array of culinary delights. It appealed to the cook in her and she marveled as they wandered the aisles. He chose the wine and paid for it. It was red wine. She never drank it these days but she remembered that it was always his colour of choice when it came to wine. She thought fondly how he used to bring around two bottles of M&S's finest Cabernet Sauvignon in the evenings when he came to visit all those years ago.

She felt relaxed as they walked back to the hotel with just a hint of nervousness. It had been a long time since she had been to bed with him and she hoped he wouldn't be disappointed. But it was clear from the way events were shaping that he wanted to sleep with her.

He uncorked the wine, handed her a glass and sat back on the bed like before sipping thoughtfully. Juliet wanted a cigarette. Alex read her mind "you must want a cigarette with that glass of wine. Why don't you open the window?" "I know they say no smoking but it is France and nearly everyone smokes, they must expect people to smoke in the room." It was one of the things that she adored about him and something they shared – the ability to break the rules, to be reckless and throw caution to the wind.

Juliet opened the window and lit her cigarette. She stood by the window drinking her wine and blowing smoke out of the open window. The wine and the cigarette were making her feel mellow. She turned to look at him. He was handsome and he had that sultry, sexy, confident, slightly cocky look about him. How she wanted him.

"I remember you being handsome but I have to · confess that I had forgotten quite how handsome you were."

He said nothing for a moment as he took this in and contemplated his next move. "Why don't you come and sit beside me when you have finished that cigarette?" he said. Her heart was beating wildly in her chest as she stubbed out her cigarette on the window sill and threw it out of the open window. She went over to sit next to him taking her half empty glass of wine with her. She knew what he was about to do, why he had asked her to sit beside him. He was always in control, you couldn't control him.

He turned to her. His clear blue eyes looking deep into hers and his hand reached out and slipped around her waist. Drawing her close he kissed her full on the lips, softly, sensuously, with his body next to hers. She hadn't been kissed like that for a long time and the memories came alive once more. He was so sexy and an exemplary kisser and he knew what he was doing. They lingered in their embrace and she was getting very aroused but she drew away from him. "I will be back in a minute," she said and slipped into the bathroom.

She took off her clothes. Jeans were not made for an afternoon of passion like this was going to be and she unzipped her bag and carefully took out the black silk chemise and put it on. It was edged with lace and had a deep slit at the neckline that was laced together with silk shoestrings. She undid them slightly. At least this covered up her stomach which in turn made her feel more confident about getting intimate. She then put on her suspender belt, lacy and deep, and very sexy Brazilian knickers again edged with lace, and cut away on the bum, just revealing a little bit of cheek. She slipped her expensive "Le Bourget" French stockings up her legs, with the sexy red and black deep lace stocking tops and then strapped on her shoes. She was still nervous but at least with the sexy outfit on she didn't feel quite so scared.

When she entered the bedroom he looked over at her and looked her up and down slowly taking her in. He had a wry smile on his face and shot her a sexy look "You look fantastic," he said "It's like Christmas," and he held out his hand to take hers pulling her towards the bed.

"I think you should take off your clothes so that we are equal," she said, as she climbed into bed lying on her side propped up with one arm watching delighted as he slipped off his long-sleeved t-shirt to reveal his large well-defined torso covered in soft blonde chest hair. She had forgotten about his chest hair and it came as a bit of a shock. So her memory wasn't quite as good as she thought it was but she was enjoying this immensely he was a vision to behold, a true treat.

Slowly he undid the buttons on his jeans and slid them off revealing his long powerful masculine legs. He kept his boxers on and climbed into bed beside her taking her in his powerful arms and pulling her tight against his body. Kissing her tenderly at first and then gradually increasing in intensity to a passion that she could palpably feel this time. She ran her hands over his back feeling the downy hairs on his smooth skin and she was transported back in time. His hands were caressing her with a gentleness and lightness of touch that sent shivers over her entire body. All nervousness melted away as her body tingled with anticipatory pleasure in response to his touch.

Chapter 4 – Montmartre.

They lay back on the pillows enjoying a glass of wine and Juliet smoking a cigarette savouring the pleasure that they had just given each other. Neither of them had come. He said he didn't want too but it didn't matter, it was the intimacy that counted. She smiled inwardly as she blew smoke into the air having given up on standing by the open window, thinking of what had just happened. It had been good, bloody good. Just seven hours after meeting for the first time in twelve years they had made love with a passion that was astonishing

The afternoon light was fading and the evening was taking over. "Where would you like to go this evening?" He said.

"Well I know you have said that you are now a vegetarian so I did a little research and have printed off some vegetarian restaurants. There is one that is really rated in the Lonely Planet guide book. It is in the Montmartre area. Why don't you have a look at the review?"

He got his phone out, "I don't mind, you don't have to do vegetarian for me," he said.

"Actually, I quite fancy their signature dish which is an assortment of salads with bread," said Juliet.

"We will go there then," replied Alex.

"I'll go and have a shower" said Juliet and with that she got up from the bed and walked towards the bathroom wearing nothing but her stockings and suspenders. "You've still got a cracking arse," he commented as she went into the bathroom. Her heart did a little leap of joy. He had always loved her bum and although her body was far from perfect it was good to know that he still liked it and it still turned him on.

They got ready and went out into the cold January evening. Paris was beautiful in the dark. It deserved to be called the city of light. Everywhere were thousands of twinkling lights. Cafes lined the boulevards with tables and chairs behind little temporary railings on the wide pavements. There were heaters outside at most of these bars under the canopies and waiters and waitresses dressed in the customary black and white expertly wielded circular silver serving trays bearing orders to waiting patrons. The Eiffel Tower was lit up like a Christmas tree as it towered in the distance. The scene was magical. He was holding her hand again and she was filled with a warmth and contentedness that she hadn't known for a long time. She felt safe with him and calm and she radiated a golden glow from the afternoon's lovemaking.

They were both absolutely starving and had set out a little after 6pm. They had been so engrossed in each other that the time had slipped by. It had always been like this before but years ago they had never had the luxury of spending so much time alone together in one session and they had rarely gone out as a couple.

Juliet let Alex navigate the Metro as before. It was such a relief to allow someone else to take control. It was also a relief to be with someone who was so relaxed and in no rush, no panic to do anything. They soon found themselves at Abbesses. Montmartre was straight out of an impressionist painting, with cobbled streets and little grocery shops displaying an amazing array of vegetables in wooden crates, crowded onto the pavement. Boulangeries were still open and selling baguettes, pain de campagne, fruit tarts and all manner of delicious looking pastries. Tabacs and bars were squeezed in between with customers sitting at tables sipping coffees, beer, and wine. Smoking, chatting and flirting. The mouth-watering aromas that drifted out from these cafes was enticing and made Juliet realise how hungry she was.

They climbed the hill towards the street where the restaurant was. It was deceptively steep and as they stopped to catch their breath they turned to look at the view behind them. Lights were everywhere, spread out like tiny diamonds on ebony velvet and here and there larger landmarks were lit up creating pools of brightness like huge solitaires amongst the smaller diamonds. "What a view," said Alex.

"I am so glad I came here with you," whispered Juliet.

"I am glad I asked you," he replied. He pulled her close to him and taking her in his arms he kissed her long and slow.

They found the restaurant without much trouble but it didn't open until 7 pm, so they slipped into a nearby bar and ordered a beer. There was no one else in there so they chose a secluded table in the corner and sat down.

"I have been offered a job in Yemen teaching English as a foreign language. It starts in a couple of week's time," said Alex as he sipped his beer.

Her heart sank. She knew it. She just knew that he would be off somewhere. She was right to think that this was just going to be a brief encounter and then nothing after. Still, she thought to herself she had prepared herself for this and she could cope. She had coped for the past twelve years when she thought that she would never see him again.

They had nearly moved in together all those years ago. They had discussed it and then out of the blue he had called the whole thing off without any real explanation. She had known deep down that it could never have been. He was a rising young professional at the time who was ambitious and had a world of opportunities before him. He wouldn't have wanted her. That was what she had told herself at the time. But then to her surprise he had contacted her a few months ago and somewhere in the back of her mind she was curious to know why.

"The salaries are higher in the Middle East for teaching English, and I will have no outgoings as there is accommodation with the job. I am hoping to save a lot of money because I would like to buy a house in France where I can retire and live cheaply. Grow my own vegetables and keep a few chickens. The property prices are cheap in France. I can't afford to buy in the UK."

"What happened, to your house in Wales?" She asked. It seemed odd that he had said what he had. When she had last known him he had one house in the North East and was in the process of buying one in Wales, a large Georgian property that she had considered moving into with him.

"Well after you moved to Oxford I went to teach at Aberystwyth University. It was only a part time position and although I had sold the house in Durham, the house in Aber needed renovating. It was swallowing a lot of cash. I did what I could but I took a job in London teaching at the Bar Council. I had to rent digs there and I travelled back on a weekend to Wales to work on the house. Although I was working in London my salary wasn't that great and what with paying for digs and the mortgage it left me very little over to play with. In the end Mom stepped in and paid the mortgage and renovated the house. I finally had enough of the Bar council and living with a landlady who I didn't see eye to eye with so I decided to sell the house and cut my losses. After I had paid Mom off I was left with 10k. I took a job prosecuting benefit fraud in Birmingham and bought a barge to live on. But that was a money pit and it drained everything I had."

Now she understood. How awful. He had really had some bad luck. The once promising young professional who had so much going for him was now as down on his luck as she was. He should have lived with her all those years back. They could have loved and helped each other.

"Oh Alex, how terrible," she said. "I didn't think your life would turn out like that." Her story was no better.

"As you know we sold the house and went to Oxford. I had little choice really. I got a job where I stayed for just over a year until my boss left and told me I had better do the same as they were closing the place down. So I got a job with some upcoming computer consultancy earning good money, but they don't pay good money for nothing. Mark would come and pick me up every night in the car after work. He would be waiting outside for me and would phone me if I wasn't out on the dot of 5.30. Well this didn't go unnoticed at work and although no one said anything I got the distinct impression it was frowned upon. Needless to sayl I didn't survive my probationary period. After that I got very depressed and felt useless. But we had a large garden which was overgrown so I got to work on it that winter and started growing vegetables. I really loved it and it saved my sanity I can tell you. I also had chickens. That was until the following November when a fox got into the shed and killed them all."

"Oh Juliet why didn't you leave him? I didn't think for one minute after all these years that you would still be putting up with his shit. I would have thought you would have left him."

"I couldn't get away Alex. I had nowhere to go and no money. It was quite obvious that my parents weren't interested in helping and to be honest I didn't want to burden them. I had three children for Christ's sake. All the money from the sale of the house was swallowed up in rent and living in Oxford in the first twelve months. It was only later did I find out that I could have claimed housing benefit and kept 18k in savings but by then it was too late and we had nothing left. When he finished his MPhil he never got a job again. He applied for some but to be honest I don't think he really wanted to work, it was left to me to look after everyone."

"I'm so sorry Juliet. I had no idea." Said Alex and he leaned forward and kissed her gently.

Talking about her life made Juliet tearful and she tried hard now to suppress the tears that were threatening to fall. The last twelve years had been truly awful and it wasn't sadness that made her want to cry but anger and frustration that she could still not escape the horror that was her marriage.

"Will that restaurant be open now Alex? I'm starving." She said, desperate to change the subject. She wanted to grab a few days of happiness before returning to the misery that was her life.

They put their empty glasses on the bar and left. Au Grain du Folie (a little bit of madness) was the name of the restaurant. It was quite apt thought Juliet to herself. The lights were on inside now and they were open. A middle-aged woman was busy inside, lighting candles on the tables. It was only a small place, quite narrow, with a front window. You could see a small bar and kitchen at the back. It was no bigger than the average living room and the building looked old. They went inside and the woman showed them to a table near the window. It was really cosy and romantic and Alex ordered a bottle of red wine. They ordered the plate of mixed salads. No ordinary dish, it came on a large white circular plate with many indentations molded into the plate. In each one of these indentations sat a small salad mixed with a different dressing. There were beetroot matchsticks with a vinaigrette dressing, exquisite in its balance of tastes, grated celeriac with a dressing so creamy and delicious, that Juliet couldn't quite work out what it was but it was delicious There were other salads, all in a similar vein. Each painstakingly prepared, and dressed in the same careful fashion. A basket of French bread accompanied the meal. It really was delightful.

They sat gazing at each other over the table, the candlelight dancing in their eyes. "You are still as lovely as you were all those years ago," he said.

"You are too," she replied. The memory of that afternoon's intimacy was still vivid in their minds. The time was passing far too quickly for Juliet's liking and she desperately tried to put thoughts of it coming to an end to the back of her mind.

They paid the bill and left the restaurant, and walked back the way they had came through the cobbled streets of Montmartre, back on the Metro and finally out into the Trocadero area. "Do you want to stop at a Café for a coffee?" he said to her.

"It's a lovely idea," said Juliet "but we are on a budget and quite frankly I would like to get these high heels off and get warm."

"But they have heaters outside the cafes," he said. "Yes, and they charge more for sitting outside," Juliet replied. As always she was practical.

"No contest, then," he said. "We will go back to the hotel."

Chapter 5 –Menilmontant

They had fallen into bed and each other's arms the night before, and had made love slowly and tenderly. Not, with the urgent passion of the afternoon, but more caring and emotional and they had fallen asleep entwined. Their passion had not been satiated for each other and neither of them had achieved an orgasm.

Juliet had slept lightly and seemed in a constant state of half arousal. Unfulfilled passion was surging through her like electricity. Several times in the night as they slept their bodies had touched and every time this had happened the touch of his flesh against hers had stirred her from her sleep. It was ecstasy and torture at the same time. She hadn't felt this alive for a long time and she certainly hadn't felt such lust for what seemed like an eternity.

It was morning now and the daylight was coming through the curtains. She looked across to see his face. He was still asleep. How young he looked. He had the face of an angel, strong and masculine. His blonde hair illuminated by the late. She lay there for several minutes just gazing at his face. How wonderful it was to share a bed with him and wake up with him. The room smelt of sex and manliness, a scent she had forgotten existed. She went to the bathroom for a pee.

When she came back into the room he was awake. "Good morning gorgeous," he said as she switched on the kettle.

"Good morning handsome," she replied. "Tea or Coffee?"

"Coffee please," said Alex. She had tea. She always had tea and he always had coffee, he loved his coffee. He got up to go to the bathroom and she admired his buttocks as he strode out of the room. What a sight in a morning she thought to herself and felt desire surge through her.

She was still in bed when he came out of the bathroom and she had no intention of moving for a while. He immediately went to the kettle to finish making the drinks for them. He was naked. Stark bollock naked. He stood there with his marvelous cock on show and she enjoyed the sight and the treat of him making tea for her. "Mind you don't burn yourself, on the steam from the kettle," she laughed. "Wouldn't want that to get damaged?" she said, gesturing towards his dangling cock.

"I'm sure you would kiss it better," he laughed.

"Well there is no need to burn it if you want it kissed," she retorted, and they both immediately fell into hysterics. That was another thing about him, he wasn't a prude. You could have a laugh about sex with him and after all sometimes sex is funny

They sat in bed with their drinks enjoying each other's presence and the peace and quiet. "What shall we do today?" He said.

"I don't mind," said Juliet. "I quite like exploring Paris. I thought Montmartre was wonderful last night."

"Let's just head in that direction then," said Alex "we need to get some breakfast."

It was grey and drizzling when they left the hotel and bitterly cold. The rain was like ice and it stung Juliet's face as they walked down the Avenue Georges Mandel towards the Trocadero Metro station. The Eiffel Tower was shrouded in grey cloud, so much so that the top was not visible. They stood waiting for the train and as they did so Alex encircled her with his arms to keep her warm. It was really cold, but he was warm.

She let him decide what route to take again. It was hard to tell what direction you were going in when you were underground on the metro, but they were going to North East Paris and they stepped out of the Pere Lachaise Metro. From there, Juliet could see the Cemetiere du Pere Lachaise. Just the right dreary grey day for a cemetery, thought Juliet as they turned left along the Boulevard Menilmontant. This was another part of Paris with a different feel to it but it still had charm and romance.

They walked along the street. It was still drizzling lightly and they came to a café. Alex stopped to look in the window. "Let's go in here," he said, "they have huge chocolate éclairs." Inside it was warm. Alex ordered himself a chocolate éclair and a coffee, Juliet just had a coffee. Juliet looked around at the seating. It wasn't the most wonderful Parisian café she had ever seen and there was an old man in the corner reading a newspaper. Alex must have shared her thoughts, as he said: "Shall we sit outside?"

"Yes, why not," said Juliet.

"You can have a smoke, with your coffee and I think I would like a smoke too. I am getting very jealous watching you puff away." replied Alex.

They sat at a table outside. It was such a dreary day no one else was sitting there. But it was nice for them to be alone. "This is absolutely lovely," said Alex, referring to his chocolate éclair. "Would you like a bite?" She took the éclair from him, and took a bite. "Blimey, you have a big mouth" he laughed. "But then, you have managed to get your mouth round bigger things." She nearly choked on her mouthful of éclair. She knew what he was referring to. He was incorrigible. He just couldn't stop thinking about sex could he? But she was glad that he did. That was what she wanted. It was what she had come to Paris for and he was making her feel sexy, attractive and desired.

After they had smoked their cigarettes and finished their coffees they set off with no particular aim in mind and after walking for a while they took a right off the Boulevard Menilmontant and up a side street. It wasn't particularly wonderful, it was just a little bit seedy and down at heel. They soon came upon a Lidl. "Well fancy that, a Lidl," said Juliet.

"You come all the way to Paris and you find Lidl." "Shall we go in?" said Alex.

"Why not," she replied. It was just the same as the ones at home and they laughed as they walked around the store.

"Shall we get a bottle of wine from here?" Said Juliet.

"We can't buy wine from a Lidl in Paris," laughed Alex. "Although, Mom had a bottle of Chateau Neuf du Pape from Lidl before Christmas at a bargain price. I kept taking the piss out of her for her pretentiousness."

They went back out onto the street without buying anything and went on their way and the time was passing quickly again.

"I think we ought to find somewhere to have lunch soon," said Alex. They walked for a while but there weren't many restaurants in this area and finding one that catered for vegetarians was not easy. They finally came across a little Lebanese restaurant and went inside. Juliet settled for Tabbouleh and pitta bread. Alex had a selection of mezze and pitta.

They had a glass of red wine each and they felt very mellow as they left the restaurant and headed back to the hotel, buying a bottle of wine along the way. It was early afternoon and it was still bitterly cold.

Chapter 6 – Sex in the afternoon

They stood at the metro station and the bitter wind came whistling through the tunnels. Finally a train came and they stepped aboard. It was very crowded and they had to stand. The sound of an accordion playing La Vie en Rose drifted from the back of the carriage. It was too noisy to talk so they stood in silence, the movement of the train jostling them as they held onto the pole in the middle of the carriage.

Juliet was thinking about Alex. There was something different about him. He seemed changed, or was it because it had been such long time since they had seen each other? It was so wonderful being with him, so easy, so comfortable. Not once had she felt awkward or embarrassed. He didn't make her feel stupid or small like Mark did.

She was painfully aware that the time was passing quickly and she thought about parting from him. She felt a sharp stabbing pain in her heart. What if she never saw him again? The invisible knife in her heart twisted. She was falling in love with him again and she knew it.

There had never been anyone else like him and there never would be. Twelve years on from their affair and the old familiar feelings were flooding back. She also remembered the pain of her heartache when he had ended it quite abruptly without warning. She could never quite let him go in her heart and she had always hoped he would come back and here she was again.

She mustn't delude herself. He wouldn't stay he was going abroad to work. Just be strong, she told herself and enjoy the moment. There was no point in being sad about it now.

The carriage shuddered to a stop and she felt his arm around her waist steadying her, pulling her close to him. He was so big compared to her, he made her feel petite in his strong arms and safe. Safe and protected, and that was something she hadn't felt for a long time. He bent his head and kissed her on the neck. Shivers ran through her body and reminded her how much she wanted him physically. They were on the way back to the hotel and she knew what was going to happen. They were going to go to bed together. To spend the afternoon touching, kissing and caressing each other. Exploring each other's bodies and pleasuring each other. And he knew how to do that. It was as if he worshipped all of her body not just one little bit. She was an instrument in his hands and her song never sang sweeter than with him.

Her heart rate was increasing and her body tingled with the thought of his touch. He hadn't let her go and she could feel his heart beating in his chest. The train shuddered to a halt again at another station and they had to release each other this time to move out of the way to allow people off the train. The carriage had emptied quite considerably and they were able to find a seat and sat together holding hands. They had held hands whenever they went out and she adored it. She felt like a teenager again, a woman. It was hard to believe that it had only been yesterday when they had met up. It seemed like they had been together a lifetime.

"I want to take you to bed when we get back" he whispered in her ear. She felt the heat sweep upwards in her neck and her heart beat faster in her chest at the thought of what he would do to her. She said nothing, but squeezed his hand tightly in a gesture of acceptance.

They got off the train and climbed up the steps of the metro station out into the afternoon. The drizzle had stopped and the cloud was clearing. The winter sun was actually peeping through the clouds as they made their way up the now very familiar Avenue Georges Mandel, stopping at the Tabac to buy more cigarettes on the way. They held hands as they walked towards the hotel, both of them full of anticipation and desire for each other. Juliet had been right in her email months ago, they never could keep their hands off each other and it was no different now.

He closed the door to the room behind them and she slid the coat from her shoulders and he took it from her and draped it on a chair. He took her hand and pulled her towards him and into his arms where he kissed her tenderly on the lips, full and long. "You're cold," he said, as he slid his hand underneath her jumper and onto the skin in the small of her back. "Come have a shower with me to warm you up." He went and turned on the shower and came back to her removing his clothing as he did so. He came over and lifted her jumper over her head and kissed her neck as he turned his attention to the buttons on her jeans. They were soon undone and as he pushed her jeans down over her hips. He lowered his kisses, down her neck towards her nipple. Her body had goose pimples all over it and her nipples were tight and erect because of the cold but he slipped his warm mouth around her left nipple and gently coaxed it with his tongue. She stepped out of her jeans and took off her socks whilst he knelt and kissed her stomach.

He lifted her up into his arms and carried her into the bathroom and set her down in the shower and got in beside her. The heat of the water soon made her feel warm again and Alex gently soaped her body all over. It was wonderful to be washed by him. She in turn did the same to him and washed him as if in some ritual, taking care to be gentle. They said nothing whilst they washed, silently contemplating what they were doing to each other. She turned Alex around to wash his back and saw the owl tattoo on his shoulder. She had forgotten completely about that. How sad. Obviously you do forget things over time she thought to herself, first his chest hair and now his tattoo. She remembered when she had discovered that he had a tattoo. The tattoo that symbolised Athene the ancient Greek goddess of war and goddess of Aries his star sign. Athene was a protector of men and she would appear as an owl in an olive tree. She has watched over you in my absence she thought.

She carefully soaped his back gently going down and doing the same to his buttocks. Obviously aroused he turned towards her. "Enough," he said and stepped out of the shower to dry himself. "Stay there and keep warm for the moment," he said and she did as she was told and stood there letting the hot water run all over her body.

He had dried himself quickly and roughly and then he turned his attention to her. He turned off the shower and enveloped her in a towel and with one fell swoop picked her up off her feet and carried her into the bedroom. He wasn't completely dry as droplets of water were on his chest and fell from his face but he was so hot that they were still warm when they fell onto her body. He laid her down onto the bed and spooned her from behind gently patting the towel to dry her. He was so hot that the heat of his body did more than the towel ever could and she was warm and relaxed.

"Do you remember what we used to do?" He said quietly.

"I remember everything we ever did," she whispered. And with that he removed the towel from her body,and commanded her to lie face down. Her body was tingling with anticipation, not really knowing what would come next. Then she felt cold droplets of oil drip onto the small of her back. Her body tensed at the cold liquid but soon relaxed again when he placed his hot hand on top of the oil and began to massage her back. The scent of sweet basil and bergamot filled the air bringing memories with it.

His hands were slow and rhythmical, sometimes firm in touch and sometimes light, using only his fingertips in circular motions. So light that they were like a feather stroking her skin over her shoulders and down her spine, back and forth gently coaxing her. They travelled further down onto her buttocks, again taking each buttock in turn in the full of his hand and then using his fingertips in that erotic light circular motion. His fingers then slowly began tracing the crease between the top of her thighs and her buttocks, working from outside towards the inner thighs and back out again. Back and forth until she thought she could bear it no longer. Her vagina was beginning to ache, with a longing to be touched and she wanted so much to turn and kiss him. She thought she couldn't take anymore.

He started to kiss the back of her neck and she could feel her erect nipples pressing into the mattress, tingling. He grasped her hip and turned her over to face him and kissed her full and hard on the lips, pressing his body into hers. She went to touch him. "Not yet," he commanded, as he kissed her neck, her back arching as her desire increased. His fingers again tracing the contours of her body in circular motions. Teasing as he went close to her

41

nipples, but still he didn't touch them. Down her neck he continued with the kissing and onto her breasts, taking each nipple in turn, gently kissing and nibbling.

Fuck that was good! She thought to herself as they lay still together, still in each other's arms. How I have missed that. There was something very raw about the way they responded to each other sexually, something she had never experienced before. It was real sex. Like it was meant to be. Not 'lovemaking' that euphemism that was used as a nice way to describe sexual intercourse. That was such an over-used phrase which could mean almost any sexual encounter, good, bad or indifferent as long as the people involved love each other. No this was real passion. A basic instinct, when two people shared the same chemistry and were excited by whatever they did to each other, even though experiencing the same act at the hands of another they might be repelled. The smell of his naked body was even good to her that was how primitive it was.

He was a most attentive lover. In her experience most men couldn't be bothered to try and pleasure you, didn't want to get you so hot you couldn't take anymore and wanted to be fucked. She had been responsible for her own pleasure with everyone else she had slept with and it was just a waste, as simple as that.

He kissed her tenderly as their bodies parted. "It is always a privilege to sleep with you Juliet," he said. Likewise, she thought but didn't say.

They dozed for a while and then Juliet woke and made a cup of tea. Being with Alex was so relaxing Juliet thought as she looked at him sitting next to her in bed.

Alex picked up his phone. Like most men loved his technology. Trust him to have the latest phone. He might be poor but he managed to keep his tech up to date. His facial expression changed. He no longer looked relaxed. "What is it?" she said.

"I have an email from Mark," he said.

She nearly dropped her cup. "What?" She couldn't take this in. How did he know she was with Alex? How did he get Alex's email address? What the hell was going on? Less than 48 hours from her leaving home, her husband had figured out what she was doing and who she was with.

Chapter 7 – The Past

Juliet was married to Mark and they had two children Alistair (14) and Guy (2). In addition Juliet had older children, Miles, Katie and Charlotte who were grown up and no longer lived at home with Juliet and Mark. Juliet's life had been awful for years. Mark her husband was an alcoholic and workshy. Quite simply he was a useless waste of space. He had cost her dearly. She had loved him very much in the beginning but looking back there were alarm bells that she just didn't see. How could she have been so blind?

Very quickly into their marriage she realised he had a problem with alcohol but he just wouldn't acknowledge it and he certainly didn't want help. Lord knows she had tried and each time he had shot her down in flames, saying "I just like a beer." That was the understatement of the year. It wasn't even that he was a nice drunk. He would suddenly turn nasty at the drop of a hat and out of the blue suddenly round on her for something or other, all petty stuff but then he would go on and on and wouldn't let go and wouldn't shut up. Verbally poking and prodding her mind when she was tired. He knew what buttons to press, often late at night, until she would snap and they would end up arguing. It was exhausting for Juliet and of course in the morning he would profess to remember nothing about the night before or his behaviour and act as if nothing had happened.

Life had been so bleak. There was never a light at the end of the tunnel and when there was a glimmer of hope Mark had immediately snuffed it out. He had never really done anything around the house, he was an academic and a thinker, not a practical man and although he had tried in the beginning he had soon given up the pretence and no longer bothered feigning interest. She had done everything from the cooking and the cleaning, shopping, looking after the kids, going to work full time to keep a roof over their heads, not to mention the gardening and the DIY. She had even replaced the brushes in the washing machine and laid a carpet in the hall stairs and landing, not that he had acknowledged or praised her for it. Mark had not worked for years and then when he finally had got a job it only lasted just over twelve months and then he had been sacked for "competency" issues, although she knew they had realised that he had a drinking problem. Whatever the reason, he had been sacked and there was no way of putting a gloss on that, and it was clear that he did not want to work again.

Over the last year, she had tried to get out. She had appliedfor better jobs with more money. She had even been successful enough to get second interviews and had made it onto the shortlist twice but she had never landed the job, which had been soul destroying at the time. She wanted a divorce but he would not let her go without making it difficult. Of course he wouldn't let her go, she was his slave. He couldn't even cook a meal for himself. Mark really was hopeless. He never gave her any affection. He never held her hand or gave her a random kiss. When she left for work in the morning he was still in bed and couldn't be bothered to give her a peck on the cheek

Going out by herself for anything other than to work was not easy. Mark was very controlling at the best of times and he did not like Juliet to go out alone. If she was five minutes late from work, he would phone her to find out where she was. He didn't do this because he loved her and worried about her safety or wellbeing, he did it because he was frightened of being alone. She had been forced to sneak out a few months ago to go to her daughters 21st Birthday Party after he had refused to let her go or to take Guy and Alistair with her. So in order to escape to Paris Juliet had concocted a lie. She had told Mark that she was going away on a training course for work and would be away for three days. He didn't like it but there was nothing he could do about it.

She had fretted about packing her bag and she knew she was taking a big risk as she had smuggled the travel kettle and more telling, the two mugs that went with it, not to mention stockings, suspenders and sexy silk lingerie. She had done this late the night before when he was drunk. And then there was the small matter of her passport. Now if he had found that was missing, it really would have given the game away but she had been careful to leave that until the very last minute and only removed her passport from the bureau immediately on waking that morning whilst he was soundly asleep.

Mark was very clever but still, she didn't understand how he had managed to hack into her email account and what had made him want to do so.

Over the few months that Juliet and Alex had emailed each other, she had opened up to him about her life. She had always viewed him as a confidante and someone who she could tell all her innermost thoughts to, so she told him about her disastrous marriage. Indeed, in one of his very first emails, he had said: *"I can't believe you are still putting up with that shit."*

On the train Juliet had told Alex about one particularly awful episode that had made Juliet realise that her marriage was dead, and she had started talking,

"I had applied for a job as a GP Practise Manager, and I was thrilled to be invited to interview. I was excited about this as it represented a real opportunity for me to get out of my marriage. If I was to get out of my marriage I needed more money so that I could move house. I had visited a solicitor earlier in the year and was told by her that given his alcoholism and his controlling nature, there was no way Mark was going to move out when I told him I wanted a divorce. The solicitor had told me I would have to rely on my parents for help but there was no way I could ask them for help, I was just going to have to get a better job and move myself and the children into another rented house, with the lease in my name only, not a joint tenancy like the one we had.

This GP Practise manager job provided such an opportunity as I would be earning £35K, not the £28k I was presently on. I had struggled a bit at the first interview but surprisingly they had liked me and had invited me back for a second interview. I had to wait a few weeks for this as the other candidate they wanted to interview had kept them waiting. However, I went for a second interview on a Friday afternoon and it seemed to have gone well, I was quite hopeful. When I got home, it was 3 pm. Mark was sat at the kitchen table watching TV, with a gin and tonic in his hand.

"Well, did you get the job?" he said.

I replied that I didn't know yet and that they had other interviews to conduct that afternoon but that they have promised to get back to me with a decision that evening.

This didn't seem to satisfy him and then the abuse started, "I suppose you think you are some fucking big cheese" he spat. As usual, it was out of nowhere, but he was pissed and he always had the potential to be like this when he was pissed. You just couldn't tell when he was going to kick off. He would suddenly snap. It was hurtful, I was already anxious about the outcome of the interview. I desperately wanted that job and I badly wanted to get away from the awful marriage I was in.

The snide comments continued all afternoon and at 6 pm the phone rang. It wasn't good news. They had appointed the other candidate. I felt disappointed, but what was pissing me off more than anything was Marks attitude. There was no sympathy, no commiseration, no consolation, just a drunken round of abusive comments designed to hurt and he carried on like this all night. At 9 pm I decided to call it a night and go to bed. He sat downstairs listening to Neil Young. That was always a bad sign. He had something on his mind and he was far from happy. Later on with hindsight, I think he had realised that if I had got that job then I would have been able to leave him, as I remarked to someone at work, ,if I get this job, then I would be like Scarlet O'Hara in Gone with the Wind, I will never go hungry again.' And this did not sit easily on his mind.

About 2 am in the morning, the bedroom door was flung open and in he staggered. He turned on the bright overhead light blinding me. He started shouting abuse at me. I asked him to stop for Guy (Guy slept in our bedroom as although he was nearly two years old Mark wouldn't let me put him in his own room.) He clearly wasn't going to shut up so I moved into the spare room away from Guy. But he was determined to have a fight and followed me in there.

When I told him to get out and leave me alone he threw a glass of beer over my head soaking my hair and my pillow. But he took no notice and continued to shout abusive comments. When I didn't respond he grabbed at my leg and pulled me off the bed. That really was the last straw and we ended up in a physical fight. The next thing I knew we were downstairs. I just wanted to get away from him but when he was like that he would follow me and continue to torment me with abusive comments. I had got used to the insults over the years and could switch them off but that night I felt disappointed about the job and I was tired and then there was a lack of consideration for Guy. It all made me so angry. I just snapped. I had had enough.

The next thing I remember, he was on the floor and I was sitting astride him with my hands around his neck, choking him. He was making a horrible noise and all I could think, was how pathetic he looked. But I became aware of someone else in the hall and looked up and saw Alistair looking over the banisters. At that moment I realised it wasn't a good idea to kill the father of my children and released my grip (not as though I could have managed it). "Get your clothes on," I said to Alistair, "and get Guy, we are leaving." I went upstairs to get some clothes on. When I came downstairs, Mark was on the phone to the Police, saying that I had tried to kill him. Kill him! True, the thought had crossed my mind but how pathetic, I hadn't and I was leaving.

Oh, of course, that was it, I was leaving and he thought he might lose me forever. That was his only motivation for calling the police, to stop me leaving. The fucking bastard, how dare he, I had had enough, so I kicked him in between the legs. "She has just kicked me in the bollocks," he whined down the phone. It was so weak, it was laughable and when I have looked back on it since, I can still picture his face and still want to laugh! Let's just get out of here I thought. We stormed out of the door, even though he tried to stand in the way. He was pissed and small and no match for us and we pushed him out of the way.

Once in the car, I decided that we would go the country route to Moms house through Chipping Norton and up through Evesham to avoid the number plate recognition cameras on the motorway. We hadn't gone far and the phone kept ringing. It was a cold November night and there was no moon. Visibility was very poor as we drove along the winding country lanes towards Chipping Norton and I was so worked up that I missed the turning to Chipping Norton. I needed to turn around so, I backed into a field entrance but when I put the car into drive the car wouldn't budge. I had put the back wheel down a ditch. Fucking typical! We were stuck there.

Then the phone rang. I answered it. It was the police asking if I was alright and where I was. I knew they didn't really want to know if I was ok, they wanted to arrest me. He would have told them I had been drinking the night before and was drunk, although I hadn't had that much and I had gone to bed at 9pm. I told them I was ok and hung up and turned off the phone. I turned to Alistair and said, "That was the police. They were obviously trying to get a GPS signal on us to see where we were. Your dad has probably told them that I was pissed up when I got behind the wheel so they will be in a rush to find us. The wanker! He will do anything to stop us from leaving." I turned the lights off on the car. I turned to Alistair. "If you see headlights coming down the road, then get out the car quick and run into the field behind. I shan't be far behind, and we will stay out there until they are gone. If I lock the car they won't be able to get in." It was all madness and a but silly but I didn't know what else to do

We were well and truly stuck. We sat there a while thinking about what to do. I hadn't got breakdown cover. I

50

tried to phone Mark, a chap at work who was into cars, to see if he had any ideas. I know it was late at night, or more correctly very early morning as it was now about 3.30am, but he was probably at his mother in laws and had no signal because it went straight to voicemail. I didn't have a clue who else to try. I didn't have any friends in Oxford. Then I thought of Nigel. Good old dependable Nigel. He would answer his phone, he was neurotic and didn't sleep well. Sure enough he answered his phone. I told him what had happened and he said he would come out.

About 45 minutes later his silver golf pulled up with him and his wife. They had a flask of coffee with them. Nigel phoned his breakdown provider and they were going to come out, although we would have to pay. He soon arrived and got us out of the ditch. I decided that as it was now after 4 am and we didn't have any clothes, and my hair was sticky, we should go home and get a couple hours sleep and then go to moms in the morning. So that's what we did. We went back home and Mark was fast asleep. I slept in the spare room and was woken at about 7 am by Mark. He was still in a foul mood.

"Oh, you're back! Well don't think of going anywhere, the police want a word with you." He said. I ignored him and went for a bath. While I was in the bath, the phone rang. I heard Mark answer and I heard him say, "Yes, she is here." He came upstairs and said, "the police are coming around for you."

I said, "why the bloody hell are the police coming here for me?"

"Because you tried to kill me last night," was his answer. "Don't worry, play happy families again and I will tell them everything is ok and I won't press the charges."

I stared at him in disbelief, it was as I thought. "You really are stupid," I said. "These days once you have made an allegation of domestic violence, the police have to investigate it. Just because you have changed your mind, it won't stop them pressing charges."

I went downstairs when I had got dressed as I realised I should wait for them and put them straight on what had happened. I put some washing in and started washing up. The doorbell went. It was two police officers. Mark let them in. I was in the kitchen. One of the police officers came into the kitchen and said that they would like to have a word with me. I said, "fire away." Then, they started talking about me assaulting Mark and they said they wanted me to come to the station to answer some questions. I said that I was the real victim of domestic abuse and had been for years. The policeman asked if the kids were alright and I replied "Yes, of course, they are alright.".

"Where are they?" said the policeman.

"They are upstairs," I replied. "Why aren't they at school?" He said, as he was walking up the stairs.

"Because it is Saturday" I shouted after him muttering 'stupid ass' under my breath. I don't think he heard me. The other police officer was in the lounge with Mark. When the first policeman came downstairs I went to go upstairs. He said, "where are you going?"

I said, "well if you want me to come down to the station, I am going to have to get my coat and put some shoes on."

"Oh, ok," he said.

When I got downstairs, I said: "Come on then, let's go."

He just looked at me and said "sit there," pointing at the stairs. I couldn't believe this. It was making me angry.

I said "why?"

And he repeated himself again "just sit down there."

Then I said, "Oh I get it, you have to wait for your friend," and suddenly it dawned on me what he was thinking.

Feeling mischievous, I said "oh, you have no need to worry I won't have a go at you. You are a damn sight bigger than he is and you are tooled up," He didn't seem amused by this but I thought it was funny, although I didn't laugh. I just kept quiet.

After a while the second policeman came out of the lounge. They took me out to the panda car and as soon as we got to the car, they arrested me! I couldn't believe it, I really couldn't. I was so angry. It was Saturday morning, in broad daylight in a middle-class street. All the neighbours would have seen me being bundled into the back of a police car. After all the shit he had given me over the years, all the taunting, all the drunken rages, all the socially embarrassing scenes, all that I had done for him. I had supported him for Christ's sake. I went to work every day and paid the bills. I was so, so very angry.

Anyway at the station, they fingerprinted me, took DNA and photos, confiscated my shoes and belt and then read me my rights. I was still shocked at this point but I had the presence of mind to ask to see a solicitor. They even asked me to take a breathalyser test and I asked if I had to, when they said no, I declined.

They stuck me in the cells for hours. It was a cold November Saturday morning and I was tired. By the time I saw a solicitor it was lunchtime and when I was finally asked to give a statement it was mid-afternoon. After they sat through my statement their attitude changed. They stuck me back in the cell but they gave me some magazines. Then they let me go. They said that Mark had been phoning them all afternoon and asking when I was coming back to cook the dinner. He had made a right nuisance of himself.

They were reluctant to let me go home and said I should stay somewhere else or with a friend. I had no friends and no money and I was concerned about Guy and Alistair. I told them this and pleaded with them to let me go home to the children and they finally agreed. A policeman took me home and although it was only 6 pm, the house was in darkness. There were empty bottles littering the kitchen table and we had to go upstairs. Alistair was in his bedroom watching TV and Mark and Guy were in bed. In bed at 6 pm. He was clearly pissed but as I said to the policeman, "he isn't going to be any trouble tonight. Not now his slave is home."

When I went into work on Monday morning after all of this I felt gutted, low and in shock. If life at home hadn't been so shit I would have called in sick but work was preferable to being with him. Nigel came into my office and asked how I was. I don't know why Alex but I just blurted the whole thing out about being arrested. I normally wouldn't have told anyone at work what had happened but I felt so low and he caught me at a moment of weakness. That was how the Nigel thing started. You know the rest.

Alex sat listening attentively and compassionately all while she talked. After all, as a former Senior Prosecutor, he had read enough case notes and been involved in enough cases not to be shocked by what she had to say.

Even so, he said "Juliet, I had no idea. I thought Mark was a wanker, but this really is another level. How many years have you put up with this? Why have you put up with this?"

If this had been any other day, with anyone else, she would have cried. But it had happened fourteen months ago and although at the time she had been shocked by it herself, over time she had learned to laugh it off although she was still not proud of what had happened. But he had driven her to it. Juliet looked him in the eye "I have told you, Alex, I had no way of getting out."

So Juliet had made Alex aware of just how bad her life was on the train journey out to Paris.

It just didn't make sense. If Mark had suspected anything about this trip he wouldn't have let her go. She recalled how he had stood on the doorstep that morning, and asked her if she really was going on a business trip. Of course she had said yes. But come on, really, he was so controlling he wouldn't have let her go if he had any firm suspicions. There had to be an explanation.

Chapter 8 –Trouble

What would he have done? He was such a control freak. She looked at her phone, three missed calls. But they were not from Mark. They were from Nigel at work and he had left a voicemail.

She listened to the voicemail. Nigel said that Mark had phoned up work and wanted to know where she was. Sue had apparently answered the phone and she had told him she didn't know. Mark had then phoned up again and asked to speak to Nigel but he had been out at the bank. Mark had then thought that Juliet was with Nigel. Mark then phoned a third time and left a drunken abusive message on the answering machine about Nigel. The Deputy Director had then called the police who apparently had visited Mark and 'had a word'.

What a mess, what an idiot, why did he do that? Now, he had made her look stupid at work. Everyone would now know about her private life. They would know that she was married to an alcoholic. It would do her credibility no good at all. They already had the knives out for her because of her position and now this would be the end. They would all be laughing at her, behind her back and she would have no authority. She could kiss that HR promotion goodbye after this. She took a deep breath and tried to stay calm. Her anger was mounting and she knew that losing her temper was not going to help the situation.

Okay so Mark had realised that she was not on a business trip, (something which she had suspected would happen) but that didn't explain how he had got hold of Alex's email address. She had not written it down anywhere, no one knew apart from her children and they wouldn't tell him, she knew that. Then a sudden thought shot through her brain, there was only one way he would know she was with Alex and have his email address. Mark must have hacked into her email account. But how? She never saved her password on the computer. He must have guessed it. It was not that complicated, but it did include numbers, even though they were her age. He was clever though and he must have worked it out, even so it was a long shot but then he had time on his hands.

Her anger began to subside. Oh well if he knew she was with Alex that would be the end of their marriage. Mark knew that she had loved Alex all those years ago and he had always dreaded him coming back to get her. Perhaps he might now accept what she had been saying for months, that she wanted a divorce. Perhaps he might let her go.

"Have you opened it?" she said, referring to the email.

"Not yet," said Alex. "Do you want me to?"

She stood for moment thinking about this. "What has he put as the subject?" She said, knowing that you could always read the subject of the email without opening it and knowing how clever Mark was, there was no telling what he had put as the subject but it would be something to catch your attention, something to make you open it and not delete it.

"A, B, C now E," he said.

It didn't quite sink in, what he had said. "Say that again," she said.

"A, B, C now E" he repeated. She thought for a moment.

Oh for fuck sake! It slowly dawned on her. He had been through her emails, all of them. He was referring to men's surnames. A for Allen, B for Baker, C for Curtis and E for Ellis, Alex's surname. Oh, Christ! The enormity of him hacking her email account was beginning to take hold. Her secret life, her private little world had been invaded by him. That was how he had got hold of Alex's email address. He knew from what he had read that Alex had the latest phone and he could access his emails on it. He knew that they were together in Paris. He had read all of her emails. Tears began to well up in her eyes and her anger and frustration increased and began to spread through her like fire on a windy day. He couldn't let her have any pleasure. He had to take that away from her. Why didn't he just let her go all those years ago? Why must he repeatedly punish her, hadn't she suffered enough?

"I'm really sorry Alex," she said. I didn't want to cause you any bother." "The shit, has obviously hacked into my email account".

"I don't mind," said Alex. "Look, you had better try and change your password on your email account before that bastard does any more damage to your life."

She breathed a heavy sigh, he was taking this better than she had expected. Thank goodness for that. He was calm and quick thinking. "I will phone my daughter and get her to change it," she said. It took several minutes of being on the phone for Juliet's daughter Charlotte to finally get into her email account and change the password. At least he couldn't get in anymore, although he had Alex's email address.

"Open it," said Juliet, talking about the email. He handed her his phone. It said:

"A, B, C now E. You are just one of a long line of suckers with that slag."

"She handed him the phone back. "He is playing mind games with you," she said. She was thankful that Alex knew most of it already but what really annoyed Juliet was the spin Mark was putting on the facts. Mark had made it sound as though she had slept with these men and she hadn't.

Alex didn't seem shocked by it, Juliet had told him a lot about her life over the preceding months. "I have a good mind to reply and tell him what a lovely time we had this afternoon" he laughed.

"He already knows that we are having a good time because we always did," replied Juliet, and they were soon both laughing together. What neither of them knew was that this was just the start of a tortuous journey, a journey into darkness and the unknown.

Chapter 9 the Latin Quarter

They went out to dinner in the evening, to the Latin Quarter and got off at the Saint Michel metro station. It was a bitterly cold night and the sky was clear and covered with stars. Juliet felt rather cold in her short skirt and stockings as they walked hand in hand along the Quai de Montebello next to the Seine, the illuminated Notre Dame casting an eerie light upon the water.

It was livelier than last night but not as pretty as Montmartre the evening before so they turned off into a side street away from the Seine in the hunt for somewhere to eat as they knew the prices would be cheaper there. The mood of the evening was quiet and thoughtful, if not just a little sombre. Tonight was their last night and Juliet was already feeling sad even though she was trying not to think about parting with Alex it was still there in the back of her mind, refusing to go away.

"What do you fancy eating?" said Alex.

"I don't really know," said Juliet but despite the stomach churning events of the late afternoon she was hungry again. They walked along the street browsing the menus on display outside of the restaurants but none of them seemed to stand out. This was rather a touristy area and there was nothing here in their price range that stood out as being wonderful. In the end hunger and cold got the better of them and they dived into one of the first restaurants they came across. Alex encouraged Juliet to have steaks frites and he would have an omelette and chips.

They sat down in the restaurant which was cosy but it didn't have quite the same charm as the night before. At least it was warm and they sat opposite each other

Alex was in a very contemplative mood as he ordered a bottle of red wine for them to share. "I have really had a lovely time," said Juliet, desperate to dispel the dark atmosphere that shrouded them. "I have loved being in Paris with you and it has been so good to see you again after all those years. It is just a shame that the time has gone so quickly."

"I feel the same," he replied. She took a gulp of her wine and she could feel the warmth returning to her toes.

"What prompted you to try and find me, and get in touch again after all those years?" she said. Time was running out and she had to know.

He swallowed his wine, "Well I hadn't had a relationship for a few years and I started to think about all the women I had been out with and you were the only one that I wanted to get in contact with again. I was shocked to find you were still married to Mark. I am really sad to think that you have endured him for all those years. He must have made your life hell for having an affair with me."

It was true he had but he had always been controlling and the affair had been a long time ago. He got annoyed about other things these days when he got pissed and angry. There was resentment on both sides. She had thought that Mark would leave her when he found out about the affair with Alex but to her horror he hadn't. She hadn't seen that one coming.

"It's not been easy," she said. "At first I felt guilty but he never got a job and after he used up my money we dipped further and further into poverty, even though I worked all the time to try and keep us afloat. It was Oxford and I never earned quite enough to get ahead. When I had Guy, he left me alone in the hospital when I needed him, I knew that he really didn't love me. He isn't capable of loving anyone else, he only thinks about his own needs. I was really ill after Guy was born and I couldn't cope, I was in bed for a week. He could hardly make me a sandwich, or a cup of tea. Alistair did it most of the time. He couldn't give me emotional support either.

Then to top it all off, he lost his job as a teacher, which I have to say in my opinion was deliberate. I was going to go back to work part-time when my maternity leave ended but I had to go full time as his job looked in danger. He was having so much time off sick. And then the incident with the Police was the last straw. I told him I wanted a divorce but he just didn't want to acknowledge it. He needs me to look after him financially and do all the chores. I am stuck and I can't get out without money. That is the end of it. My parents are now too old and I cannot burden them with all this".

He looked at her compassionately and said: "That's really sad."

They finished their meals and they were soon discussing the email that he had received that afternoon. "What did he mean, by A,B,C in that email yesterday?" Alex asked. Juliet put her wine glass down. "He was talking about my emails. He obviously is trying to put doubts in your mind about me. He didn't email or phone me as he knows I want a divorce so there is nothing he can do to hurt me. But he can get to me through you and make you think that you are just one of a long line of lovers. I wouldn't mind but I haven't slept with all of them.

A is for James Allen, a young man that was my assistant at work a few years back. He had a Ph.D. and the job was really only a stop gap but I keep in touch with him and he has given me a reference for a job. He helped me a great deal when I had Guy and was an emotional wreck and Mark didn't want to know. And ok, yes, I fancied him but he was twelve years younger than me. We ended up in a snog once but there was never anything more than that. He was really sweet and kind.

B is for Nigel Baker, the accountant at work. Well, that is a long story but after I had been arrested that time fourteen months ago I went into work on the following Monday. I didn't want to go but I had to. He came into my office and asked me how I was. He knew nothing, about me being arrested on Saturday so I told him. I don't know why but I was still in shock. He was absolutely stunned. He said he had no idea how awful my marriage was. But then said he loved me and had done so for the last six years. It was my turn to be stunned. I told him that he had no idea what I was like and he couldn't possibly love me on just knowing me at work.

He said he was rich and his parents were millionaires. I just laughed and said, "You are married." But I knew he was unhappy. It just snowballed from there really and he kept pursuing me.

A month later in early December, he sent me a text and said that he had seen a pair of pearl earrings whilst out Christmas shopping. I had recently lost one of mine and was finding it difficult to replace. He told me, that the ones he had seen were £2,500. I laughed and just thought this was a joke. But then at the Christmas lunch (we had gone to Brasserie Blanc) Nigel had drunk too much and he didn't usually drink but he kept feeling my knee under the table and I had to keep saying "stop that." When the meal ended a group of us were walking back towards town and I usually go and do a bit of Christmas shopping after the works Christmas lunch but I suddenly realised, that everyone else had peeled off and I was left with him.

We came to Bonn square and I was desperate to shake him off so I said: "I have to go and get some dinner from Marks and Spencer's."

Then he said; "don't you want to go and look at those earrings?"

Well I thought he was joking and I said 'oh, that is just pie in the sky' and shot across the road to M & S. But he followed me all around the food hall. I finally managed to ditch him when I came out of M&S and saw my bus so I said, 'there's my bus, bye.' And, I shot across the road. On the way home I kept receiving texts from him, saying that I would never have to worry about money, that he would buy me anything I wanted, how he would take me on holiday wherever I would like to go and how much he loved me. I was appalled and I turned off my phone. When I turned it back on the next morning there were multiple messages about what he would do for me. I was horrified. I deleted them all so Mark wouldn't see them.

On Monday morning I went into work and there weren't many people in as it was the start of the Christmas holidays. He came to my office. I was so angry; I tore a strip off him and said I was so cross with him. I didn't want to talk to him. I told him that if Mark had seen those texts he would have thought I was having an affair and told him of how much trouble it would have caused me. I reminded him about the incident where I had been arrested just a short while earlier. He apologised but I was not convinced that he had got the message. But at least he left me alone for the rest of the day. However I had a suspicion that wouldn't be the last I heard from him although thankfully I had nearly two weeks off over Christmas when he would have time to cool off.

On my return to work after Christmas he came into my office and stood in front of me. I could see that he was nervously making grasping motions with his hands in his trouser pockets and I can honestly say this was really making me cringe.

"I have missed you he said."

"Don't start that again," I barked.

"I have thought about you all Christmas" he continued, and then he produced a small posh looking bag and said "I want you to have this."

I stared in disbelief at the bag. It was marked with 'Rowell's,' on the side. Rowell's is the most expensive jewellers in Oxford. I suddenly realised, that he had bought the pearl earrings. "You haven't," I said. "Did you buy those expensive pearl earrings?"

"Yes," he replied.

"Take them away," I said. "I cannot possibly accept them."

He argued with me for a while saying he couldn't return them so I told him to give them to his wife. But in the end he took them away. He finally admitted that he could return them and he had warned the jeweller that I might not like them and in which case, he would need a refund. He knew I probably wouldn't accept them.

When I had calmed down I had a laugh to myself. Weeks later, I could see the potential in this and perhaps use him to get out of my marriage. After all I was running out of options and getting another job was taking forever. Give him a little of what he wanted in return for being a guarantor on a rented house. It was the only way of getting away from Mark. I had visited a solicitor again after the incident where I was arrested. She had told me that I couldn't get Mark out of our rented house as it was in joint names and I would have a tough time. I would have to live with him while I divorced him and that he would use me and drain me of everything I had. So I suppose I used Nigel but quite frankly it hadn't gone quite to plan as I couldn't stand him and he must have guessed I wasn't genuine, as he wouldn't act as a guarantor when I pushed him five months ago.

Things have gone quiet between us since then and I haven't had a lot to do with him apart from work-related stuff.

C is for Andy Curtis. You remember Andy, I went to Uni with him and I had lost contact but he found me through Friends Reunited a few months ago and we have emailed each other. Although I am not interested in him and we have never met since he got in contact. He is married and it is nothing more than friendship.

"I see," said Alex. "How did he hack into your email account?"

"Well that is what I want to know," said Juliet. "I never save my password on the computer." But she had asked Alistair to log on for her over Christmas and she had told him her password. Perhaps he had saved it. That could be the only explanation. She was angry about it but what could she do now? It was too late and the damage had been done but then again Alistair knew how miserable her life was, he had told her to get out of the marriage to his Dad months ago. "Of course he could have worked it out," she said. "It wasn't difficult and he had plenty of time on his hands".

Alex paid the bill and they hurried back to the metro station. They wanted to be alone together for their last night together. They didn't say it but they both knew that is what they felt. At least they didn't have to rush in the morning as their train didn't leave Paris until 4.45pm. It was still bitterly cold and they sat silently holding hands on the metro.

Chapter 10 – Revelations

They sat on the bed with their usual glass of red wine. Thankfully they were now both warm and much more relaxed. Alex turned to look at Juliet, "there is something I want to say to you Juliet," said Alex.

Oh God, she thought, what on earth can it be?

"You know, I am going to Yemen to save money to buy a place in France?" said Alex.

"Yes," she replied.

He continued, "Well I would like it very much if you would come with me and share my life in France. It will take me a few years but when I do I would like to do it with you. We won't have a lot of money but we will own the house and the land outright and you like growing vegetables, you have kept chickens and your experience would be a real help. I regret my decision all those years ago not to make a life with you. That is why I got back in touch. I had thought about you often and then when I looked for you on the internet and found you on your work's website, I just had to email you"

She couldn't believe what she had just heard. A lump had formed in her throat and now tears ran uncontrollably down her face. He just turned and cupped her face in his hands and kissed her on the lips as he had done before, and mopped up her tears with his lips. "I don't understand why you are crying," he said. "Have I upset you?"

She laughed "Oh, goodness not in the slightest, I am just so shocked. Are you sure you want this? This isn't lust talking is it? After all, you have been celibate for five years."

He laughed now and said "no, it isn't lust talking, although I have to admit the sex has been incredible. I mean every word of what I say. I am sorry that I left you with him and I am sorry you have had to endure all of that shit." Then he took her in his arms and kissed her with tenderness and love. "I love you, Juliet," he said.

"I love you Alex. I always have," she replied. She was overflowing with joy and felt as though a ray of sunshine on a cloudy day had just covered her cold body and filled it with warmth. The light at the end of the tunnel had just appeared and was beckoning her towards it and she was going to go to it.

They slept soundly, their bodies always close and touching and she awoke before him and lay quietly in the early morning light thinking about all they had said to each other the night before. She was determined now that whatever happened over the next few days, weeks and months, she would not veer from the path that they had chosen. Her marriage was well and truly over and there was no way that Mark could deny it.

Alex awoke and they lay there holding each other silently not wanting to let go. This was their last day together and they didn't know when they would see each other again. "What would you like to do this morning?" he said. "Would you like to go and look at the Degas collection in the Musee D'Orsay?"

They had both been fond of Degas all those years ago and he had once sent her a billet-doux on the back of a postcard that was a copy of an erotic Degas drawing of a reclining nude. He had said that the woman in the drawing had reminded him of her and she had been extremely flattered at the time and still was.

She was quiet for a moment and then replied "Alex, you know that I love Degas but I want to spend the morning in bed with you. There will be another time to see the Degas but today I don't want to waste a moment when I could be in bed naked with you."

His hand started to caress the naked skin on her stomach and then he moved his hand upwards to cup her right breast in his hand. It hadn't gone away, and it had not been quelled. Their desire for each other was as strong as it had been all those years before. But today, now after he had said he loved her this was moving onto a higher realm. She knew that she had loved him when they had first had their affair but he had never said he loved her. Now he just had. Her body thrilled to his touch and she started to buzz all over when he began kissing the back of her neck and gently nibbling her ear. Her nipple grew hard as he caressed it with his fingers and she could feel a tingling between her legs. Oh God, she wanted him so much.

They spent the next couple of hours, exploring each other's bodies, teasing, stroking, sucking, licking, biting and kissing until they were so aroused, they couldn't take it anymore and finally made love with an intensity and sensuality they had not known before. They lay holding each other for the last time. She would never forget Paris with Alex it would stay with her until she died.

Finally they had to accept that the time had beaten them and they had to leave so they got out of bed, showered, dressed and packed their bags.

As they were ultimately headed for the Gare du Nord, they decided to have one last visit to the area around

Montmartre where they could have a last drink in a Parisian café and grab a sandwich to eat on the way home. It was in the direction of the Gare du Nord and besides, they were running out of money.

The sun was shining even though it was a cold day and it was lovely to see Paris in a brighter light but parting was looming over them like a dark cloud. The time had flown by and Juliet had enjoyed every minute of it. They got off the metro at Abbesses, where they had done so on the first evening of their trip, the memory of everything they had done, and said to each other vivid in their minds and walked along the narrow, cobbled streets admiring the shops and taking in all the sights, sounds and smells. Paris really was a city for lovers there was no doubting that, thought Juliet. She had loved it the first time she had visited but it was in shallow comparison to how she viewed it now that she had been there with Alex. She felt truly alive for the first time in her life and awake for the first time in years. There was a future. There was something to look forward to. A future with Alex and she wanted to grasp that with both hands.

Despite their cumbersome bags they held hands and soon found a wonderful little square, with a myriad of lovely little bars. They found one with a gorgeous view, and a little marquee erected adjacent to the main building where they could sit and smoke and still be warm. Alex ordered two bier blonde and they sat opposite each other as they had done so often over the past two days but Juliet was brooding, and Alex sensed this. "What are you thinking about?" said Alex.

Juliet paused for a moment. Of course, she could tell him everything, unlike in the past with others where she kept her innermost thoughts private, for her only.

"How lovely this has been," she said "how lovely and relaxed and easy it is with you and how I wish it would never end. I don't want to go back home but I have to. I dread to think what awaits me. He is going to be a right shit."

Alex sipped his beer and she knew that he was thinking. "I know he said, I have loved every minute with you too but be strong Juliet, we can do this. I have no money at the moment but it will be different soon I promise. I love you, and realise what a fool I was all those years ago to let you go."

Although what he had said was comforting it couldn't dispel the growing doom in her heart. But she could be strong, she would be strong, she had been in the past but with his love she could be even more so. She would have to be because there was a storm brewing and she knew it.

They stopped and bought a couple of baguettes on the walk back to the Gare du Nord. She had difficulty keeping up with his large strides as they walked and he bent down and took her bag from her. Her heart somersaulted with love and admiration. When had someone else done this for her? Never. She had even had to wrestle the suitcases off the carousel at the airport on the one and only holiday that she had had in the last few years with Mark whilst he stood with the luggage trolley and that was five years ago. "Are you sure you are ok carrying a girlie bag?" she laughed. And then quickly realised how nothing could make a man who was as masculine as Alex look feminine.

"I am fine," he said, "it is the least I can do."

They were soon at the Gare du Nord, and as they passed through passport control the girl on the desk looked at Juliet, and then at her passport. "Please stamp it," said Juliet. The girl did as she was asked with a proud look on her face.

Alex said "why did you want it stamped?"

"There is no going back and I want to remember this forever, I want to have that as a souvenir," she said.

They sat melancholy on the seats waiting to board the train. They were both tired. Physically and emotionally exhausted, holding hands as they had done all of the last three days. Juliet felt a sorrow creeping into her heart. The sunlight was streaming through the windows even though it was late afternoon. It was late January and the seasons were on the turn, the days had begun to grow longer again but in her heart there was an icy chill.

They climbed wearily aboard the Eurostar and ate their baguettes. The train departed the magnificence of the Gare du Nord and Juliet took one last look out of the window as if to take a photograph to keep in her heart forever and then watched slowly as Paris slipped away through the suburbs complete with slums and graffiti and out into open countryside. Alex watched all this too and then tired and lulled by the motion of the train laid his head against Juliet's shoulder and fell into a contented sleep. Juliet was comforted by his physical presence on her shoulder but was too anxious to sleep herself so she stared out of the window at the passing French countryside and thoughts filled her head and love filled her heart. A single tear slowly made its way down her cheek. Her life was never going to be the same again she knew that and she was so glad.

It was dark when they got to London and they left the Eurostar, headed out of the station and walked along the Euston Road. Alex's train to Birmingham was leaving from Euston at 9pm so they had an hour to sit and have a coffee at the Library before they would say their goodbyes. The time flew by so quickly and they were soon at Euston. Juliet felt so sad but they had both said that they would have a weekend together once she had been paid,as Alex wasn't going to Yemen until sometime in February. It would be their last chance to spend some time together for a while.

"I had better go now," he said.

"I know" she replied, "I shall miss you very much". They held each other tight and had one last kiss. They didn't want to leave each other and they lingered until finally Juliet broke away and said," I am going now before I cry. I won't look back, but know that I am sad, and that I love you."

Alex nodded and said, "Ok, know that I love you too." And with that she picked up her bag and turned and walked out of Euston Station into the darkness with tears stinging her eyes, keeping her word and not looking back.

Chapter 11 – 'The affair'

It was a 9.30pm, when Juliet finally climbed aboard the X90 bus from London to Oxford. It was warm on the bus and she sank into her seat alone and stared out into the night. She had a lot to think about. So much had happened in the past three days. She had thought that it would be just a brief encounter but she had been wrong, it had been more than she had ever hoped for, certainly more than she had expected, and now she was going home to start a new chapter of her life.

She would tell Mark straight, he was bound to be drunk and abusive when she got home. After all, he had found out what she had been up to, not as though she cared, she knew before she went to Paris that he would find out about her not going on a business trip but she hadn't cared at the time and she cared even less now. She shut her eyes and her thoughts drifted back to the affair with Alex all those years ago.

'Part One' – March 1997 - Juliet had first met Alex in March 1997. He had been a colleague of Mark's. Mark had brought him home with him for dinner one day and when she had opened the door and saw Alex standing there she had been rather surprised. In fact her first thought had been 'God, he's handsome.' When he said 'hello' in his deep sexy voice, she had gone weak at the knees. She had then regained her composure and had banished these thoughts from her mind. She was a married woman. And that was that.

Alex proved to be thoroughly charming and he and Juliet shared a lot of things in common but most of all he was her age (well two years younger) and he also originated from the West Midlands. Mark had always made fun about her slight accent and joked about how parochial she was. Although the jokes were meant to be funny, they weren't and it was as though she wasn't good enough for him. He was such a snob.

His visits became more frequent and he always brought a couple of bottles of good Marks and Spencer gold label red wine with him, either merlot or cabernet sauvignon or one of each. He would open one straight away and hand her a glass whilst she was cooking. Mark was always in the lounge watching the TV.

Alex would ask her how her day had been and actively take an interest in her. He was always so appreciative of her cooking and often asked for second helpings. It made a refreshing change as Mark had the appetite of a mouse. She started to make an effort for him when he visited, making sure the meal was extra nice and always making a cafetiere of coffee for after dinner. She always remembered to buy the cream he loved to have with his coffee and sometimes he would stay overnight on the camp bed in the lounge.

Her marriage was not wonderful. They had recently spent twelve months in America with Marks job but it had been a struggle. She had been told she could work out there and as she had just finished her degree this is what she would have liked but when they got to America it was a different story. She felt Mark hadn't told her enough about what exactly would happen in America. He had wanted to go so badly that he had overlooked a lot of important details and when she had asked him about things he had just said that it would be alright.

The accommodation was scarce and expensive and instead of the clapboard house Mark had promised, they ended up in a high-rise apartment on the sixth floor with pensioners as neighbours. They had had to rent furniture. It had been a disaster from start to finish and Mark struggled to cope with his job and began to drink heavily. It was the first time that she had realised he really was an alcoholic, not the social drinker she had previously thought he was. She had questioned him about it but he didn't seem to want to know and didn't care. He also spent heavily on credit cards much to her dismay as she knew he was storing up trouble for them when they got home. He also insisted on going out for meals all of the time which quite frankly she felt were just a waste of money as Katie was six, Charlotte was five and Alistair was not yet one and they didn't want to sit in some fancy restaurant for two hours.

On their return home he become even worse. The drinking had not decreased and he would have 'episodes' late at night where he would become abusive and shout at her, insulting her, and being threatening. She was at her wit's end with it all and didn't know what to do. She asked someone from Aquarius the local charity for people with alcohol problems to come and see him but she listened as Mark had made the counsellor feel small and told him he hadn't got a problem. He didn't even want help or admit he had a problem.

They had struggled on like this for months. She was looking for a job but it had been over twelve months since she had finished her degree thanks to America and she was struggling financially. Mark didn't seem to care and never gave her any money. All he said was "if you need anything then let me know and I will get it." But he always questioned her as to why she wanted it. It was food for Christ's sake not a Michael Kors handbag. She took a job in the coffee shop at the local supermarket in order to have a little money so she didn't have to ask him for any.

He had said that it was his job that made him drink. She couldn't really understand this as he was a Senior Lecturer and had worked at the University for twenty years. He actually did very few hours, no more than ten a week teaching and he had been doing it for so long he didn't have to do any preparation. There was absolutely no stress involved. He had no idea what life was like in the real world. He had said he wanted to study Egyptology as this was his real passion, and because she was desperate for him to stop drinking she said that he could give up his job and return to study if she had a job earning 15k which was not a lot of money in those days but the mortgage needed paying and they had to survive.

He agreed to this and to her horror he applied to Oxford University. Hold on a minute, she thought to herself and said so to him, "I haven't even got a job yet, you can't give up your job yet."

All Mark had said was; "well if I get in, I can defer it to next year." That was alright in principle but he was offered a place on the Masters course and he couldn't resist and he accepted.

He came home one day in July and said, "I have handed in my notice."

Juliet was stunned. She felt that the bottom had dropped out of her world. "How are you going to pay for your fees?" she had asked.

"I shall sell my car," he had replied. But he didn't care, he was doing what he wanted. What has happened to our agreement, she thought to herself. It had been conditional upon her getting a full-time job. They would never survive. He had just committed financial suicide. She had felt betrayed at the time but he didn't give a shit. She felt sick with worry and alone. There was nothing for it, she had to find work and bring in some money so she started to apply for any jobs that she could.

Alex had been to Oxford University as an undergraduate and Mark asked him to come with them on a day trip one weekend. They all went. Alex, Juliet and Alistair and had followed Mark about as they went from pub to pub watching him oblivious to Juliet's disbelief at what he had done, far away in his own little world of selfishness, delighted by the thought of studying there.

They sat in a pub and whilst Mark was up at the bar, Alex turned to Juliet and said "how are you going to survive financially?"

"I don't honestly know. I am so angry at what he has done, I don't think he cares about me and the children at all, I am desperately looking for a job."

Alex had said, "I will give you a reference if you need one."

Mark had organised a leaving party at home and had invited everyone from work to turn up. It was on a Saturday and Juliet had made lots of food in anticipation of a house full of guests. It was supposed to be a 'drop by' party at any time from midday to evening but by about 6 o'clock it was apparent that no one was going to come.

There were just a handful of people who had turned up and two of those were Juliet's friends and of course Alex was there. When Mark had realised that he was universally unpopular he threw a tantrum and went to bed and it was only 7 o'clock.

Left alone, angry and pissed off with Mark, Juliet had started to flirt with Alex. She had made up her mind. Mark had betrayed her and so she would betray him. The little thought that she had first put to the back of her mind on meeting Alex was fetched out and allowed to grow. She would sleep with Alex. It was the ultimate betrayal. She didn't care if her marriage would be over. He hadn't cared when he had resigned from his job.

She had thrown her arms around Alex's neck and said tearfully, "I am sorry he is behaving badly, he has caused me so much stress but you will still come around for dinner when he has gone to Uni, won't you?"

Alex had immediately understood the implication of what Juliet had said and he replied "yes of course."

When Mark had been delivered to Oxford and his digs like an eighteen-year-old, she had not hesitated in calling up Alex and asking him to come to dinner.

It was a Friday night and she remembered it vividly. She had purchased smoked salmon and prawns for a starter and had rushed back home at lunchtime to do some food prep for the evening but she was so nervous that she had left her keys in the house and shut the door behind her when she had returned to work. When she had come home later that day she realised what she had done and she had to get her father to break into the house. She had fed the kids hastily and hurried them to bed so that they would know nothing about what she was doing.

She had been so nervous that evening that the time dragged but Alex had arrived at 9 o'clock as requested and brought his usual two bottles of red wine. They chatted and ate but as the evening went by Alex had not given her any indication that he wanted to sleep with her.

She was bemused but thought that she had got it wrong. He didn't fancy her after all. After the meal when she had made coffee she suggested that they drank it in the lounge and she put on some Beethoven which they both liked. He sat on the other sofa away from Juliet which confirmed her thoughts that he didn't want her. And then just when she had given up hope he looked at her and said.

"Do you want to sleep with me?"

She was shocked at the directness of this but she knew that there was only one answer she could give to his question.

"Yes," she replied. He had then stood up and took her by the hand and led her upstairs to the bedroom.

That first night had been a discovery. It had been a revelation and his kisses blew her away in their sensuality. His touch was equally as gentle and despite his size he was not heavy-handed or rough and it was like nothing she had ever experienced before. That marked the start of their affair in October 1997.

He would phone her twice a week and once a week he would come around for dinner, always arriving at 9pm with two bottles of red wine. It was a mission for him as he had to hang around at work and travel by bus from Wolverhampton over seven miles away and then walk for about a mile. In the morning he would leave at 6am so the children didn't know.

And then there were the billets-doux he would send her. Little thank you notes for a lovely evening, always saying something lovely about her. She always received them with surprise and delight when she returned from work. She had never had anything like this before. She kept them, but she knew it was dangerous.

He started to bring massage oil with him, scented carefully with essential oils and he would lavish her body with them. He said she worked so hard and looked after the kids (including Mark, who behaved like a child, bringing his washing back at weekends so that she could launder it for him) that she needed pampering. They stayed up late into the night until the early hours when they would finally sleep, just snatching a few hours before he had to leave.

It was exhausting to say the least. Mark didn't stop drinking and his childlike dependency on her didn't abate. He would phone her on an evening and he was usually drunk. He didn't seem to care that she was having a rotten time. Alistair had to go to nursery full time and as he had been with his mother since birth he was not happy with the disruption. He didn't complain about going to nursery but when they arrived home on an evening he would throw himself onto the carpet in the hall and have a fit of crying and be inconsolable.

The only little pleasure was Alex's once weekly visits. He told her to stop cooking and he would bring Indian takeaways for them to eat so that she didn't have to go to any effort. "I can't take you out," he said, "but I don't want you to cook, you need a bit of time off."

Late November and the end of term was rapidly approaching and she knew that her little trysts would have to be put on hold and she didn't like the thought of that one little bit.

That weekend she had her hair done and Mark had been pissed when she arrived home. Why did he have to come back every bloody weekend? He wanted to go to

Oxford. Why did she care if he was lonely? It had been his choice to put them in this bloody mess, he should at least enjoy it. And he hadn't given up drinking. She felt even more betrayed. It had just been a rouse to do what he wanted. It was exhausting and he never once asked how she was coping.

She had been forced to take some shitty job as a purchase ledger clerk where the pay was 9.5k just because of his folly. She was barely covering the bills and she knew it. The nursery fees for Alistair alone took half her salary. She was angry and she resented him. They started bickering, she was tired and she didn't want to cook so she suggested a takeaway. Mark never ate takeaways. "I don't want a takeaway Juliet. I don't know why you can't cook? You have been at the hairdressers all afternoon doing nothing."

This statement made her anger bubble over like a volcano exploding. She had had quite enough of him. Weeks of picking him up on a Friday evening at the train station, weekends cooking and cleaning and doing his washing and ironing, and he always insisted on wearing shirts. Then having to get up and get Alistair up extra early on a Monday to drop him off at the train station.

"You don't care about me at all do you Mark? Well I don't care about you anymore. Alex treats me better than this. At least he brings a takeaway when he visits me."

He didn't seem to have heard what she had said as he didn't react at all and then he said "what did you say?"

"You heard me Mark. Alex brings a takeaway when he visits and then we sleep together. I have taken him as my lover."

Stupid and she knew it but she wanted to hurt him, to shock him into consciousness over what he had done. But of course it didn't, he just went mad and became physically aggressive. He searched the bedroom from top to bottom and found her billets-doux and shredded them into tiny pieces.

Not the Degas she had thought, please not the Degas. She had treasured that billet doux. It was such an erotic drawing and it symbolised Alex's desire for her. She never got compliments from Mark anymore just criticisms.

Mark continued his rampage and ranting, calling her a cheap slag and any other derogatory terms he could think of. She had to get away from him. She could take no more of his torture so she fled to her mothers with the kids. All her Dad could say was "what the bloody hell did he expect, bringing a younger man home."

She had stayed the night at her mothers and thought that her marriage was finally over and he would leave but to her astonishment she was wrong. He didn't go back to Uni that week but stayed walking around the house playing the victim and saying he was heartbroken. She ignored him for the most part and went to work on Monday morning. Someone had to play the grown up. It was no different when she came home Monday evening. He was drunk but she again gave him a wide berth. She hoped he would get the message and leave.

Then she came home from work on Tuesday lunchtime because she had forgotten her lunch and he was lying in bed with an empty bottle of whisky beside him and pills scattered all over the bedroom floor. It was an attention seeking act, she knew it. The scattered pills were designed to give the impression that had taken loads of them but if he had they wouldn't have been all over the floor. She felt nothing but contempt for him and she had little time for this pathetic acting display.

"You stupid arsehole how can you do this? I have kids to think about."She had said.

She couldn't very well leave him there for the kids to find when she returned home from work so she bundled him in the car, dropped him at A and E and went back to work.

Alex knew all about thi, because Mark had phoned the house where he rented a room and threatened him. Alex had phoned Juliet at work and told her how concerned he was for her but that he was ok and not frightened of Mark.

A spell in the hospital and a chat with a psychiatrist who wanted to section Mark, brought Mark to his senses and he then played a different game. He composed himself and told her that he forgave her and went back to Uni. Forgive me! Forgive ME! How dare he, she thought to herself, he started this by his betrayal.

She saw Alex one last time before Christmas but she knew he didn't love her. She knew that for him she was just a passing phase. He had too much going for him, he wouldn't want to live with her and it was such a mess, with the house and the kids and some crazed psychopath of a husband. So she wrote him a letter and said that she didn't want to see him again. She was falling in love with him and she knew it. It was getting messy and she would end up getting hurt.

Christmas was awful. Three whole weeks of Mark who was at his grovelling best. He even did ironing for her but none of it mattered. Her heart was sad and like lead, she was heartbroken, she was grieving.

Christmas went and he returned to Uni and she returned to work. She was hollow and missed Alex like hell. He had written her a letter telling her he understood her decision and that he was going on a trip to New Zealand. He wished her well.

Then in March she had another bombshell. Her period was late and she felt sick. She was pregnant. She was horrified. It was Marks she knew it was. She had had a period after she last slept with Alex and they had been very careful, using condoms, so it could only be Mark. She only slept with him to keep him quiet and stop the rants that still continued when he was drunk.

She didn't want it and she was angry. It was his fault, she had been careful. (Now sitting on the bus all those years later she realised that he had purposefully made her pregnant and he had done it again years later with Guy, when he thought he was losing her. What an idiot she had been.) She had to get rid of it. No way was she having another child with him in these circumstances. They really would be on skid row.

She needed someone to talk to and so she went to see Alex. She knew where to find him, she knew when he had evening classes so one Tuesday evening she went to the University and waited outside his class for him to finish.

He came out and when saw her he realised she was in a state so he booked a hotel room for them both and took her there. He bathed her carefully and listened to her woes. He made her laugh and she felt immediately better. In the morning he kissed her goodbye when they parted, and made her laugh saying, "you only like me because I have a big willy," of course there was more to it than that.

He went off to New Zealand in the Easter break and she had an abortion. She hated the fact that she had been placed in this position because of Mark.

In mid-MayAlex sent a love letter to Juliet's mothers and they started up their affair again.

This time it was different and he fell for her although he never told her he loved her. He was going to work in Aberystwyth and he was buying a house there. She wanted to move in with him and leave her marriage behind and divorce Mark and for a while he bought into this and said he had been thinking about a life with her.

Then out of the blue he asked to see her. She knew it was the end, she knew it was over, and he delivered the blow without an explanation. She sat calmly and stifled back the tears, she wasn't going to let him see she was hurt, that would be humiliating. She just said "let's go to bed just one last time as friends" she had to have the last fix of his love. So they did.

After then she decided that as she had no option but to stay with Mark and they would have to sell the house. Well it was either that or for it ultimately to be repossessed. No one cared, she was on her own. She would get a job in Oxford and they would move there to a rented house because there was no way they could afford to buy there given the property prices.

So that was what they did. Mark knew he had won and she was utterly and totally miserable.

One morning she was in the kitchen and Mark was asleep in bed. She felt devastated and all the pent-up emotion came pouring out and she sobbed and wailed with grief and heartache. The door to the kitchen opened and Mark stood there watching her. "Crying for that

Bastard are you?" he said. She turned away from him and said nothing. Drying her eyes she pushed passed him, and locked herself in the bathroom.

She got a job in Oxford and they moved there at the end of July. A ramshackle old house with a rambling overgrown garden and her life continued miserable as ever with no light at the end of the tunnel. She thought of Alex often. No one can invade your thoughts or take away your memories she said to herself.

Mark finished his MPhil but he never got a job and the little pot of equity from her house was swallowed up and she had struggled to go on. That was twelve years ago. She heard nothing from Alex until he had contacted her last October. But he had come back. He had come back and he had made her happy and they were going to have a life together.

Back on the bus she was woken from her memories as her phoned beeped with a text. Probably Mark, she thought and looked at her phone. No, it wasn't Mark it was Alex. She read it;

"It's a jolly holiday with Mary!" – "Thank you for a wonderful few days. Be strong and know I am with you in spirit. Love Alex XXX"

She smiled. Mary Poppins, she thought. He had remembered her bag and what the girls had said about her being Mary Poppins. If only she had her magic.

They pulled into the Oxford Park and Ride stop. She had to get off at the next stop, she was nearly home. Time to face the music, she thought.

Chapter 12 – Fallout

She put her key in the front door and opened it. The house was illuminated and lights blazed in almost every room which was unlike Mark as he usually moaned at her for leaving the light on in the hall on an evening. It was after 10.30pm but he was still up and so were the boys. Alistair would be as he was 15 but Guy was in the playpen in the lounge and he was not yet 3 and should have been in bed hours ago. There was washing up piled up in the sink and toys littered the floor.

"Oh here she is, here is the slag herself," said Mark.

"Leave me alone Mark." she said. He was pissed, as she knew he would be. "Why is Guy not in bed?"

He said nothing, "Oh never mind," she huffed and went and picked Guy up and gave him a big hug. She made him a bottle of warm milk, and took him upstairs and changed him ready for bed, and laid him in his cot. He was soon fast asleep. She put on her pyjamas and climbed into bed and lay down to sleep.

Mark came in and started. He was loud when he was drunk, "well, enjoy your trip did you, with him? I phoned work up and they know all about you," he said.

Juliet roused from her dozing wearily "Mark, I don't want to argue with you this evening, I have work in the morning and I am tired and Guy is asleep."

Despite Guy being nearly three, Mark had not let Juliet move his cot out of their bedroom and into his own room. Juliet was infuriated by this but every time she had mentioned it Mark had complained and said Guy wasn't ready for it. But it didn't stop him coming in and turning on the main ceiling light and shouting loudly when he was drunk.

She was going to move into the spare room tomorrow but tonight she was too tired to make up the bed with bedding so she would stay here. Mark climbed into bed next to her and started ranting, to himself mainly but she knew it was for her benefit. At least his voice had quietened a little. Don't let him goad you, she thought, he is trying to get you to argue. He had done this many times before and she was used to it. Although he knew which buttons to press to provoke her she kept quiet.

When he could see that his words were not affecting her, he stretched out his arm and made a grab for her tit. "Leave me alone" she barked. "Don't touch me," she may have had to share the bed with him tonight but he was never, ever going to have sex with her again. He turned the light on and got out of bed. He stood there in his nightshirt. He looked terrible.

His hair was a mess. His face was ruddy and bloated from the drink with broken veins all over it. He was skinny and had no muscle tone. He was 56 and not in great shape. He had abused himself so much with smoking and drinking and apart from walking he never did any exercise. She felt repulsed. She remembered after her affair with Alex all those years ago how she had hated Mark touching her and she had endured sex with him only to stop him from getting angry. Well not anymore, it was well and truly over. She wouldn't be doing that again.

He stood looking at her. "I want a divorce Mark," she said. "It is well and truly over."

He started to cry. It was not attractive and it repulsed her even more. He always cried when he was pissed, it really was rather effeminate. She shot him a look of disgust. "I don't want you to touch me ever again," she said.

He sobbed a little which sounded fake and contrived and then said angrily; "what, had an extra 3 inches of cock have you?" She was disgusted. It was not about that and he knew it. It was not just the sex, it was the caring.

"I shall move into the spare bedroom tomorrow Mark but for now I need some sleep. I have to work tomorrow." He seemed to accept this thankfully and climbed into bed. She was tense and wary but he soon started to snore and she was so tired that even her tenseness and anxiety couldn't keep her awake and she drifted off.

The next day her voice had nearly disappeared. She knew it was the stress of it all. Mark was still asleep when she got up but he woke before she left for work. "You will come home tonight? Won't you?" he asked.

"I have nowhere else to go Mark and you know it. I don't have a lot of choices. It is bad enough that you have made a nuisance of yourself at my work and I have to go in and face that today, so keep away I warn you." she said hoarsely and at that she left the house and took Guy to the nursery and then went to work.

Work wasn't as bad as she expected and no one asked her any questions. She had a chat with the Director and he seemed genuinely concerned although he had a soft spot for Juliet as he had relied heavily on her when he had started there and everyone else had been against him. No one at work knew her husband was an alcoholic despite having worked there for six years. She had kept it a secret until the last couple of days and now it wasn't a secret anymore. She soon logged onto her emails when she had a chance.

There at the top of her emails was *Alex;*

"When Mary holds your hand, you feel so grand, your heart starts beating like a big brass band"

She smiled to herself, another Mary Poppins reference, from the song that Bert the chimney sweep sings. She opened it and read it.

"Hi Juliet, I hope you are ok. I am worried about you and that shit. I want you to know that I love you and really hope we can be together one day. I really want to see you again, and soon. Let me know you are ok. I stayed overnight at a friend of Bill's in Birmingham and shall probably stay here over the weekend, but I can access my emails.

Love Alex xxxxx"

A surge of emotion swept through her. He was so lovely and she wanted to see him more than ever. She replied to his email and told him what had happened the night before. Then a thought occurred to her. If he was in Birmingham she could go up and visit her family in the West Midlands and she could then go and see him. Her mom and dad were on holiday in Tenerife so she could stay at their house. Her daughters and her eldest son Miles lived there anyway. She could stay in the caravan that they kept on the drive in the winter. She could take Guy and that way she wouldn't have to be stuck with Mark all weekend trying to wear her down. Yes she thought, this was a good idea. So she emailed him. He soon replied with a firm yes, he would stay the weekend at his friend's house. She would travel there on Saturday morning. She was not up to it today. She was absolutely exhausted and she had lost her voice. It was stress and she knew it.

Everyone at work seemed concerned. Even the miserable old Deputy Director came in and asked if she was alright. He had borne the brunt of Marks venom and had received various threatening emails and it was him who had called the Police. Everyone that is except Nigel. He had given her a wide berth thankfully. She really didn't want to see him. He was about as clingy as Mark and equally as effeminate, if not more. Perhaps he really had got the message, finally. He had blown the opportunity he had with her when he wouldn't be a guarantor on a rented house for her. Since then she had shut him out in the cold.

She went home that evening. Mark was pissed as usual but he wasn't aggressive. He had moved into game playing mode. She told him that she was going to see her older children at the weekend and would be taking the car and Guy and Alistair. She didn't let him know what her real motive for the trip was. It was none of his damn business anymore. He asked her about her voice, but it wasn't a genuine concern as he couldn't resist a coarse comment about her 'sucking prong," he really was vile, she thought to herself, just because he didn't like fellatio.

Surprisingly he didn't complain about her going away for the weekend with Guy, it was unlike him, he usually put up fierce resistance to her going anywhere alone, or with the kids as he hated being left on his own but he was playing mind games. She made up the spare bed and after dinner and after putting Guy to bed she went and shut herself in there and locked the door and went to sleep.

The next day, Juliet, Alistair and Guy travelled up to the Midlands. Miles, Katie and Charlotte were happy to see them all and after a while she left them to go to Birmingham to see Alex.

She hadn't long set off and her phone started ringing, her heart gave a little leap, it was probably Alex but when she glanced briefly at her phone, she saw it was Nigel (who she jokingly called Mr B). Fuck she thought, not that wanker. It was just typical of him, he hadn't bothered with her for months but now that he knew she had someone else, he was getting jealous. What a hypocrite! He was married. He had no rights over her so what the fuck was he thinking? Did he realise that she could make a great deal of trouble for him if she told his wife what he had been up to? She had saved his bacon more than once, but that didn't mean she wouldn't tell his wife. The only reason she was reluctant to do this was that she felt sorry for Jackie, the poor woman had enough to put up with.

She ignored her phone but it hadn't gone two minutes and it rang again. Again, she ignored it and then a text message pinged to announce its arrival in her phone. She pulled over to look at it.

"I know you went to Paris with someone else. Does that mean you don't love me anymore?"

What a child she thought, he really is stupid. How did he think I ever loved him in the first place? She put the phone down and then it pinged again. She picked it back up and looked at the message.

"Why won't you answer the phone? I need to talk to you."

He really was a nuisance and she knew he wouldn't stop so she replied.

"I have nothing to say to you, stop bothering me."

Another ping and this time she ignored it and carried on driving. More repeated pings but she just ignored those as well.

She got lost in Birmingham so she phoned Alex and he asked her where she was.

"Wait there," he said, "you are not far away and I will come to you," She sat in the car, and saw him come around the corner, a thrill shot through her. She was overjoyed to see him again so soon, and he climbed into the passenger seat, reached over and gave her a long slow kiss.

"I have missed you," he said.

"I've missed you too," she replied. They sat in the car chatting for a while, mainly about Mark and then he kissed her again. "Would you like to go for a coffee?" he suggested.

"Yes, I would like that Alex I am gasping for a drink."

They went to a nearby coffee shop and then she drove him back to her parent's house to meet her grown-up kids and Guy. No skulking about anymore, she thought to herself, I am not having an affair, my marriage is over, it has been for a while and Alex is the new man in my life for the rest of my life. They had a lovely evening and they all got on splendidly. Alex was amazed at how much like Alistair, Guy looked. Alex had remembered Alistair when he was the same age as Guy and he had spent many hours entertaining Alistair when he used to come over for dinner and Mark couldn't be arsed and Juliet was cooking.

Sunday morning soon came, and she dropped Alex off at his friends. They had a long lingering embrace and parting was such a wrench. They had spent too many years apart and now it was truly awful to leave each other, but she had to go home and she had work.

"Why don't we meet up next weekend somewhere such as Ironbridge" Alex suggested. "We can stay in a hotel, and you can meet me at Telford train station. I shall be off to Yemen in two weeks, and I want to see you again soon before I have to go, I still have some money."

"That would be really lovely," she replied.

During their time together, Alex had warned Juliet to be careful with Mark. He had warned her that he was clever and calculating, even if he was a drunkard. And she intended to be so but she knew it wasn't going to be easy. "Call the police if you have to, if he steps out of line," he had said. She didn't look forward to going home but she had to, she had nowhere else to go.

All that coming week they emailed every day, and spoke on the telephone every night. She locked herself away in the spare room after dinner, after she had given Guy a bath and had put him in bed. Mark didn't say a lot, in fact he was rather worryingly quiet. He made a few little nasty snide comments when he was drunk but mainly he kept quiet. He constantly tried to pretend everything was all right between them and acted as if this was some passing fad. Juliet was glad for the peace but she knew that it wouldn't last once he realised that she meant business, that she really did want a divorce. Just keep quiet for now she thought to herself. Once Alex has gone to Yemen it will all kick off but I can be strong and it will happen.

Friday morning came and in the post at work, came a little package for Juliet. It was a DVD of Mary Poppins. She smiled, Alex was still as sweet and thoughtful as he had always been. She took the afternoon off and left work and travelled up the motorway to meet Alex, stopping off at her parents to drop off Alistair. He hadn't wanted to stay at home with his father. Juliet didn't blame him, she felt sorry for Guy but Mark hadn't let her take him. She just hoped he would be alright.

Her mother was in when she dropped Alistair off. Juliet asked her mother about her holiday.

"Oh it was good Juliet. Good to have a break but I have been having this niggling pain in my stomach. Some dog jumped up me when we went to the country the weekend before we went away and it hasn't gone." Juliet was worried but hoped her mother would get better soon.

Juliet kissed her mom goodbye and set off for her rendezvous with Alex. His train was getting in at Telford station at 3pm. It was a sunny but bitterly cold day and every now and then little of flurries of snow appeared as she made her way along the motorway.

Juliet was so excited to be seeing Alex again and as she pulled into the car park at the train station it was starting to snow heavier. She sat in the car watching the flakes of snow swirling around and around settling on the ground and covering it with a white blanket.

She sat in the car until 2.55pm and then got out and went to wait on the platform. She didn't have to wait long and the train pulled in from Wales. She held her breath as the doors opened, and there he was all 6'3" blonde, manly sexiness, walking towards her through the snow. They embraced each other and kissed. God it was good to see him. He was huge and gave her a big bear like hug. "Hello," he said in that deep, masculine sexy voice. She really couldn't get enough of him.

It continued to snow as they made their way to the little riverside inn in Ironbridge and parked the car on the opposite side of the road and checked in. It was a lovely spacious room in a building adjacent to the pub on the second floor with large windows and a view of the river. The naked branches of the dormant trees framed the view. It was warm in the room and there was a Velux window through which they could see the snowflakes settling, melting as they hit the warm glass. It was getting dark with the snow as it was late afternoon.

No sooner had they put their bags down he immediately swept her up in his arms and carried her over to the bed.

"I really want you," he said, "I have been unable to think about anything else all week," as he laid her down carefully on the bed. He held her in his arms, caressing and kissing her and undoing the buttons on her blouse. He slipped his hand inside to touch her warm skin. She responded to his touch with a burning passion. She too had been unable to think of anything else but him all week but she was too busy kissing him to tell him that. She needed him to fuck her and she needed it now. She grasped at his clothes and he helped her free himself of his jeans, boxers, and socks. He then removed her clothing and they got under the covers. She could smell him. It was a distinctive masculine smell, musky and sexy. He never wore aftershave and she was glad he didn't, because he smelt sexy enough without it.

Her senses were aroused. His smell, his touch, his chest hair brushing up against her nipples, his large erection pressing against her thighs was overwhelming. She had never felt this way with anyone else, it was just so natural, so right. She hadn't felt this alive sexually for years. In fact she had never felt like this. It wasn't dirty, it wasn't sordid, it was entirely natural. She would never grow tired of this. He put his hands gently between her legs and found what he was looking for.

He didn't need a map or guidance, he had just the right touch and soon he was driving her wild. Her body was tingling all over and she couldn't take anymore. "Fuck me please," she begged and he did as he was asked and gently entered her, his largeness completely filling her, but she was ready, she was dripping and swollen and god it felt good for him to be in her. He kissed her as he moved back and forth, gently at first, his left arm wound tightly around her shoulders, but then his movements grew in strength and forcefulness and he soon burst and groaned with a climax. "I love you, Juliet," he said. "I love you Alex" she replied.

Passion satisfied, for now, they lay back. He held her close and they drifted off to sleep.

Chapter 12 – Ironbridge

They only dozed lightly and when they awoke it was just after six pm. They were hungry and they needed to bathe. To their utter joy, there was a large bath in a spacious bathroom. Alex ran the bath and poured Juliet a large glass of wine. They sat in the bath together relaxing in the hot water sipping their wine while the weather outside grew icy dark.

When the bath had begun to grow cold Alex got out and roughly dried himself and then held out a large towel for Juliet to step into.

He carried her into the bedroom and set her down on the bed and dried her. This was heaven for Juliet. She had not been pampered like this for a long time and because Mark was so small he never picked her up. They were the same size and his strength had gone a long time ago. Alex's powerful manliness was just the perfect antidote she needed for years of abuse and neglect.

The snow was still falling outside and there was a blanket of snow on the ground that sparkled in the light from the street lights as they walked up the hill to the Indian restaurant they had chosen. Alex adored Indian food and he had travelled to India many times when he was younger and although he was now vegetarian there was enough variety on the menu to satisfy his needs. It was quiet for a Saturday night in the restaurant, although it was still early and they enjoyed just sitting and chatting.

"I am concerned about you and what Mark is going to do," said Alex. It was true, it was worrying that Mark was taking it so calmly and Alex thought he was just playing for time. He suspected that Mark was thinking that Alex's relationship with Juliet would blow over when he went to Yemen.

"So am I," said Juliet, "he will dig in his heels and without getting another job with more money to move myself, I can't force him out of the house as it is a joint tenancy. The solicitor told me that months ago when I went to see her about getting a divorce."

Mark had moved in on her all those years ago when Alex had called it off and Alex thought that this was what he was waiting for now. "I am glad you have moved into the spare room," said Alex "but I don't trust him at all, he is too clever and manipulative and you do realise that you have been the victim of domestic abuse for years, Juliet. He may not have hit you but the abuse has been mental, you know that. He has been bullying and controlling."

She nodded. She hadn't thought of it like that but now that Alex had said it, she knew that it was true. "Are you still cooking for him?" said Alex. Again she nodded, she had a mouthful of the most delicious chicken tikka. "Oh Juliet, you really should stop doing anything for him. I know you have been conditioned,but you are still sending signals that you care for him."

"I know Alex, it just seems petty not to, but I understand I will stop. I suppose I am scared of him kicking off and I am so tired when I come back from work that it is easier to keep him happy." she said.

"But where will it end Juliet? What if he pesters you for sex?" She was irritated by this statement as she couldn't bear to have Mark touch her but she knew that what Alex had said was a fair comment. "I can see that he will wait for me to go to Yemen and then he will step up his game and before you know it you will be bullied into sex to keep the peace. I want you to promise me that you will not sleep with him."

She was angry about what he had said. "Of course I am not going to sleep with him Alex. It is just such a mess. I don't know how I am going to get out of this marriage. I have been trying for the past twelve months to get out but he just won't accept it. I suppose I thought that when I came back from Paris he would accept it as he knew you were on the scene. But I suppose you are right, he is going to fight to keep his slave. He has nothing without me, I pay for everything." She knew it was not going to be easy and she had focused all her attention on Alex for the last couple of weeks since Paris, but she knew that Mark was good at playing games. "I wish you weren't going to Yemen," she said, "but I know you want to earn money to buy a place in France."

They finished their meal and paid the bill. "Let's not talk about this anymore tonight Juliet. I don't want to think of him when I am with you."

The rest of the weekend went by in a flash and they had a wonderful time together but like Paris it was tinged with sadness, as they knew this would be the last time they would see each for other for many months. Parting at the train station on Sunday morning was hell and they clung to each other until the last possible moment before he had no choice but to hop onto his train back to Wales.

When she got to her mother and fathers house they were just finishing their Sunday lunch. Her poor mother looked very tired. She did a lot of running about for her father who still owned his own business, and showed no sign of retiring even though he was 73.

All the three generations of women, Juliet, her mother, and her daughters sat in the 'snug' as her parents called it after lunch. The snug was the old dining room. It was an open plan room that was adjacent to the kitchen but her mother had done away with the dining table a long time ago and had now got a small two-seater sofa and an armchair in there complete with a TV, so that she could watch the programmes she liked that her husband didn't.

Juliet's daughters Katie and Charlotte were in their early twenties and lived with their grandparents after they had moved back to the Midlands (after an abortive attempt to live on their own). The girls wanted to know all the salacious gossip about the weekend but Juliet just smiled a girlie smile when they asked how Alex was. She couldn't help but think of all the wonderful toe-curling sex they had shared over the weekend.

"Your mother is in love," said Juliet's Mom. This surprised Juliet. She didn't think her mother was perceptive to these things but clearly she was. After much tittering by the girls and a little chat Juliet had to leave to go back to Oxford. She kissed her mother goodbye.

Alistair was good company in the car and they soon got home. The house was surprisingly tidy and Guy was pleased to see her. Mark knew that she had been to see Alex but he didn't make any comments, snide or otherwise.

Alex was right thought Juliet, he is up to something. She had booked a day's leave on Monday a few weeks earlier, as Mark had an interview for a job at a local senior school. It was very uncharacteristic of him as he made no attempts to disguise the fact he hated teaching and he didn't want to work. He was hanging on for his teachers' pension at 60. But he was making a show of looking like he was doing something. I don't like this one bit thought Juliet, he is up to something.

The next day when Mark went to his interview, she phoned Alex and they spoke on the phone for a long time. It was clear that Alex had much on his mind. "I don't want to go to Yemen," said Alex.

"I don't want you to go either," said Juliet "but you need the money."

"But how are you going to cope on your own Juliet. I don't think you will manage it. I think you will wind up back where you started with him. He is going to make your life hell. I don't know what to do?"

Juliet didn't know what to do either and she came off the phone feeling very sad. How on earth were they going to get her out of this marriage?

She had decided to cook a roast dinner as she had missed out on one the day before and she was largely doing it for Guy, who although he was not quite three loved his food and especially his roast dinners. But she did as Alex had asked and did not make one for Mark.

When Mark came home from his interview she was just finishing her first glass of red wine.

"Where is my glass?" said Mark. "Drinking red now are we, because of Alex? You know I dislike red wine." He sneered at her.

Who did he think he was? He didn't turn up a penny. She had told him she wanted a divorce and now here he was demanding, criticising and sneering at her. Her anger immediately fired up, thinking of what Alex had said at the weekend. Yes she had been a little naïve and yes she had been abused for years, even conditioned by it but she wasn't going to stand for it anymore.

"Well, actually Mark you are not having a glass of wine. I paid for that and I pay for everything here. You are not having any of the meal I have cooked either, you can get your own. I shouldn't even provide food for you to cook given that you haven't worked for months on end."

His face turned red with rage. He stepped closer to her and forced her back onto the counter and pushed his face into hers so it was almost touching. She could smell alcohol on his breath. He must have gone for a drink in the pub when he had come out of his interview. "You fucking bitch," he spat as he spoke and she felt his rancid foul-smelling spit spatter over her face. Her heart was beating faster now; she never knew what he would do next. "I suppose he has put you up to this," Mark said. He hadn't moved and she was pinned to the kitchen counter.

He wasn't strong and she could push him off but she had been arrested once because of him and she didn't want to touch him again. The knife block was within her reach. "Back off Mark," she said, placing her hand on the handle of the large carving knife. She didn't want to draw it out of the block, she might use it in anger and she knew that would not only be stupid it would also be fatal. He saw her hand go to the knife and knew that she meant it. He stepped back and turned to the fridge. He got out a beer and opening it he retreated to the lounge and put on the television.

She breathed a sigh of relief and was shaking with anger. This is not going to be easy, she thought to herself.

Mark stayed in the lounge and only came out now and then to get more beer. He said nothing and she fed herself and the kids. She bathed Guy and got him ready for bed. She decided that Guy should sleep with her in the spare room from now on, especially as it looked as though Mark was going on a bender tonight. She could hear music coming from downstairs. Neil Young and she knew that was a bad sign. Mark always played Neil Young's sentimental melancholy pap when he was like this.

There was a good chance he would flip tonight. In any case he was in no fit state to look after Guy if he woke up in the night. She didn't want to have to go into their old bedroom to see to Guy. If Mark was in there and drunk, going in there would be a very bad move. There was not enough time to dismantle the cot and move it into the spare room so she just took the mattress. She held Guy close in bed and read him a bedtime story, he was soon fast asleep. She was tired too and although she had promised Alex she would phone at 10pm, she soon fell asleep.

She was woken by the sound of banging on the bedroom door. "Where is Guy?" Mark slurred from the other side of the door. She said nothing, she was half asleep. "Let me in." Mark shouted.

She woke up fast. "I have got him in here with me," she said, "he is asleep, go away and be quiet."

"Let me in you bitch, I want my pup," he shouted loudly. It sickened her the way he called Guy 'his pup'. He was not right in the head. Guy had been born on his 54th Birthday and Mark had said he was his twin born 54 years later. That was sick and twisted.

She ignored him and then there was a loud bang on the door, he was thumping the door with his fists. Then he

106

kicked the door and it flew open. It was an old door and the lock wasn't very strong so it didn't take much to kick it in. He had wrenched the keep from the door frame. The noise had woken Guy and he was crying. Mark staggered into the bedroom "I want my pup," he shouted.

"Just go away Mark, you have just woke him up" screamed Juliet.

"I am not going without him," shouted Mark back. Juliet got up and stood between Mark and Guy but he pushed her back onto the bed and picked up Guy and took him into his bedroom. There was nothing Juliet could do. She didn't want to tackle Mark when he had Guy in his arms, and she didn't want to upset Guy further by trying to stop him, she could hear him crying and Mark trying to console him.

She couldn't believe what Mark had just done. He didn't care about Guy at all if he was willing to do that, but there was no reasoning with Mark when he was sober, and so you had no chance of reasoning with him when he was drunk. She hated him with a passion.

She looked at her phone. To make matters worse it was 11 o'clock and she hadn't called Alex. What the hell would he think? She was tired by all of this and it had only just started.

It was alright for Mark, he didn't work but she did and she worked full time. She lay there in the darkness thinking about the hopelessness of it all. What would she do when Alex had gone to Yemen? It would be really difficult. She had to get some sleep, she had to go to work in the morning. There was nothing she could do about it now she thought to herself and emotionally drained she drifted off to sleep.

Chapter 13 – Confrontation

The next day at work, she logged onto her emails. As she expected there was one from Alex. Alex had asked her to phone him the night before rather than the other way around. He knew that she had Guy in the bedroom with her and he didn't want to wake him up with the sound of the phone ringing. Juliet didn't have a phone that received emails. She was still stuck in the past as far as technology was concerned. He had sent an email as she had expected;

Alex "Are you ok? You didn't call at 10pm as promised and I was worried. Let me know you are ok as soon as you see this. Love Alex xxxxx."

This wasn't good. He was already concerned about Mark bullying her into sex and not phoning him late at night would look bad. She could have phoned him last night after the fracas with Mark but she had been so tired, and needed her sleep. She emailed Alex back telling him what had happened with Guy and Mark kicking in the door. It hadn't gone five minutes and she received a reply.

Alex "let me know when you can take a call, we need to talk."

She messaged him back *"Five minutes,"* she said.

Sure enough Alex called, and she answered her phone, taking it outside to have some privacy.

" Juliet I have had enough. Things are not going to get better with Mark, they are going to get worse and I am worried sick about you, God knows what he is capable of."

Juliet agreed "I know Alex. I don't know what to do either."

Alex continued "he is a nasty little shit Juliet and we don't know what he might do next. Do you want me to come to Oxford?"

Juliet was stunned by this, what did he mean?

"I don't understand Alex," she said, "I thought you were going to Yemen on Thursday."

Alex replied "I was, but quite frankly I don't think I should go and leave you to face this alone. I could come to Oxford and stay in the house with you, to keep him at a distance."

This was all confusing. What Alex had just said was completely messed up and wrong but then what she was enduring with Mark was crazy, messed up and wrong. Nothing was right anymore but at least he was willing to protect her from him.

"Juliet, are you still there?" Alex said, "You have gone very quiet."

She didn't know what to say. "Sorry Alex, it is just a bit of a shock, what you have just said."

"Do I take it you don't want me to come there?" Alex said brusquely

Juliet panicked, he thought she had something to hide, he thought she wanted to stay married. "No Alex, of course not, I don't know why I was quiet, I was just thinking about it. He does have his name on the tenancy agreement, couldn't he kick you out?"

There was a pause as Alex thought, "Not if you write a letter and sign it saying that your name is on the lease and you grant permission for me to stay in the house as your guest. After all Juliet you have been paying the rent out of your salary for years. He hasn't contributed a penny."

Juliet could see the sense in this. She felt quite flattered that Alex was willing to take this step and protect her but even so it was a little sudden and there was something not quite right about it that made her feel uneasy. She felt she really didn't have any choice. She couldn't risk losing Alex, not now, not after all those years so she just said ,"yes, ok Alex, come and live with me," and after a pause added, "and him."

She received an email about ten minutes later from Alex saying that he would be arriving at Oxford station at 3.30. She replied and said she would meet him there. It was not busy at work and most people were working from home, besides she didn't care anymore. She then typed up the letter as he requested and printed a few copies, signed them and stuffed them in her bag.

She got to the train station with 5 minutes to spare and waited. It was a cold afternoon and it was cloudy and dark, and it looked as though it was threatening rain or even snow. She had travelled by bus, it really was the only way to travel to the city centre in Oxford unless you were mega rich and she wasn't. A throng of people began to spill into the station from the platform, a train must have arrived. She managed to pick him out of the crowd and thankfully he was wearing his glasses this time, not like at St Pancras. He saw her waving frantically over the hordes of people and pushed his way through them to her. They hugged but it was clear that they were both tense about what they were about to do.

"I have the signed letters," she said "I made a few copies just in case."

Alex looked at her "that's good," he said, "don't worry Juliet, everything is going to be alright."

She felt slightly relieved at this but was not entirely relaxed about the situation. She dreaded the confrontation between Mark and Alex. They had been friends once but that was a long time ago. Alex had said during their affair, that he wasn't scared of Mark. Of course he wasn't he had no reason to be, at least physically. Mark was 14 years older than him, he was nearly a foot shorter and he was a slim build and was weak. Alex would easily win in a fight. No it wasn't a physical fight she was worried about. It was how manipulative Mark would be, how cunning and how devious.

The sat holding hands on the bus. It felt good to be with him again she had to admit it. And at least with Alex there, it might speed up the process of her divorce. She had been worried that it would drag on for ages once Alex had gone to Yemen. Not because she would have held up the process but she knew that Mark wouldn't let her go easily and he would drag his feet every step of the way, hoping she would change her mind.

They got off the bus and walked down the street holding hands. Juliet felt as if the curtains were twitching and all the neighbours were watching her. A wave of embarrassment washed over her. First being taken to a police car by two policemen and arrested on a Saturday morning in full sight of anyone who had happened to peer out of their window at the time and now walking down the street holding hands with a clearly younger man who was not her husband. Oh, fuck them! She thought to herself. No one came to help me over the years with that

111

shit did they? I never belonged here with these pretentious people anyway.

She opened the front door and Mark came out of the kitchen and he immediately saw Alex behind her. The look on his face was priceless. He looked like he had just seen a ghost.

"What the fuck is he doing here?" Mark said. He had been drinking.

Before Juliet could open her mouth, Alex replied. "Hello Mark, I am a guest of Juliet's and I am here to make sure you behave yourself."

Juliet could see Marks face turning red with rage. "Get out of my house," said Mark to Alex.

Alex just stood there and said "This isn't just your house, it is Juliet's too and she has been paying for it for years. I am not going anywhere," and he handed Mark one of the letters Juliet had prepared earlier.

Mark stared at the piece of paper and said nothing. He had been outsmarted this time and he knew it. He withdrew to the kitchen and gulped down a beer. They all stood there for a while and then Alex went to the bathroom and Mark seized his opportunity.

He cornered Juliet in the kitchen "what the fuck are you thinking bringing him here you old slag?

Juliet looked at him, he was horrible. How had she managed to get through all of those years with him?

"Last night Mark you kicked in the door on my room. I have told you I want a divorce and you don't want to acknowledge it and you won't leave me alone. You kicked down the door whilst Guy was asleep in there.

What you did with Guy last night was the last straw," she said.

His face flushed with rage and he knew he was being outwitted. "You are not having my pup," Mark said.

Alex came through the kitchen door and saw Mark with Juliet cornered in the room. "Mark, leave Juliet alone." He said in a strong voice. "You have bullied her for years and it has to stop now."

Mark spun round to look at Alex, "Oh is that what this whore has told you?" He sneered "you shouldn't believe anything she has said. She is a serial liar as well as a slag. She has slept with most of the men she works with." Juliet couldn't believe what she had just heard, although she could, she was used to his insults and insinuations and he had wasted no time in trying to put more doubts into Alex's mind.

"Don't listen to him Alex?" she said, "he is just an alcoholic." Mark was annoyed, she had wounded his pride and he spun out the usual old line he was so fond of; "there is nothing wrong with liking a beer" and as if to add further gravitas to it he said, "Would you like a beer Alex?"

Juliet was outraged. He was actually trying to make friends with Alex? Thankfully Alex didn't rise to the bait. "No Mark, I wouldn't like a beer, and I think you have had quite enough. I would have never slept with Juliet all those years ago, if I didn't think you were a wanker. You were then, and you haven't changed at all. You still are a wanker."

But Mark didn't go. It was as if he was watching a piece of theatre and it was too riveting to leave the room. He sat on a kitchen chair and watched Juliet as she prepared dinner for herself, Alex and the children. Every so often he would make some snide remark, but he was careful as to not overstep the line and outrage Alex and all the while he drank.

Guy was liked Alex, as had Alistair when he was young. Alex was engaging with children, and they enjoyed his company. He could engage with them on their level. He hadn't lost his inner child unlike Mark who viewed them as extensions of himself.

Alistair had soon got fed up with Marks limited attention towards him when he was younger knowing that if he, Alistair wanted something different to Mark's wishes he was soon met with disapproval.

Juliet had been his salvation and she did 'manly' things with Alistair. The sort of things that boys like to do with their Dads, only Mark was not a typical Dad and he didn't want to do such things. They had rebuilt the pigsty wall together, Alistair and Juliet. She didn't have much idea but her Dad had told her how to mix mortar and she and Alistair had done it together when he was eleven. Yes it was a bit wonky and not exactly level but it still stood there and it stopped the neighbour's dog invading their garden.

At forty-one Juliet to her surprise had found herself pregnant. She had thought she was going through the menopause early.

She had been beginning to sow the seeds of getting out of her relationship with Mark. Katie had left school and had returned to the Midlands and was now living with her grandparents and Charlotte had been at sixth form. Juliet herself was thinking that finally there may be a light at the end of the tunnel and then she had found herself pregnant.

She was immensely flattered that her body at this age could still produce a child. But she had been confused as to what to do. She didn't really want to tie herself to Mark but she thought that she could still get out of her marriage after all she had virtually raised her children singlehanded. Mark had never changed a nappy or had given a bottle. When she had told Mark she was pregnant, he was overjoyed. He had always said he wanted another child but she had always said no.

They weren't financially secure and he didn't work but this time she saw an opportunity and told Mark that she would only have the baby if he got a job. He had a PGCE, a teaching qualification and he had always maintained that it was only for students over sixteen, something Juliet had not believed. But on finding herself pregnant she had rooted through the bureau and had found it and she had phoned the relative authority and had been told that it was for all ages, not just further education.

So she made a bargain with him. They were crying out for secondary school teachers and he could go on a return to teaching course and get a job at a secondary school. He was reluctant but he wanted Juliet to have the baby so he agreed. Juliet even completed the application form for him and he was accepted onto the course and by the Christmas when Juliet was six months pregnant with Guy, he was offered a job as Head of RE in a secondary school.

They tried to offer him a meagre salary but again Juliet told him to stay firm and request more money as they were in a tight spot and wanted him to start as soon as possible. They finally agreed and gave him the salary he requested.

At that time, Juliet thought that everything was going to get better but it didn't last long and he soon started taking time off sick with any old excuse and he didn't attend the meetings after school, he couldn't wait to get home and have a beer. Then Guy was born. That was another episode of trauma for Juliet.

It had been twelve years since Juliet had given birth but she was still fit and had envisaged a home birth as she had done with Alistair. She had gone into labour nearly two weeks overdue and from the outset it was different from all her other labours. She was in intense pain, so bad that it shot down her legs and left her breathless with each contraction.

It was a Saturday morning. In fact, it was Marks' fifty-fourth birthday. She woke him and told him she was in labour and he needed to get up as she was going to call the midwife. She needed gas and air and she needed it now.

When the midwife came Mark was in the bath and the midwife was useless. She didn't have the gas and air with her and Juliet was aghast. She was in so much pain but the midwife didn't seem to care and told her that if it was that bad then she should go into hospital.

When Juliet informed Mark of this he was angry "why do you have to go to the hospital? I thought you were going to have a home birth. I haven't had any breakfast, can't she take you?" referring to the midwife. When Juliet had replied no, his mood turned foul. He didn't even care about Juliet and the pain she was in. "I know Mark," she replied, "but there may be something wrong and it is better to be safe than sorry."

Reluctantly he got dressed and got the car out of the garage and he drove to the hospital which was only a mile away. Every bump in the road was agony for Juliet and he saw her into the room and left her there, he didn't even carry her bag for her. She had begged him not to leave her.

She was scared and needed support.

"I have to go and get Alistair and my camera," he said.

"Don't get Alistair" she had begged. She thought there might be something wrong and Alistair was safely at his friends. She had phoned his friends' mom to let her know what was happening. She was a local nurse and so understood that it was better for him to stay there. He was only twelve at the time.

But over an hour went by and Mark had returned with Alistair. She was leaning over the back of the bed at the time with a hospital gown on and her arse on show to the entire world. Mark had opened the door to the room and she had turned around to see Alistair standing next to him .What a fucking idiot, she had thought at the time, allowing her twelve-year-old son to witness that.

"Take him out of here," she had yelled, "this is no place for a twelve-year-old."

She had then realised that Mark was scared and was using Alistair as support. It was hopeless. He wasn't going to hold her hand through this and she was in it alone.

Several hours went by and no progress had been made with her labour and she had begged for an epidural which was so unlike Juliet and her other labours. Even the anaesthetist thought it was odd given she had previously had four children but then finally the registrar came in and examined her and she then declared that the baby was facing the wrong way and was stuck. Juliet could have an epidural and she needed forceps, so they wheeled her into theatre.

"Do you want your husband present?" said the midwife oblivious to what Marks was like. Knowing he had been useless so far and was prone to panic, she had firmly said "No." He would be about as much use an ashtray on a motorbike.

Once in the theatre the anaesthetist commanded that she keep perfectly still so that he could put the needle in her spine. She did as commanded and soon the pain disappeared.

"Will you marry me?" said Juliet to the anaesthetist . Everyone laughed. "But I bet all the women say that to you," she added and they laughed again.

Ten minutes later Guy was delivered safely. And what a little bundle of joy he was just lying there, 7.5 pounds of loveliness and she had fallen in love with him as soon as she set eyes on him.

When she had been tucked up in bed on the ward Mark and Alistair had come to see her. The first thing Mark said was "is that your wee bag?" referring to the catheter and bag that hung on the foot of the bed. He didn't ask how she was or give her a kiss. Just nothing but then he was pissed. He had been drinking throughout the day.

The days after were no better. Juliet was bruised badly from the forceps and she had been cut down below. She could hardly stand and once home, she lay in bed just feeding and changing Guy. Her nipples were sore as hell and she felt about 80. Every time she stood up she felt like her bottom was going to drop out.

The first day at home, she was starving but Mark and Alistair had gone out shopping for gifts for Guy. When they came back she had to shout downstairs and ask for a cup of tea, and could she possibly have a sandwich.

Mark never cooked and he wasn't of a caring nature, so he struggled for five days to get dinner for them all, they were mainly microwave meals and Alistair took pity on his mom and made her tea and a sandwich for lunch every day. It came to something when a twelve-year-old was more competent than a fifty-four-year-old male.

By the end of the week, she felt marginally better, and she got up on Saturday, eight days after Guy had been born. At least she felt half human. Mark didn't ask her how she was, all he said was "does that mean I am relieved of my duties now?" She never forgave him for that episode. Guy was his child too and it proved to her that he didn't love her; if he had, how could he be so cold and uncaring? The writing was on the wall.

Over the next few months, he repeatedly had time off work sick, so much so that by the September, he had been sent to Occupational Health. She had returned to work in December, and even though Mark was still having time off work she thought everything was ok and then in April she was looking for a bill in Marks briefcase and came upon a letter from the Headmaster at his school.

She stared in horror as she read the letter. Mark was being taken for competency proceedings. It was the end. It referred to a meeting in December that Mark had had with the Headmaster. He had told her nothing about this. It looked as though he would lose his job for sure and yet again he had been weak and been deceitful. She was furious. He didn't want to work, he didn't care about her or the kids, he just wanted to do nothing but drink. She had been deceived and she knew it.

Chapter 14 – Madness

Alex and Juliet made their bed in the spare room. They put the single mattress on the floor and some pads from the sun loungers next to it and topped it off with an old duvet to lie on. It wasn't the world's greatest bed but at least they could lie next to each other in relative comfort and it was a good job Alex wasn't precious like Mark so he didn't complain.

Once warm under the duvet, they kissed and cuddled for a while and then chatted, Alex made tea for them and they smoked numerous cigarettes. It was like being a student, only they weren't students and she had work in the morning.

"He has got worse over the years" said Alex. "I remember him being an arsehole all those years ago, and to a certain extent I thought you were exaggerating about him. The things you have said over the past few months, and in Paris but if I hadn't come here and witnessed it for myself I wouldn't have believed it."

Juliet sighed, "now you understand how awful it has been. I mean, to the outside world Mark presents himself as some pretentious snob, just like the rest of the people here. He goes out with a shirt and tie on, or a bloody bow tie like he is some Oxford Professor and all the time he doesn't earn any money and lives off me. If he ever meets anyone he tells them he is an Egyptologist! That wouldn't have been so bad but he doesn't love me. To be honest, I don't think he ever did.

He does nothing around the house. I do everything. He has misbehaved and caused a scene at every family social occasion we have been too. So much, that we are now not invited to any family social function. My father says he is no better than a pimp, living off the earnings of a woman."

Alex looked Juliet in the eyes softly and tenderly, "I promise never to be like him, Juliet. I want to look after you. We have to get you out of this." They held each other close and drifted off to sleep. It was past midnight and Juliet didn't usually stay up this late, she was exhausted.

Juliet went off to work the next morning and gave Alex a key to the front door. He was going to go into town and keep out of Marks way.

At work it was the same old usual stuff and Juliet still received emails from Alex throughout the day, telling her what he was doing which brought her joy. Although she had an underlying thought of niggling worry, everything was so stressful and just how resilient was Alex? Could he really withstand Mark's attempts at manipulation? Would he believe all the things he kept saying about Juliet being a slag? Would he doubt her?

Mr. B had been quiet since the texts after Juliet's return from Paris and he had largely kept out of her way, although they had to have some interaction because of some of her job duties. He was still creepy though. He came and sat close to her in the meeting last Friday, and she wished he hadn't because she could tell he was watching her.

There weren't many people in at work that day and he came into her office. They were alone together, but curiosity was killing him.

"I knew you were going to Paris," he said "you left a printout of a map on your desk. Is it that man from years ago that you met? The one you told me about? The one you had loved deeply?"

Why did he have to do this? She thought to herself. He hadn't bothered her for months, and now all of a sudden because he thought there was someone else, he was getting attentive and worried.

He hadn't received a response from her to his texts weeks ago when she was on her way to Birmingham and he had to know.

"Yes, it is," she replied, and said nothing more, leaving a silence in the air as he thought what to say next.

"I know I messed up," he said.

She didn't reply, she had nothing to say to him and she didn't want to discuss this with him. It was over, he meant nothing to her and she wished he would just accept that and move on.

He stood around nervously waiting for her to say something, but she didn't.

"Don't you love me anymore?"

What a bloody stupid childish question, of course she didn't, she had gone to Paris with another man, one who Mr. B himself had admitted she had loved deeply years ago.

"I think you know the answer to that question," she said, and then added, "I thought we were done months ago".

He looked crestfallen. "But, but," he stammered.

But before he could say anymore, Juliet said "I don't wish to discuss this, the matter is closed now please leave my office if you haven't come here for work purposes," and with that he stood for a moment not knowing what to say next. She didn't look at him, she just carried on typing so he turned and walked out of her office closing the door behind him.

Alex met her from work and they walked home together stopping by the shops on the way home to buy food for dinner. Juliet was a good cook and she was enjoying her new challenge of vegetarian cooking so they selected the ingredients for that evening's meal. Alex loved her cooking and he always complimented her on it. He insisted on carrying her bags as they left the supermarket.

When they got home, Mark was sitting in the kitchen, with his usual drink in his hand. Where was he getting his money from? Thought Juliet, she had stopped giving him any.

This infuriated Juliet. Why did he have to sit there in the kitchen? He knew she would be cooking food and Alex was with her. However Alex was unnerved by this so he sat opposite Mark at the kitchen table.

"Can I help you with anything Juliet?" said Alex.

Mark sniggered, "ooh, she has got you well trained," he said snidely.

"What slop are you cooking tonight Juliet?" Mark said in a mocking voice.

"Why should it matter to you Mark? You are not having any," she retorted.

"What am I going to do for dinner?" he said, suddenly in a self -pitying tone.

"I have no idea," she responded, "but I am no longer cooking for you, or giving you any money. From now on, you and I are separate do you understand?"

She could see he was not happy with this but as Alex was there he did nothing about it. If Alex hadn't been there things would have got very unpleasant and she would have ended up giving him food to keep him quiet.

They ate their meal in silence and then went upstairs to the bedroom. Juliet went and got Guy ready for bed and read him a story and put him in his cot. The cot was still in the bedroom Mark slept in. He had steadfastly refused to let Juliet move him. Juliet didn't like going into that room but she thought Mark was downstairs and she would be safe.

She didn't see Mark enter the bedroom behind her.

"Get rid of him and let's be friends again," he said to Juliet.

She jumped when she heard his voice and felt fear spread through her but she tried not to let it show as she turned to face him. "Mark, I am not going to do that, and you know it, we are finished, just accept it."

"I won't accept it," he replied.

She tried to get past him to get out of the room, but he blocked her way, "Let me out Mark," she said.

"I won't let you go," he replied.

Alex must have heard this altercation as he soon appeared in the doorway. "Let her go Mark," he said calmly, and Mark stood aside to let her pass.

They went into the bedroom after Mark had gone to bed. Alex made tea and they talked for a while and then Alex kissed her. It was approaching midnight and Juliet was tired. "Alex, I am really tired, I love you and I adore sex with you but I am really knackered tonight to do anything like that."

He kissed her gently on the cheek and gave her an Eskimo kiss, rubbing her nose gently with his.

"Hey, listen, Juliet, I know you are tired and I know how hard you work and that beautiful meal you cooked for us tonight was delicious but it took a lot of effort. I also know how tiring it is to deal with Mark. He is a major piece of work so I don't want to do anything either. I would like to give you a massage though, that is all, just a massage. I still have some of that wonderfully scented massage oil that I had in Paris in my bag. Are you sure you wouldn't like a massage?"

Well how could she refuse? He was just the master of massage. She turned over and lay on her front and murmured "well, if you insist," and felt the drops of cold oil drip onto her back followed by his warm hands gently caressing and massaging her back and she relaxed in no time at all and fell asleep.

The next few days were the same as the ones before, but then on Friday when Juliet came home from work with Alex the car had gone. They went into the house and Mark wasn't there and neither was Guy.

Alistair was in the kitchen "he has gone to see Grandma," said Alistair.

"How do you know? Did he tell you?" said Juliet.

"Well no butI heard him on the phone to Grandma this morning and he was doing all the usual moaning stuff Mom. You know the sort of stuff he says about how horrible you are being to him."

"What a cheek," said Juliet, "she doesn't know what he is really like."

"I know," said Alistair. Alistair knew full well what his dad was like. He had told her the year before. He had said, "Mom, you have to get out, all you do is look after him, and you will be doing that when you are old. He doesn't care about you, he is too far gone with the drink."It was quite a revelation coming from someone so young.

Juliet laughed, "he is probably going to try and get some money out of your grandma, you know what he is like," she said to Alistair. "Never mind, at least we can have the house to ourselves for a couple of days."

They relaxed and made a fire in the grate in the lounge and bought the first bottle of wine they had shared since Ironbridge. They all ate pizza and watched TV.

"I have an idea," said Alex "why don't we put a lock on this door and move in here and use this lounge as our room. That bedroom is far too small up there. We could sleep on the floor at night, using the pads from the sofa as a bed. Mark wouldn't be able to use the computer then or get access to the internet. After all, Juliet, why should he? You pay for it."

"Why not," said Juliet, so that is what they did. The next day they walked to B&Q,and got a lock, and Alex fitted it to the door.

It had become apparent to Mark that he was not going to win. Not whilst Alex was helping Juliet. As long as

Alex was there Mark could not get Juliet alone and bully or manipulate her into submission as he had done in the past. So he had to be smart. He was far from happy when he came back from visiting his mom to find out that they had moved into the lounge.

He was now living on some money his Mom had given him but that wouldn't last long, and he needed to do something else. Quite what that was, Juliet had no idea.

On Monday evening he gave Juliet a letter in an envelope. "What is this?" she said.

"It is from my solicitor," said Mark. Juliet opened it and read it. It was just the usual Solicitors letter saying that Mark proposed having custody of the kids. It also said he wanted a divorce from her on the grounds of adultery.

Juliet was fuming. She said nothing to Mark for now but later on when Alex and she were alone, she talked to him about it. "Alex, Mark says he wants custody of the kids, but you have seen what he is like with them. Alistair is old enough to make up his own mind, but Guy, really, Mark never wants to change a nappy. I have come back home from work before now when Mark has looked after him, and have found Guy sitting in his playpen watching TV with a soiled nappy on. And you know what Mark is like, he can't even cook a meal. I don't want him to have custody, I don't think he is capable."

Alex sat silently thinking about this. "He has been to see a solicitor," said Alex, "he knows that you are not going to back down about having a divorce at least, that is a good thing. But he also knows if he has the kids with him then he will have the house but I can't see a judge granting him custody with his alcohol problem."

Juliet looked at Alex, "what are we going to do?" She said. "I don't know," said Alex, "we will have to think about it, but for now Juliet we need to get you a solicitor, and fast. I think I know just the one." She was someone Alex had known when he had been a Senior Prosecutor some time ago, he said he would email her and see if she still practised.

The next day at work things took a strange turn. Mr. B came into her office "Juliet I can't go on, I miss you, I realise I made a mistake," he said.

"Stop," she said, "don't go on, nothing you can say will make me change my mind."

"Are you sure about that?" he said, and he reached into his pocket and pulled out something. "Will you marry me? "He said, proffering a ring.

"What?" she gasped. "Don't be so ridiculous, how can you ask me to marry you? You are still married, put it away."

"Don't you even want to have a look at the ring?" he said.

"No, I do not," she barked and walked out of the office and went to the ladies. She waited there for a while until she thought it was safe to come out. After she had calmed down, she laughed to herself. This was getting nuts. How could he ask her to marry him when he was still married the silly sod? And, she didn't see the light sparkling off a huge diamond in fact, come to think of it she didn't see the diamond at all it was so small. Cheapskate, she laughed to herself. At least he kept out of her way for the rest of the day. It was a shame he finished at 3pm because Alex always met her when she finished work, perhaps if

Mr. B saw how big Alex was, he might think twice about pursuing her.

That evening when they were alone, she told Alex what had happened at work with Mr. B. Alex was not happy, in fact, he was fuming. "I thought it was all over between you two," he said. Juliet was taken aback, she only told him because it was so funny. But Alex hadn't met Nigel and she could see that he might view it differently as he wasn't aware that Nigel was such a first-class prat. In a way it was protective and she should be flattered but instead she was irritated.

"Look Alex it was all over between us, I don't know what he is playing at and quite frankly I don't care. I don't want anyone else but you but I am a bit sick of it, he doesn't seem to want to give up." Nigel was getting on her nerves and she tried to avoid him but it still played on her mind and she had enough problems dealing with Mark.

The problem was that Mark who was very good at manipulating people was playing a dirty game with Alex. There were times during the day when Mark and Alex would be at home together.

At first Mark had given Alex a wide berth and ignored him, he had even locked him out on one occasion by putting the bolt on the door but Juliet had made it perfectly clear that she would call the police if this happened again. Then Mark had adopted a different tactic. He became friendly towards Alex as they had been friends years ago. Mark had engaged Alex's attention by talking about current affairs and politics, something they both had an interest in. Slowly he started to introduce the topic of Juliet. He was very clever and at first he painted a rosy picture of Juliet, listing all of her virtues and praising her, but then slowly he had led Alex down the garden path and told stories of Juliet's misdoings.

Mark was very good at playing the victim and the stories he told about James Allen and Nigel Baker were second hand and all gleaned from things he had read in her emails when he had hacked into her account. The stories he told were not entirely true but Mark had made them compelling and they were entirely believable. Alex was already in over his head and the seeds of doubt that Mark had planted in Alex's mind about Juliet were beginning to sprout.

Juliet could now see what was happening as Alex was overreacting to Nigel's pathetic proposal. She couldn't understand why he was so jealous of Nigel, he clearly didn't know Nigel at all but it may be about Nigel's wealth. Of course Mark would have told Alex about the jewellery Nigel had bought her and about how he had money and that would have made Alex insecure. Bloody Mark, he really was an arsehole. He knew that Juliet really loved Alex and that nothing would stand in her way of being with him, but he could make Alex waiver in his love for Juliet.

"And what about the jewellery he bought you?" Said Alex.

God this was turning into an argument, thought Juliet. "What about it?" said Juliet "It means nothing to me it was all part of a game, to see how much I could get him to do. Nigel started it with those pearl earrings, I just carried it on. I wanted to get out of here and he had stupidly said he had loved me for the six years I was working there so I thought let him put his money where his mouth is, if he really feels like that, then perhaps I can get out of here. You know the ultimate goal was for him to be a guarantor on a rented house because my credit is fucked thanks to Mark."

Alex looked angry, "so you manipulated a man who said he loved you. Will you do that to me?"

Juliet was getting exasperated with the situation. "Alex, you know I wouldn't. If I had wanted Nigel I wouldn't have gone to Paris with you. Look, I know what I did wasn't nice but he didn't miss the money. I was way out of his league anyway, and he knew it. It was as you would say quid pro quo."

Alex looked even angrier "Juliet that makes you sound like a prostitute! I want to see your phone," said Alex. This really was another level, she couldn't let him see that. He shouldn't ask but she knew she had to appear as though she had nothing to hide. This was getting dangerous and she was frightened so she let him look at her phone. There were messages on there going back a while and Alex had a field day with her. He must have been bloody good at his job when he was a prosecutor, as he questioned her relentlessly and twisted every answer she gave him.

She was gripped with fear, this was all going wrong and she was scared of losing Alex. She couldn't win, he was making her look terrible and she was really angry; this was all Marks doing.

Alex was agitated and his deep voice was getting louder, she knew Mark would be listening in the next room. "Please be quiet Alex," she said, but he was angry and he didn't take any notice.

It was after midnight, she was tired and to make matters worse they had run out of cigarettes. She needed to calm down. It was not going to do any good getting angry in a situation like this. "Look, Alex, I don't want to argue with you. I am going to walk to the petrol station for some cigarettes, alone, I need to calm down."

She left the house to walk half a mile to the petrol station in Headington. It was cold out, but it helped her relax a little. What a mess, she thought to herself as she walked. I have to find a way out of this, I cannot lose Alex, not after all these years, not after I have come this far.

She knew that she would not be able to get away from Mark on her own, she knew if Alex left then she would be back to square one and life would be hopeless again and she would be heartbroken. If she blew it with Alex now there would not be another chance with him. She had to be bold, she had to seize this with both hands, and she had to take a risk and suddenly she knew what she had to do.

When she got back to the house there was a police car parked in the street. What the hell is going on she thought to herself and hurried to put the key in the front door. The lights were on in the kitchen, so she went in. There in the kitchen was Alex, Mark, and a policeman. "What's going on?" said Juliet.

"I heard you arguing with Alex and then you left, so I called the police as you clearly don't want him here anymore," said Mark. He really was a shit, thought Juliet, he was playing games, there was no doubt about that but he wasn't going to outsmart her.

Juliet calmly went over to Alex and kissed him gently on the cheek. "Whatever gave you that idea Mark?" she said sweetly. "We weren't arguing and I certainly don't want Alex to go. I only went out because I needed some more cigarettes."

The policeman looked confused. "I am sorry you have been called out on false pretences," Juliet said to the policeman "my husband was wrong but then he doesn't want Alex here so that is probably why he phoned you." The policeman got up and said, "Well if you are sure everything is ok?"

"Yes, I am sure," replied Juliet, and he left. Juliet just shot Mark a withering look of contempt. He knew better than to say anything and went upstairs to bed.

Alex turned to Juliet and laughed in that deep sexy way of his "You were brilliant Juliet. What you just did was amazing. I thought I was done for then."

She smiled at him, "it is Mark. He is one little nasty, manipulative shit. Do you think for one minute I am going to let him win? The argument between us was nothing. I love you too much to let a trivial thing like that stand in our way."

He went over to her and took her in his arms and gave her a long sensuous kiss that told her he felt the same way. "Anyway," she said," I have an idea. I am going to go to the doctors tomorrow and get myself signed off sick with stress. Nigel is being a pain and Mark is stepping up his campaign, I cannot leave you alone with him. It will buy us a little time but we need to find somewhere else to live, we need to get away from him. When we go he won't be able to stay in this house, they won't give him enough housing benefit and he will end up with his mom in Oswestry." Juliet was convinced that she would get custody of Alistair and Guy.

Chapter 15 – Wales

It wasn't hard to convince the doctor to sign Juliet off work with stress. She was actually very stressed and that stress, coupled with late nights and a vegetarian diet meant that she was losing weight. Her clothes that had previously been quite snug were now loose on her but she didn't mind, she had needed to lose a bit of weight. She had tried before Christmas in readiness for Paris but she hadn't been able to shed more than a couple of pounds, now the weight was dropping off her. And there was all the sex, mind-blowing wonderful sex, night after night. Her stomach muscles were getting toned not to mention her pelvic floor muscles with all that activity.

It happened that the solicitor Alex knew was in Newtown in Wales. He had worked there for a while when his mother had an antique shop in Llanidloes. They set off early on Tuesday morning to see the solicitor. Alex had arranged for them to stay the night at his Uncle Bill's house in Newtown, and he wanted to show Juliet off to Bill. Bill was renowned for his appreciation of the female form. Indeed, his hobby was carving erotic figures of naked women out of wood.

It was a frosty day but the scenery was spectacular as they crossed over the border into Wales. Miles upon miles of hills with pine forests clothing them. The odd sheep here and there, way up in the hills, so small that they looked like little white dots against the green. They were happy, it had been a wonderful idea to sign off work with stress and she was enjoying being with Alex 24 hours a day. She didn't tire of his company at all and they still found plenty to talk about.

They arrived in Newtown at about 10.45am and her appointment was at 11 o'clock. Faith was a very nice woman, the solicitor that Alex had recommended, she was in her mid-forties and she was a homely woman, definitely not a sex kitten. She talked Juliet through the divorce proceedings and didn't offer much of an opinion and in turn Juliet told her about how they were going to find somewhere else to live. They had thought about Shrewsbury so that they would be near Oswestry so that Mark could see Guy and this seemed like a plan, they would also be near enough to The Midlands so that Juliet would be near her Mom and Dad and her daughters. Juliet left the office and found Alex waiting for her. He handed her an envelope. In it was a card, on the front it said

'*You brought me love*' and inside he had written "*My beautiful Juliet, I am so happy to have the opportunity to make up for the lost years. I know that this calls for sacrifices and I am so very flattered that you are willing to make them. I consider it an immense privilege that you wish to share your life with me. I love you more than I thought it possible to love anyone, more than words could possibly express. I love you. Alex XXXXX*"

Juliet was truly touched by his written confirmation of his love for her and she vowed to keep the card safe forever, to look at when she was old.

So they went to meet Uncle Bill, walking through the park on the way. It was beginning to snow and soon it became a snowstorm with the snow swirling around them. It was very romantic and as usual, they held hands. The snow was sticking and there was a film of snow on the pavement when they arrived at Bill's house. Bill was a nice old man and he liked Juliet immediately and they were all soon happy chatting and planning dinner.

"Your Mom is in Newtown today isn't she Alex?" Bill said.

Juliet was taken aback, Alex hadn't mentioned this to her. She had never met his mother. "Yes, she is bringing my suit," said Alex. Oh God, Juliet was going to meet his mother. She had heard so much about this woman and she knew she would be judged.

Alex had told Juliet that it had been his mother who had put him off having a relationship with her all those years ago. Juliet wasn't entirely happy about this woman who was ready to judge her without meeting her. Still, face the tiger head on thought Juliet, she could stand up and be proud of herself. When the doorbell rang she was ready.

She stood up and proffered a hand when Jean was shown into the room. Jean eyed her with suspicion and she clearly hadn't been expecting to meet Juliet "It is lovely to meet you Jean," said Juliet, "I have heard so much about you," she added.

"I hope you know what you are taking on with Alex," she replied.

What on earth did she mean by that? Thought Juliet, but Juliet wasn't going to be defeated, "I love Alex very much, and have done for a long time. I am sure we can make a go of it," responded Juliet. What a cow thought Juliet.

The next day they went for a walk in the town, stopping to look in an estate agents window. There in the corner of the window was a little black and white half-timber cottage for rent, at a bargain price of £250. "Hey," said Juliet, "look at that."

Alex peered through the window, "that is cheap," he said, "and it is only just a few miles out of town. Do you want to go and look at it? It isn't too far from Oswestry here and it is handy for the solicitors."

Juliet jumped up and pecked him on the cheek "yes why not." They soon arranged to meet the estate agent there in an hour. 3 Gilfach Cottages was a quirky little place on the road between Newtown and Llanidloes. It was nearer Llani than Newtown and it was in a row of three cottages which must have been originally built to house farm workers who worked in the fields. There was a parking area behind, a few outhouses, plus what looked like an orchard at the rear of the cottages. The house itself was the end house and when they went inside it was like a dolls house.

"Mind your head," Juliet laughed to Alex, as they climbed the stairs to the first floor. It only had one bedroom but there was a huge landing area which could be partitioned off to be a second bedroom. The shower was in a cubby hole at the top of the stairs. Juliet wandered whether Alex would be able to fit in there. "I like it," said Juliet, "it is a bit like a dolls house but we could do something with it and I like the location, not to mention the price."

It was placed in a valley between two ranges of hills, where the road wound its way. "I like it too," said Alex.

"Let's say we will have it then," said Juliet, so they said they wanted it to the estate agent.

"Come back to the office and we will fill in some forms then," the estate agent said.

In the ca, on the way to the estate agent's office, Juliet turned to Alex, "obviously I am going to have to hand in my notice at work if we are going to move here. They will probably want to do a credit check and I might not pass but for this amount of rent I can pay six months up front out of my salary and they should go for that." They filled in the forms but they told the estate agent they would pay six months up front. The landlord was happy with that and they agreed to move in on the 9th March, just under two weeks away.

They drove back to Oxford with a sense of purpose. They wouldn't have to endure Mark much more and she could leave Mr. B behind and not have to suffer him either. They spent that evening making plans about hiring a van and Juliet typed her resignation notice and emailed it to her boss. She would never have to go back there again.

Alex arranged to borrow his half of the rent from an old friend. He said he didn't want Juliet to bear all of the costs herself. They would apply for jobs when they were in Wales. Juliet had already accumulated a lot of boxes from work, for packing her stuff up in anticipation of moving out a few months ago but it had come to nothing. She wrote a letter to the landlords, telling them that she was terminating her part of the tenancy and that she was leaving Mark. Things were moving now, for the first time in years and she felt relieved that it was actually happening, but she had overlooked one important detail. Alistair. How would he feel about moving?

Alistair had known about their plans to leave Oxford and move nearer the Midlands and he seemed quite enthusiastic about it. He knew that his father wouldn't leave as he had nowhere else to go and he knew that they would have to move. However he was only fifteen and Newtown was not exactly the Midlands but he agreed to move with them.

Mark was becoming more and more possessive with Guy and wouldn't let Juliet and Alex take him out anymore. It was ridiculous but Juliet didn't want to upset Guy by arguing with Mark. Mark had signed on to receive benefits and he was still drinking albeit cheap cider. He went out in the day a lot and always took his flight bag with him. Juliet never asked him where he was going but she knew he was up to something.

The day before they were due to move out soon came. They had hired a van from Welshpool which was near enough to Newtown. They would travel by Megabus to Birmingham and get the train to Welshpool from there to collect the van. They would next drive to Newtown to sign the lease and then they would go back to Oxford, and park the van around the corner from the house so that Mark knew nothing about it. They would get up early the next day to load the van and then leave before Mark was awake. They had deliberately not told Mark about the exact day they were leaving Juliet thought it would be better not to give him any notice as she didn't know what he was planning.

It was 2.30pm when they finally arrived at the van hire place. They were hiring the largest van they could (one with a tail lift), and they had originally planned for Alex to drive it but he had lost his glasses a few days before, so Juliet was going to have to drive it.

When she saw the van she was horrified, it was huge. The place they hired the van from was a bit rough and ready and they just handed the keys to Juliet and Alex. "How am I supposed to drive this?" She said as she climbed into the driver's seat.

"You will be fine," said Alex. She was as scared as hell, this was too much and she was shaking with fear. She turned the key in the ignition to start the van and it shook into life. She was used to driving an automatic and now she had to virtually stand on the clutch to get it into gear. She was petite and the gear stick was miles away.

The van shuddered into forwarding motion as she took her foot off the clutch and she carefully made her way out of the yard of the hire company then she changed gear. "You have just hit that van," said Alex referring to a van parked on the side of the road.

"What?" screamed Juliet, "I didn't feel anything??" She carried on driving.

"Aren't you going to stop?" said Alex. "No" replied Juliet. "I have no money and we are running out of time, we have to get to Newtown to the estate agents and sign that lease."

She was really shaken now. She was scared to start with and now she had hit a van and she had to negotiate the narrow streets of Welshpool. Who else would she hit? The visibility was absolutely appalling and she had not got used to the size of the van. "I can't do this Alex," she said with a rising panic in her voice.

"Yes, you can Juliet," he said calmly. "I have every faith in you," then he laughed and said, "plus, we don't have any choice." Juliet's heart was pounding in her chest with fear but this made her feel a little calmer, plus she had just successfully negotiated a set of traffic lights and had managed to go 500 yards without hitting anything or running anyone over. Soon they were out of town and she was settling into driving the van.

It took seemingly ages to get to Newtown and they were stuck in traffic edging its way into town, it was Friday afternoon. "This will take forever," said Alex, "we will be quicker walking," so they parked up and walked into town. It must have been just over a mile away and it was 4.00pm when they finally got to the estate agents.

They had expected to be given the keys but to their horror, the estate agent had said that they would have to collect them from the Llanidloes office tomorrow morning, but they shut at midday. "Shit," said Juliet "that doesn't give us much time, we will have to get up at the crack of dawn."

It took them ages to get back to Oxford, the van had a limiter on it and the fastest it could go was 60mph, plus it was Friday and the traffic was horrendous. Negotiating the street and turning the van round was a bit of a nightmare, especially in the dark but Juliet finally managed it. She was exhausted, it was nearly 9pm.

They lay in bed talking. They were going to get up at 4am and bring the van around to the house and start loading it. Alex had already unplumbed the washing machine and they had made sandwiches for the next day. Alistair would be giving them a hand to load up the truck but he had gone out to a party that night although he had promised he would be back to load the van in the morning.

They didn't seem to have been asleep for long when the alarm went off on Alex's phone. It was 4am. This was it! They were going to move out. Juliet threw on her clothes, made them drinks and then she went to fetch the van. It took them nearly twenty minutes to figure out how to work the tail lift but they soon started packing the boxes of stuff onto the van. They had a cut off time of 9am and they would have to go then whatever happened in order to get the keys to the cottage. Juliet had a sinking feeling in her heart. This was going to be a disaster.

Oh well, she thought to herself, I am just going to have to leave some stuff behind. "We need to pack the most important stuff on the van first," she said to Alex and they frantically piled things in the van, including toys for Guy. There was still no sign of Alistair and Juliet was getting annoyed about it, she had tried ringing his phone a couple of times but there was no answer.

Mark came walking downstairs in his bathrobe "moving out today, are you?" He knew that they were going to move but he didn't know when. They had kept him in the dark about that. He also knew that Juliet had resigned from her job and that she had given notice on the lease. He was annoyed about it but how on earth did he think he was going to keep that house? Juliet had always paid the rent and the council wouldn't pay £950 per month in housing benefit for just him.

"Yes," was all Juliet said.

"Does that mean you agree to me having custody of Guy then Juliet, because you never replied to my Solicitors letter?"

Juliet's temper started to rise, "no Mark, I do not agree to you keeping Guy. Your solicitor should have had a letter from my solicitor by now. Guy is coming with me."

Marks face was filled with anger. He was already red in the face with alcohol but now he was furious "you are not taking my pup," he said.

Juliet just carried on filling the van with boxes of stuff. Where the hell was Alistair? They had to leave soon and it was rapidly approaching 9 o'clock. It hadn't gone ten minutes and a police car pulled up and two police officers got out.

What happened next seemed to go by in a blur. Juliet could not comprehend what was going on. The police told Juliet that she could not take Guy with her. Juliet couldn't understand why they were taking Mark's side in all this.

Over the past few weeks they had repeatedly called the police out to Mark when he had been drunk and abusive. On one occasion the Police had removed him and taken him to the other side of Oxford supposedly to spend the night in a travel lodge but he had just walked back. He was well known for being a drunkard, so why then were they taking his side here? Juliet had even told one police officer of her plans to leave and suspecting that Mark would call the police had asked him if they would allow her to take Guy, now they had completely changed position. None of it made sense.

Juliet tried to appeal to the police officers but they were having none of it and said that she couldn't take him. They made her get the toys out of the van. Juliet was in absolute shock, what the hell was going on? She was numb. There was nothing she could do.

Alex was equally shocked; he didn't know what to do either. He just went and held Juliet's hand. Juliet felt as though a knife had been plunged deep into her heart. "We have to go," she said to Alex. She went to hold Guy and the police officer stopped her "I only want to cuddle my little boy," she said, tears running down her face. They wouldn't even let her cuddle him. "Goodbye Guy, Mommy loves you remember that and I will be back for you." Guy was crying, despite being nearly three he didn't really say much yet but he was clearly upset and distraught.

Chapter 16 – 3 Gilfach Cottage

Words could not describe how Juliet felt. She was in shock. She felt in pain, she felt that the world had ended, she was angry. But she drove on in silence.

Over an hour went by and she didn't say a word. Alex knew that she was absolutely gutted. He was equally stunned by what had happened.

"I can't take in what just happened back there," she said finally. "How can the police act as judge and jury? Mark is the bloody alcoholic, not me. All the times over the last few weeks we have called the police and they had assured me I could take Guy. And where the bloody hell is Alistair?"

Alex put his hand on her thigh and squeezed it. "Juliet, I don't know what to say. I am really sorry about what has happened we must get onto Faith first thing on Monday morning." True, she thought to herself there was nothing she could do about it now, so she just drove.

It seemed to take forever in the van even though it was flat out at 60mph most of the time and they were going to be late for the estate agents. Alex had phoned them and they said they would leave the keys at the newsagents next door. Thank God for the trusting nature of rural Wales, you wouldn't get that elsewhere thought Juliet.

They finally got to Llanidloes at 1pm and picked up the keys to the cottage. They went on to Alex's mother's house to collect his stuff. Juliet was annoyed by this as it was already late and Alex had only just thought to mention this to her.

His mother lived in a remote location and it took over an hour after passing the cottage to get there. The street where his mother lived was narrow and Juliet had to reverse the van. She had to stand on the clutch and Alex had to force the gear stick into reverse.

Jean seemed a little pleasanter with Juliet today but was shocked when she realised they hadn't got Guy. Juliet didn't need to be reminded of this and felt annoyed, as the tone of Jean's voice seemed to be insinuating that Juliet was at fault and Mark was the wronged party.

"Alex should have never come to live with you and your husband Juliet. It was not proper. I can understand why the police wouldn't let you take Guy." Juliet was stunned by this judgment. did she not know about Mark?

"Mark is an alcoholic Jean and as such he is not fit to look after a child. He has been abusive to me over the years and stepped it up when I came back from Paris. Alex was just trying to protect me." She felt like crying, but she held back the tears. Alex sensed she was about to cry.

"Look, Mom you have no idea what Mark is like it is not fair to make a judgment like that," he said. How could she bloody criticise them? She had hardly been a saint in her life but then her second husband had left her for another woman, so Juliet could partly understand why her sympathy lay with Mark.

They left quickly and drove back to the cottage. By the time they arrived there it was dark. They opened the back door to the cottage and Alex carried Juliet over the doorstep as they had planned but it was not with the joy that they had envisaged when they had planned it.

They unloaded the van and drove all the way to Welshpool to drop off the van. They only just made the last train from Welshpool and it was 10 o'clock. It was dark and cold when they finally got back to the cottage. They had used most of the little cash they had left to get a taxi from Newtown. They made a makeshift bed out of a thin camp bed mattress on the floor next to the wood burner, lit a fire and fell asleep in each in other's arms. It had been a very long day, and they were both exhausted.

There were no curtains in the lounge and it was daylight. The fire had died long ago in the wood burner. It was only the warmth of Alex that kept Juliet from freezing.

She lay there thinking about yesterday. Her feelings were no better. She felt awful about it all. What a nightmare. She went over it all in her mind, thinking about how she could have done it better. She should have taken Guy first and then gone back for the furniture, why hadn't she done that? But then that would have been upsetting for Guy.

She was torturing herself now. Hindsight is both a wonderful and a terrible thing. How was she to know that the police would take that position? It was no use, what was done was done and she couldn't change it, but it didn't stop the sick feeling in the pit of her stomach.

She got up to make some tea. Alex did not stir. How could he sleep? It was bloody freezing in the cottage. There was a hard frost on the ground outside. The cottage did not have central heating, it only had a small wood-burning stove in the lounge and you had to get really close to that to keep warm. And the mattress they were lying on was one from a camp bed. It was thin and not very comfortable.

This was shit, everything was shit, everything was a mess and she felt too numb to cry anymore. Yes numb, cold and empty inside. They had also made a vow to stop smoking and they only had two fags left. She lit one up with her cup of tea. God it is cold in here, thought Juliet. She had put her fleece on over her pyjamas and she still wasn't warm. I had better make a fire in a minute, she thought to herself.

How can he sleep? It was after 10am. She looked around at the boxes in the room. They had brought hardly anything. They had been in such a rush and so shocked.

She made a fire and lit it and at least it provided some warmth. Alex stirred a little, thank God he is finally awake she thought.

"Come here," he said, "get into bed with me, you must be cold." She did as he asked and snuggled up beside him. He put his arms around her and she began to feel warm. His hands started wandering underneath her top, and up to her breasts. He started gently fondling her breasts and started kissing the back of her neck.

How could he feel horny after what had happened yesterday? But she knew resistance was futile. She was under his spell and he was a master with her body and she was beginning to get aroused. He gently played with her nipples until they grew hard and tingled. She could feel his erection in the small of her back.

Sex was the last thing she wanted now and she hated herself for thinking of her own pleasure at a time like this but the more he kissed her the more she fell under his spell.

148

His hands moved down her back and he put them inside her pyjamas and gently stroked her bottom. This fanned the flames of her ardour and she wanted him to take her pyjamas off. He read her mind and pushed down her pyjama trousers. He was naked of course, he always slept naked and no matter how cold it was he was always hot. He gently parted her legs and explored her wetness with his hands.

She was in a dream like state. How could he manage to do this to her? He was an exemplary lover. He knew just how to play her body. Which parts to touch and in what order, and he never rushed. He took his time and paid great care and attention to each movement and each touch. His fingers were light and featherlike. He grasped her breasts and buttocks firmly in turn. He was enjoying himself, she could tell. His face and his shallow breathing said more than any words could.

She had learned not to rush and with him there was no need, she wanted it to go on as long as it could, her arousal growing more the longer they continued. It was divine.

She was growing sexually she knew it and she was enjoying it immensely. She was casting off all inhibitions with Alex, nothing was dirty or wrong, she was discovering new pleasure, a pleasure that she had never known before. No man had ever made her orgasm. She could make herself come and had done so since she was young, but another man, no that had never happened.

When she was younger at University, she had seen a sex therapist. There was nothing wrong with her the therapist had declared. She suffered from anxiety a little, but that was all. She had taught Juliet how to do relaxation exercises but still no man had made her come.

Her mother had been a prude and had caught Juliet masturbating when she had been young. Juliet had not known what she was doing at the time, but she knew it was pleasurable. Her mother had been appalled and told her it was dirty. Juliet had felt ashamed, but it didn't stop her doing it when she was alone.

"I want to make you come," said Alex. "I know you find it difficult, but please let me try. We are quite alone here and there is no one to interrupt us, we don't even have a telephone," he laughed gently.

" Ok," she said, and surrendered herself to him. He tried but it became too much, she couldn't take anymore and she begged to be fucked.

He obliged and after when they lay together, she said "I am sorry Alex, it just becomes too much. It is really wonderful but then it becomes painful and I can't bear it" said Juliet.

"Well I am going to make you come, I want you to enjoy sex fully and I know that I can make you come. What about if I use my tongue? I am really good at that. My first girlfriend Janet made me do it all the time, and I soon became an expert. She is probably a top lawyer with a city firm and a Prada handbag now. She was such a cow, I am sure she is a lesbian she loved cunnilingus that much. She had me at it night and day," he laughed.

"Oh, you poor love," laughed Juliet. "I'll consider it, but I will have to bathe first. I want to be clean and we haven't had a shower since the day before yesterday, so not now as we have too much to do." She was nervous and she didn't really like anybody using their tongue on her clitoris, but for him she would give it a go. She really thought it was an issue of trust. She never trusted men enough to let them have absolute power over her and

150

giving them the mastery of her pleasure signified that power to Juliet. But now she realised that she loved Alex so much. He had rescued her from her marriage when no one else had and he had come back for her after all those years. She wanted to give him that power, so she would let him try.

They got up and got dressed and tried to make sense of the boxes, at least they managed to unpack the kitchen, and Juliet cooked lentil Dahl. It wasn't wonderful but it was a one pot meal, and it was warming.

There was a frost outside and it had not thawed all day, and it was still bitterly cold. Juliet put on a woolly hat as she cooked in the kitchen. How was she going to adapt to this cold? She really didn't like being cold at all, and that bed, it really was inadequate but then she thought of Alex and his love and suddenly she didn't mind, she was feeling a little more hopeful. She knew this was a bit shit but things would get better, it was early days yet. "I am going to draft an email to Faith," said Alex "about what happened yesterday, she should be able to do something surely. I know nothing about family law but she is very good, she will help."

The heartache over Guy had not gone away but Juliet was a fighter, and she had to keep going and not give up. She would never give up.

The next day when they awoke Juliet was in turmoil again over Guy, about everything. She felt guilty about the sex she had enjoyed yesterday, and she was feeling more than irritated. The lack of cigarettes didn't help.

Alex was equally agitated and they were niggling each other. They had no money to buy any cigarettes either, they had used up the last of her salary on Saturday, and with all the stress now really wasn't a good time to give up smoking.

Alex made fun of her "I think someone needs a cigarette," he said laughing.

Juliet flipped "how can you be so silly at a time like this? Everything is a mess and I am heartbroken without Guy."

Alex looked at her "calm down, perhaps sex would help."

This did not calm Juliet down at all, and she shouted "is that all you bloody think about?"

"Mostly," he replied laughing again. Juliet's temper rose swiftly and without thinking she threw her mug of tea over him. Thankfully, the cottage was so cold the tea was not hot. As soon as she had thrown the tea she realised how silly she was being.

"I'm sorry Alex, I don't know what came over me," she said. At least Alex had stopped laughing

"I've never had a cup of tea thrown over me before," he said.

"Really," said Juliet, "I am surprised, you are such a shit at times," and they both started laughing.

Alex started to mop himself off with a tea towel "Juliet, I was serious about the sex. If you had an orgasm you would be much more chilled."

Juliet sighed "Yes, I know Alex, and I appreciate it very much that you want to give me one but now is really not the time. I have to sort out some of this shit, so I am going to walk to the phone box and phone my Mom, we need help."

Alex wasn't happy about this, as he didn't know what she could do but he knew Juliet had to try so he just said: "ok, I will come with you, there is no footpath and that stretch of road is treacherous."

He waited outside the phone box while she phoned her Mom. She had to reverse the charges as it was a card only payphone. Alex had said that phone boxes in rural areas in Wales were repeatedly robbed so they had moved a lot over to card payment. Neither of them had a penny. They would have to sign on but that didn't solve their immediate problem.

She came out of the phone box after talking to her mom. "Mom is going to put £200 in my bank account, so we have to walk to Llanidloes and the money should be in my account by then. We can have some lunch, and then I am going to get the bus to Newtown and get the train to Wolverhampton. I shall stay at moms tonight, and tomorrow I shall hire a smaller van and go to Oxford and try and get Guy. I shall tell Mark I have come for the rest of my stuff and when he is not looking, I shall take Guy. I shall try and get Alistair to come as well."

After lunch at a café in Llani they waited at the bus stop for the bus. It had been a three-mile walk and it had tried to snow on the way. It was a walk that they would do many times over the next few months. They got on the bus sat down and held hands "Be careful Juliet, and phone me tonight please," said Alex.

"I shall miss you," said Juliet and then Alex got off the bus and went back to the cottage.

She got to her mother's around 5 o'clock. It was lovely to see her parents again and their house was lovely and warm. She talked to her Mom after dinner. She was sympathetic and understood why Juliet had left Mark, and she seemed to know how much she loved Alex.

"Do you remember I said I had that pain a couple of weeks ago Juliet?" said her mom "Yes, I do mom, have you been to the doctors about it?" Her mom looked worried, "yes, I did and they want me to see a consultant, they think it may be cancer."

Oh god no, not her mom, not cancer, this was awful, everything was going bad. "Oh no Mom, well it may not be cancer, right?"

Her mom looked at her "well that is always a possibility. I am trying not to get down about it until I see the consultant."

Juliet hugged her Mom. She didn't want to lose her. All the years that she had missed out on seeing her Mom as often as she had liked because of Mark. And now she might lose her. This was just another blow. But she hadn't seen the consultant yet, there was no point worrying about it at the moment and she had something to do tomorrow, something that gave her hope.

She showered and phoned Alex. She thought about him in the cottage alone, in the cold and she wanted him here but she knew that what she had to do tomorrow, she had to do without him. She was going to take her eldest daughter Katie. Katie was going to take her car and would bring Guy back to her mother's and she would then take Guy to the cottage in the van. That was the plan, whether it would work was a different matter but she had to try, she had to give it a go.

Chapter 17 – Fool's Errand

She was on her way to Oxford in convoy with Katie. She had managed to rent a transit van, and it was much easier to drive than that awful large van she had hired on Friday. Her mom had taken her shopping first thing and bought her a new phone. She had left the other one in the hire van in Welshpool and she was cut off without it. It would be three weeks before the landline was connected the cottage was so remote and the mobile signal was weak because of the surrounding hills but she would need a phone today.

What she was really annoyed about was that the phone she had left in the van had all the contact numbers in it and it had over ten pounds of credit on it which would have been really useful. God knows how long it would be before they got any benefits and it was three weeks until she would get her final pay from work.

They arrived in Oxford and parked up in the street. They had discussed it earlier and Katie was going to wait in her car. It would be easier to make a quick get away with Guy if she did so.

Juliet opened the front door as she still had her key and Mark soon appeared in the hallway. He looked rough and the house was a mess. He immediately got angry when he saw her "what are you doing here?" he said.

"I have come to get some of my things I left on Saturday but first, I want to see Guy." Guy had heard her voice and he came running towards her shouting

"Mommy." She went towards him but Mark held him back. They were in the hallway and Juliet knew she had to act fast.

"Please let me hold him," she pleaded and Guy was struggling in his father's arms to get to his mom. She went to reach out to Guy and Mark pushed her back against the wall.

"You are not having my Pup," he shouted. Guy screamed. What kind of deranged person was he? Thought Juliet, he really was not in his right mind, how could he do this to her.

Mark took Guy into the kitchen. "Get your things and piss off," he shouted to her. She started to get her belongings to put in the van. She hadn't given up, she was just biding her time. She had only been doing this for ten minutes and the police arrived.

Two sodding panda cars! What the fuck! She thought. What the hell has he told them to get this level of response? She was busy packing the van and went back into the house to get some other stuff and a policeman followed her in.

"What are you doing?" he asked Juliet.

"I have come to get some of my belongings," she said.

"I want you to come outside with me," he said.

What the hell was going on? She had done nothing wrong but she didn't want to antagonise him so she did as she was asked. He then asked her to sit in the panda car with him. "I don't really want to if you don't mind," said Juliet, memories of being arrested before came flooding back into her mind. "Look I don't know what he has said to you," said Juliet, "but I don't know what all this is about. He is an alcoholic and I have repeatedly called the police over the last few weeks out to him and one of your colleagues assured me that I could take my son when I left, but on Saturday they wouldn't let me take him."

The policeman didn't seem a bit interested in what she was saying. "I need you to get your stuff as quickly as possible and get out of here."

She couldn't believe what she had just heard. Could he do that? Who was he to tell her she had to hurry up? "He just assaulted me in there," she said referring to Mark pushing her against the wall.

"Well if you want to press charges, you will have to come to the police station," the policeman said.

It was clear to Juliet that she didn't have a leg to stand on. Mark had been up to his old tricks and had been telling tales about her again. This was just ridiculous, it felt like bad dream, like one of those thrillers where the victim is the only person telling the truth but everyone around them thinks they are a murderer. Even if she did go to the police station and press charges what would happen? Nothing and she still wouldn't have Guy.

She went back and continued to get her stuff. All the while a policeman followed her around the house. He even questioned what she was taking. This really was taking the piss. Most of the stuff was hers. When Mark had first come to live with her all he had bought with him was his bloody records, his many boxes of slides and a shabby old bureau. "Have you finished yet?" said the policeman.

"No, I haven't" she replied, but she was feeling increasingly pressurised to do so. Why hadn't her Dad come with her? He would have done something.

"This is the last box," Juliet said to the policeman. "I would like to see Guy before I go," and she went towards the lounge where he was with Mark and two other policemen. Two bloody policemen, this was outrageous. Mark must have said some seriously bad shit about her for this level of security. She went to pick up Guy.

"Don't do that, you can't touch him," said one of the police officers.

God, this really was the next level. She looked at the policeman in disbelief "why ever not?" she said.

"Never mind why not," said the policeman "just say goodbye." She couldn't believe what was happening but Juliet said goodbye to Guy who was now crying and walked out of the house.

She walked down the street to Katie who sat in her parked car. She hadn't the foggiest idea of what was going on. "Come on, we had better go back," she said to Katie "I will tell you all about it when we get home."

All the way back to her mothers' house, Juliet was trying to make sense of it all but the more she thought about it, the more it didn't make any sense. What had happened on Saturday, and now this. The police and their attitude towards her. Why had there been two lots of police cars?

The only explanation was that Mark had been telling lies to everyone about her. He had been going out a lot with his flight bag over the last few weeks but she suspected that he used that to keep his secret stash of booze in, for drinking on the bus. How could they all be so blind to him she thought, he smelt of booze all of the time? She kept coming back to the same conclusion. He must have been telling lies about her, seriously nasty lies.

158

She didn't stay at her Mom's for very long. She wanted to get back to Alex. She told her family what had happened and left, there was nothing they could do to help her but at least her mother had given her an old sofa and another £100, which was a big help.

She needed to get a move on, as she would have to drive the winding roads of Wales in the dark and she didn't fancy that one bit. She stopped to put fuel in the van and phoned Alex "I am on my way back now" she said, "I should be with you around 8 o'clock."

It was not a nice journey and she decided to take the direct route and go over Clows Top. It had been a sunny March day and as she got to the top of Clee Hill the sun was setting. She felt that she was not making much progress at all and was beginning to wish she had taken the motorway to Shrewsbury but it was pointless turning back now. She just had to keep pushing on so she drove a little faster. She was coming down the other side of Clee Hill and it was now dusk when suddenly something flew straight out in front of her. She could just make out that it was an Owl before she heard a thud as it hit the top of the van. She felt very sad and hoped it was alright but it was an almighty thud and she feared the worst and knew she had probably killed it. How awful to kill such a noble and wise bird. That was a bad omen she thought to herself and remembered Alex's owl tattoo and Athene the goddess of their star sign, Aries.

It was dark when she hit the road out of Newtown to Aberystwyth and there was quite a lot of traffic. She had to keep her wits about her as the cottages came up suddenly after a bend and she would have to indicate pretty quickly as the turn up the drive was quite a sharp one. It was a very dark night and the stars weren't out and there was no moon.

She rounded the bend and saw a flashlight. As she got closer she realised it was Alex. He had come out with a flashlight to guide her home. Madman, she thought to herself. There was hardly any verge there and he could have been hit by a truck but she was truly glad he cared enough to do that for her.

"Come inside and have a see what I have done," said Alex. Juliet was amazed. He had emptied all of the boxes and he had moved their bed upstairs into the bedroom, the cottage looked a little homelier than it had done when she had left yesterday morning and he had made some soup for dinner. Soup was not really dinner food, thought Juliet but she was still grateful that he had made it, it was more than Mark had managed in all the years she had been with him.

The bedroom was a little more intimate than lying in the lounge by the fire. There were no curtains in the bedroom either but at least someone couldn't peep in without getting a ladder. Juliet had a pair of kitchen curtains that would be just the right size for that window and she could put some lining in them to add to the warmth.

She had remembered to get the winter weight feather duvet when she had returned to Oxford so they wouldn't be cold and Alex had set up his portable gas fire. At least it wasn't Siberia temperatures anymore and she was surprised by how cosy it seemed. They had put the feather mattress topper on the top of the thin camp bed mattress and it certainly was an improvement on the first couple of nights they were there.

"Alex, you have done wonders while I have been away," she said, as she put her arms around him and kissed him.

"I am glad you like it," he said "I have missed you. Why don't you have a shower and come to bed, I seem to remember that you said I could try to make you come, and I really want to try." A little shiver ran up her spine and her stomach lurched. She had said she would consider it and yes she did want to let him try. She was going to do her very best to try and let go and surrender herself to his control but so much had happened today that sex was the furthest thing from her mind.

She showered and the water warmed her but as soon as she turned off the water it was freezing, she ran quickly to the warmth of the bedroom and the gas fire. Alex was already in bed.

"Come and get into bed and I will dry you," he said, and she did as he commanded. He dried her tenderly and warmed her with his body and kissed her again and again, murmuring how lovely she was. He stroked her hair and his hands moved down her back. "I want you to be completely relaxed," he said, "so I want you to do nothing to me, just lie there and concentrate on relaxing and I want you to lie on your front."

She turned over, and lay face down with the duvet still on her to keep her warm and shut her eyes and did as he said and tried to relax. His fingers were playing lightly over her shoulders in small circular motions then moving up and down her back towards her buttocks. This was nothing new, he had done this many times before. It was pleasurable and she was enjoying it very much. It was calming and relaxing.

She wasn't anxious. He had done nothing but give her pleasure in bed over the past few weeks and he was always very careful and gentle with her body. He started to blow gently in her ear, and then he started gently

161

nibbling and playing with it with his tongue. It was very erotic and she was enjoying the sensation. He gently lifted her hair out of the way and started kissing the nape of her neck, and then licked and kissed it. All the while she lay perfectly still and surrendered herself to this pleasure.

His hands still moved gently up and down her back, as he moved across the top of her shoulders with his tongue and nipped lightly on the base of her neck where it met the shoulder. It was just the right blend of soft and hard, soft gentle kisses and tongue flicks and a little nip with the teeth.   She was getting really turned on but she lay still and kept her eyes shut, just concentrating on the pleasure she was receiving.

His tongue and his lips moved down her spine to the top of the crack of her arse. It was getting really sexy and she could feel her vagina throbbing in anticipation, but she took a deep breath and just lay still. He licked the buttocks of her arse, taking each buttock in turn and then took his finger and stroked the crack of her arse all the way from the top down to inside her thighs.

She thought he was going to touch her vagina but he didn't, he stopped before he got there. He was teasing her now but she had to keep very still. He traced the line along the crease where her arse met her legs with his tongue and she gently parted her legs for him and he stroked the inside of her thigh with his fingertips. She knew that he was moving his position and the anticipation was nearly unbearable. She wondered what he was going to do next and then she felt his tongue on the inside of her thighs gently, little circular motions as it moved nearer and nearer to her vagina.

He grasped her thighs with each hand and firmly parted her legs further, and continued licking the top of her inner thighs, and then finally he plunged his tongue into her wetness. "My god, you are dripping," he said in his deep sexy voice "turn onto your back" and as soon as she did so, he plunged his head between her legs and immediately found her clitoris with his tongue.

At first, she found it too ticklish and knew that there was no way she would come like this "Stop, Alex, please stop." He stopped what he was doing. "It is just too ticklish," she said.

"Ok, Juliet, but I am not going to stop, I want to make you come. Most women adore this and I am very, very good at it. I will try a different technique," and this time he used light little flicks that were barely perceptible and it was more bearable. She was longing to come but just when she seemed to be edging towards it, the moment was lost and the sensitivity would move and what he was doing was just no good anymore.

Her body was crying out to for release and she desperately wanted to come. "Why don't you come and lie next to me and try using your finger," she suggested "I need a little more pressure than you are applying with your tongue. "Ok," he said and he soon took her in his arms and his finger had found her clitoris.

"You are so fucking sexy," he whispered in her ear "tell me what you want me to do with my finger, direct me, because I really want to get you to come."

Oh god she thought, he really is a sex god. This was much better and she spread her legs wider so he could access her clitoris easier. She moved his finger gently with her hand to position it better on her clit and she could feel her wetness trickling down her buttocks, and her legs began to shake. She was going to blow soon, she could feel it.

First she thought she was and then he lost it again. This was all too much, her heart was pounding hard in her chest and her face felt flushed, she was so close to coming it was unbelievable but then it disappeared. She repositioned his finger again and they went through it all again, finally after the third time of nearly getting to the point of orgasm, she begged him to fuck her. "Please fuck me "she begged. "I can't take anymore."

He couldn't take anymore either, he was so turned on that he was rock hard and he had little beads of come on the tip of his penis. He didn't need to be asked twice and he fucked her hard and fast.

They lay quietly for a while and then Alex said: "I thought I had it then, I thought you were going to come."

Juliet exhaled "so did I, I was so close but I was on the edge for a while and then it would just go."

Alex looked at her and smiled "I am not going to give up," he said, "I am going to keep trying."

Juliet laughed, "Not tonight though please, I'm shattered."

Chapter 18 – Damaged goods

It was Wednesday and they still had the van for a day. "After we have unloaded the van, let's go and get some shopping and sign on at the Job Centre while we have transport, because I have to take it back tomorrow. I shall get a car at the end of the month when I get paid, as living in the middle of nowhere without a car is just hopeless."

"Good Idea," said Alex "and we will drop in on Faith, she hasn't replied to my email."

It was a cold crisp day but the sun was shining over the hills and down the valley where the road snaked its way towards Newtown. The daffodils were out in the hedgerows and the sheep were in the fields awaiting the arrival of their lambs and you had a feeling that spring was just around the corner. It certainly was different from Oxford but she was no stranger to change and indeed it was good to shake up the snow globe of life now and then and experience something different. It really was very picturesque here but the wind really blew down that valley. Juliet had already made a mental note of little things they needed when she got paid, and a washing line was one of them. That wind would dry washing a treat.

They did their shopping at Tesco and signed on at the job centre although they wouldn't hear anything for a while, and went into the solicitors to see if Faith was about. She hadn't got a client with her and came out to see Juliet and Alex. "You have to send me your statement for a divorce petition" she said to Juliet "I can't do anything until I file for divorce."

They told Faith all about what had happened on Saturday and she didn't offer any explanation as to why the police hadn't let her take Guy but all she did say was "you need to get the name of a school where Alistair will go and you need Alistair to come here soon. Without him you have no chance of getting Guy as the courts like to keep siblings together."

They left Faith's office and Juliet was not happy. "I am not happy with what she has said Alex. She didn't offer any explanation as to why the police behaved as they did, and she didn't appear to be very worried about it either. My son is left behind with an alcoholic and she didn't seem the slightest bit concerned. I know Mark is up to something."

Alex looked thoughtful, "I have to agree Juliet but she did say that she has written to his solicitor, although she hasn't yet received a reply and you must try and write up your divorce petition statement."

"And something else I am not happy with," replied Juliet "is Alistair. He said he would come with us but the fact is he wasn't there on Saturday morning and he wasn't there yesterday either seriously worries me. Although I spoke to him on the phone and he said he would come to the cottage soon. I suppose he is worried about leaving Guy alone with his Dad. That is the best way of looking at it."

"You had better apply some pressure on him to come here soon then," said Alex.

The next day she took the van back to the West Midlands and after a brief chat with her Mom she took her to the train station in Wolverhampton and she got the train back home. Alex met her at the station in Newtown, and they walked to Bill's for a cup of tea.

It was a cold day but it was dull, unlike yesterday when it had been sunny and cheerful. "Hello you two lovebirds," said Uncle Bill as he opened the door to them. He was such a sweet person and he made for intelligent conversation.

They went into the kitchen and admired Bill's latest handiwork, a beautifully sculptured backside of a young woman. "What do you think?" he said nodding towards the sculpture. Alex immediately ran his hands over the smooth wooden arse, caressing it as if it were Juliet's. Juliet blushed when she saw him do this and turned away so Bill wouldn't see her. "Very nice," said Alex and then laughed that deep sexy dirty laugh he did when he and Juliet were intimate together. He really was just sex on legs she thought and that wonderful massive cock of his was the best she had ever seen or experienced. She really loved him, and apart from the ache in her heart over Guy, she was ecstatically happy.

"Would you like some rabbit stew?" Bill asked Juliet. She had never eaten rabbit before and it had been weeks since she had eaten meat, but she was absolutely starving, she hadn't had any lunch and it was now 3pm.

She looked at Alex as she knew he had chosen not to eat meat on welfare grounds but he didn't mind her eating it although she had chosen not to for simplicity. It was simply not an economical use of resources or time to cook two separate meals. So she accepted Bill's offer and tucked into the rabbit stew.

Bill gave them a lift back to the cottage and he was playing Rodriguez Concerto Aranjuez, which Juliet instantly recognised. Alex was quite taken aback with her knowledge of classical music.

Alex had insecurities and he had experienced a difficult childhood. His mother had divorced his father when he was six. His father had been a serial womaniser and his mother had found out he had been cheating on her. There was him, an elder brother and a younger sister. Then his mother had met someone else but she was 28 and he was 18 and she fell head over heels in love with him. It was a lot to ask for an eighteen-year-old to take on three kids and he must have found it difficult.

Alex had told Juliet that he remembers being shut outside in the garden by his mother. He also said he had walked in on his Mom and stepdad having sex on more than one occasion. Whatever had happened, it was clear to Juliet that Alex had been starved of his mother's affection and his stepfather found it difficult to cope with three children that weren't his own.

Alex felt that his stepdad hated him and it was obvious that they had a difficult relationship. Then to add to the mix his mother had twins by his stepdad, which must have compounded the lack of attention Alex received from his mother. He told Juliet that they were always poor and they moved house a lot.

But Alex was bright and he flourished at secondary school under the guidance of a teacher who encouraged him. School was his salvation and he found joy in going to school escaping a miserable home life. Then one day he came home to find his mother on the phone shovelling pills down her mouth and crying. His stepfather had left her. He had been cheating on her with someone else and she was on the phone to the other woman. This must have had a profound effect on a sixteen-year-old but it didn't stop there. A few days later his grandmother came to the school, she took him to one side and spoke to him "you have to come home with me, she has had that Bastard back," was what she had said.

His stepdad had returned to his mother but on the one condition that Alex went and lived with his grandmother. He stayed with his grandmother until he went to University and of course his stepdad left his mother a few years later never to return.

Alex's first girlfriend Janet, (of the cunnilingus training fame) had made Alex go to counselling, saying he was excessively jealous but he had never completed his course of counselling. Alex knew he had issues with his mother and this had subsequently impacted on his relationships with women. He had never married or settled down despite having had many relationships with seemingly beautiful, well-educated professional women, and he had often pondered on this himself.

His previous relationship before Juliet had ended five years ago with Bernadette. He had lived with her for two years and his mother had liked her very much, although she differed somewhat from his usual choice of intelligent woman and hadn't been to University and had worked as a secretary. He had moved in with her after two weeks, presumably because he had nowhere else to go and he had then thought to himself "What the fuck am I doing here with her?" Alex had told Juliet this and despite not loving Bernadette, he had continued to live with her for two years.

Apparently Alex had felt bad about this afterward and that was why he had been celibate. He knew he was damaged and his behaviour and attitude towards women was not healthy. He had hurt Bernadette deeply.

There had been a couple of times over the last few weeks where Alex had displayed extreme jealousy but then Juliet knew that they had been through extreme circumstances. She hadn't envisaged Alex wanting a relationship with her when she had agreed to go to Paris otherwise she would have cleared her pitch before she had gone. No Juliet had expected to come back from Paris and never see him again and therefore she had a lot of loose ends lying about that needed tying up.

Mr. B had been a source of jealousy for Alex, probably because he had been generous with his money and Alex didn't have a job but of course, Alex needn't have worried. He absolutely blew Mr. B out of the water on every other front and in bed they were incomparable, the difference was that great.

Then there had been Mark, who had played games, nasty little games. First hacking into her account and reading her emails and then sending emails to Alex, then his little chats around the kitchen table which had been designed to put Alex off Juliet and indeed Mark had sowed the seeds of doubt in Alex's mind. Juliet had thought that giving up work and leaving Oxford would go some way to ease Alex's insecurities but only yesterday he had questioned why she had been annoyed about leaving her phone in the hire van. It was only because they hadn't yet got the landline connected and there was over £10 worth of credit on that phone but Alex had interpreted the root of her annoyance differently, he thought it was because of the telephone numbers she had on there.

Juliet did her best to convince Alex of her love and she understood why he was jealous. She absolutely adored him and knew that he was the only man for her. She had never, and would never, love anyone like she loved Alex.

170

She would do almost anything for him. But she had to admit to herself that his behaviour and extreme jealousy was unwarranted and bordered on the paranoid. It caused her a lot of anxiety and it was like walking on eggshells, as she never knew what would set him off or when his mood would change.

When they got back to the cottage Alex seemed to be in a mood. Juliet could just tell. His facial expression changed, and he radiated hostility towards her. "Do you have to flirt with Bill?"

Juliet couldn't believe what he was saying. "Flirt with Bill? What on earth do you mean Alex?" she replied.

"Don't come the innocent with me, Juliet, you know what I mean. All that 'Is that the Rodriguez Concerto Aranjuez Bill?' Flutter, flutter of your eyelashes."

Juliet was astounded by what she had just heard. "Alex, you are talking rubbish. Bill is a sweet old man and he is old enough to be my father."

Alex was clearly not convinced. "Bill is not a sweet old man Juliet, he sculpts nude women, young ones and you have clearly made an impression on him. What have you said to him when I have been out of the room? Offered to model for him, have you?"

Juliet felt shocked and sick at the same time. Where was all this coming from? She had not flirted with Bill, not knowingly and she was old enough to know when she was having an effect on a man.

"I have done no such thing Alex and you are being ridiculous." Her words did not seem to be having any effect on him, indeed his anger appeared to be growing.

171

"How can I believe you, Juliet? You have consistently lied to your husband, lied to Nigel Baker and you have probably lied to me, your morals are completely skewed Juliet. You shagged about behind your husband's back and you will probably shag about behind mine." She was stunned.

Nothing had happened and he was just completely going off at a tangent. "That was completely different Alex. I didn't love Mark and I didn't love Mr. B, you know that. My life was completely stuffed and as you have said, I suffered domestic abuse. How can you make a comparison like that?"

Juliet felt gutted he thought these things but Alex didn't seem to believe what she said. "How do I know you love me, Juliet? Perhaps you just needed me to get you out of your marriage, perhaps you are lying when you say you love me. After all, you must have said it to Mark and probably said it to Nigel. You are just a slag like Mark says."

Now he had gone too far and she was really very, very, angry. This was all bullshit and she couldn't contain her temper any longer. "How fucking dare, you," she shouted at him, standing up and projecting her voice with a force that was seriously impressive. "I have given up everything for you. I have left my job, my home, and my son behind. How much more fucking proof do you need of my love for you? If I had wanted Mr. B, I could have had him but I didn't love him. Twelve years I thought of you, through all the shit. I didn't ask you to live with me you invited yourself but I am here now with you, not with them. Doesn't that say anything to you?"

He was shocked, he had never seen her this angry before. He smiled a sexy smile at her "Wow, you are so sexy when you are angry, did you know that?" He said.

But now she was angry and he wasn't going to calm her down with that. "Do you want me to go back to my husband?" she said.

"No, I don't," he replied, "I want to fuck you, you are so damn sexy. Come here and get your knickers off." How could she resist him? She loved and adored him and he was just the best fuck she had ever had.

Chapter 19 – Doubts

They spent a lot of time in bed at the cottage. Well it was cold for a start and they didn't have any central heating. They didn't have a TV, no landline, so no internet, no jobs, and no money. There really was very little else to do. But most of all, they were madly and deeply in love with each other and they had wasted twelve years where they could have been together and they needed to make up for lost time.

They became very intimate with each other and Alex persevered on his quest to give Juliet an orgasm. She in turn, became master of his pleasure and she had relished discovering every little erogenous zone on his body in the devotion of her love for him.

Juliet had been shocked by Alex's jealousy but she understood how difficult it was for him to love her. Not only because of the issues surrounding her but he was damaged as well and he had actually opened his heart and loved her, and love her deeply he did. They adored each other with a passion. Juliet vowed to be very careful in the company of other men in the future, how she acted and what she said. She wanted to make him feel secure and for him to understand that she really did love him.

They did a lot of talking as well as having a lot of sex and Alex started asking a lot of questions about Nigel. At first it seemed innocent enough and Juliet didn't hesitate to answer his questions but then the questions started to get more probing and Juliet felt like she was being cross-examined by a top barrister. A lot of the questions were about the sex she had with Nigel. Questions he really shouldn't have asked Juliet. The trouble was that if she said nothing, Alex would take it that she had something to hide. He had obviously been very good at his job as he was relentless in his questioning. It got worse and he even accused her of lying. This caused friction between them and arguments. It was often late at night and she was tired. She couldn't understand why he had a fixation on Nigel. It was so frustrating, he didn't know Nigel and hadn't met him .If he had, he might have realised what an idiot he was. He was insecure, deeply insecure but he had no reason to be so. Juliet loved him more than anyone she had ever loved

The truth was Alex was having doubts about Juliet, partly fuelled by Mark. The seeds he had sown a few months ago had not only taken root and sprouted, they were growing at an alarming rate. Juliet was deeply distressed about Guy not being with her and she was haunted by that, and although she loved Alex and she was being taken on a sexual journey and was revelling in it, that in turn fuelled her guilt about Guy.

Alistair arrived with her daughters Charlotte and Katie on her birthday; Juliet's 44th birthday. Katie was 22 and Charlotte was 20 and they could both drive. Juliet had baked a cake for her birthday. It wasn't really for her but for her visitors. She expected them to be happy to see her but instead, they were hostile.

"What do you think of the cottage?" Juliet asked the girls. She could see from the sneering look on their faces that it met with their disapproval.

"It is so small," said Katie.

"You haven't got any curtains," said Charlotte.

Juliet was not expecting this from them. Why were they being so unkind and hostile? "Well," said Juliet, "it is a work in progress, we shall have it straightened out soon. Alex is decorating upstairs and is going to partition it to make a second bedroom."

They didn't seem impressed. What the hell was the matter with them? Thought Juliet, they know we have no money but things will be different when we get jobs.

Alistair sat there looking sullen. Alex had been upstairs when they had arrived and he had come downstairs to say hello but had gone back to his wallpaper stripping when he realised that they were in a hostile mood. Juliet was angry that he had left her alone with them. He ought to be there with her, fighting her corner.

"What about Guy?" said Charlotte.

"What do you mean?" said Juliet "you know I wanted him to come with me and I tried to get him again but I couldn't take him."

"Well it is just as well," said Charlotte, "because this place is awful." Juliet was fuming. This was not how she had brought them up, why were they being so snobbish?

"I have a solicitor," said Juliet "and she is applying for an interim residency order on my behalf but it all relies on Alistair staying here. The fact he didn't come with me on the morning I left has not helped but he is here now and that is all that matters."Alistair looked singularly unimpressed.

"Where is Alistair going to sleep?" asked Katie. "Well, he can sleep in the lounge for now, or he can have the bedroom and we can sleep in the lounge."

The girls said nothing for while leaving a hostile silence hanging in the air like a bad smell.

"Why did you leave Mark?" asked Charlotte. Juliet couldn't believe her ears. He wasn't the girls' father and he had been consistently unkind to them throughout their formative years. They knew he was mentally abusive towards her so why did they even say that?

"You know why I left him," Juliet screamed. "I wanted to see you both and it is my birthday but you have been nothing but horrible towards me and Alex. If you don't want to be here, then just go."

It was of no use, it was a bad situation and there was no redeeming it. They hadn't even wanted a piece of birthday cake and neither of them had bought a present, not so much as a bottle of wine. They left.

When they had gone, Alex consoled her. Juliet cried. "I don't know why they behaved like that Alex? It is as though everyone is turning against me. They hated him as much as I did."

All Alex could say was; "I don't know Juliet, perhaps it is me they don't like."Alistair was no comfort either, he just sat there trying to tune in the TV he had bought with him.

The girls had brought a birthday card with them from Juliet's Aunty Pat (her Mothers twin sister), and it was lying on the kitchen counter unopened. "Aren't you going to open the card?" Alex asked, so Juliet reluctantly picked it up and opened the envelope.

To her joy there was a crisp £10 note in there. "Why don't we walk to Llanidloes and get a bottle of wine?" said Alex, "I think you could do with a drink."

"Why bloody not," said Juliet.

It was no mean walk to Llanidloes, in fact it was a treacherous stretch but they had done it a few times before, over the last few weeks. First you had to traverse a narrow verge in the face of oncoming traffic and around a difficult bend, then you had to climb a five barred gate into a field to follow the narrow footpath next to the river, which twisted amongst tree stumps and was difficult to say the least. Then you encountered three more five bar gates. The next step was easier and you crossed a field but that could be marshy and muddy. Then for the next mile you had a wide grass verge although this had long uncut grass which was wet and arduous to travel. Finally when you hit the rugby club, there was a mile-long path that took you into Llani. All in all it was three miles and took an hour. The light was still good although it would be fading on the way back. It was the 21st of March, the first day of spring which should have bought hope, but there was none today. Juliet was in a foul mood, she hoped the walk would help her clear her head.

"I am so angry," she said as they walked. "Why were they being like that?"

Alex was quiet for a while. "I was angry too, that is why I stayed upstairs. I couldn't believe what I was hearing. They were not very nice to you and I know what you have been through, but they were awful, from now on I am going to dub them the two ugly sisters." Juliet laughed, as her daughters were far from ugly, they were quite beautiful but at least he knew how to make light of a situation. He knew what turmoil she was going through. She was on her own, apart from Alex. It was bleak.

They arrived at Llani and brought the cheapest bottle of red wine at the Spar they could. A bottle of house

Chilean red. They hadn't drunk wine for months. At least I will get pissed tonight and forget all my troubles Juliet thought.

The walk back was more arduous than the way there, they were battling the fading light and the last stretch on the narrow verge was in the dark but at least Alex had bought his torch.

Alistair had already made his bed in the lounge and Alex stoked up the wood burner. They chatted for a while and the red wine hit Juliet's head quicker than she imagined and they went up to bed. She soon fell into a deep sleep with Alex holding her tight.

She woke with a start. It was daylight. She looked at her watch, it was 7.40am and it was Monday, family allowance day and she had it paid into the joint account. She had to get to Llani to the cash point as soon as possible.

They had no money and no food in the house. How was she going to keep Alistair with no money? She needed to make sure that Mark was not going to get his hands on that. It would be at least 9 o'clock before he hit the cash point. It is him or me she thought, so she threw on her clothes and went downstairs.

Alistair was still asleep and the fire was dying in the wood burner so she threw some more coal on and left the house as quickly as she could.

She rounded the bend by the river café and looked at her watch, Fuck! It was after eight and it took an hour to walk to Lani. She wouldn't make it in time, he would beat her to the cash point. It couldn't happen, she would not let it happen. Think quick, she thought to herself.

There was a lorry driver just pulling out of the Riverside Café and he was indicating to go towards Llani so she flagged him down. There was no danger, she was over forty and could take care of herself. What was the worst that would happen? If he tried it on, she would scream like a banshee. She waved her arms frantically at the lorry driver.

He stopped and opened his cab door. Thank god she thought, he looked ok and was a lot older than her. "Are you heading past Llanidloes?" she asked.

"Yes," he replied.

"Could I have a lift there?" she asked. He hesitated and looked concerned. Juliet supposed that he thought she might make an allegation of rape or something. God, men really were getting wimpish these days, she thought to herself.

She made up some bullshit about having to be in Llani by 9am to get to the doctors and he swallowed it. Finally he said, "yes, climb aboard," So she did. In no time at all, they were on the outskirts of Llani. He dropped her at the roundabout that branched off towards the centre. It was 8.30 when she left the lorry and in ten minutes she was at the cash point.

Please let there be cash she thought to herself as she slid her card into the machine and sure enough there it was, £130. They had been surviving on crisis loans for the past three weeks and handouts from Uncle Bill and this was like manna from heaven. Today we shall eat, she thought to herself.

She walked all the way back after stopping at the Spar to buy bread and bacon and veggie sausages for Alex. It was 10am when she got back to Gilfach and

Alistair and Alex were still asleep. She stoked up the wood burner and the smell of sizzling bacon soon woke the sleeping men.

"We are off to Newtown on the bus today," she exclaimed. So that is what they did. Boy did they make that £130 cover some ground. It paid for bus fare, and a trip for food around Tesco's, they went to Jewson's and ordered some wood for Alex to partition the bedroom off. Alex had laughed to Juliet and said that Newtown's answer to Johnny Wilkinson was behind the counter. Although Juliet laughed as she had the hots for Johnny Wilkinson she knew that Alex was her sex idol.

They then went to Lidl for more food and caught the bus home. They very nearly couldn't carry all of the stuff they had bought. Although Alex and Juliet were burdened down, Alistair was still in a sulky mood and didn't offer to carry anything. Alex got off the bus early to order some coal and a bottle of gas from the coal merchants in Llandinam so they could be warm. When they got home Juliet cooked up a storm.

But still Alistair had a face like a wet fish. As if Juliet didn't have enough on her plate. Alex had scolded her about the family allowance. Although she had said that it was for Alistair (Mark had received last months), Alex still thought it was wrong. He was suffering from guilt too. Juliet was between a rock and a hard place. What was she to do? Everything was going wrong.

For the next three days, Alistair didn't want to do anything and he was permanently in a sulk. Finally on Friday, Juliet had had enough. Alex wasn't his usual self and Alistair was clearly not happy.

It was a lovely spring day. The first nice day of weather that they had had for months. Juliet asked Alistair to go into the orchard with her for a chat.

Juliet couldn't bear to see him unhappy, and she knew he was desperately unhappy. What was the point in her happiness if it made him or anybody else she loved unhappy? And with hand on heart, she chatted to him.

"Look, Alistair, I know you are unhappy and you don't want to be here. I know you are miles away from your friends and the thought of going to a different school for the last twelve months of senior school is not a good one. I also realise that life is a little bleak here at the moment and we don't have any money or jobs, so if you want to go back to your Dad in Oxford then I am letting you go."

Alistair's face changed in an instance. He wasn't expecting this from his mom. "But what about Guy?" he said to her "If I leave and go back to Dad it will seriously damage your chances of getting Guy."

She looked at him. She loved her children dearly, and Alistair was special to her. He had borne the brunt of his father's abuse to her over the years and he had told her to get out, something that was quite remarkable given his age at the time and the fact that it was his it father he was talking about. She knew that would be the case if he went back, that it would not help her get Guy but she couldn't make him unhappy, or risk further damage to him at this time in his life.

"I know that," said Juliet "and it is a chance I am going to have to take. It is far from ideal here but it is the best option I had, the only option so if you want to go, then you can. You can catch a bus and a train to Wolverhampton, and Katie can pick you up from there and take you back to your Dads. I will phone and let her know". He put his arms around his mother and gave her a big hug, "I love you mom," he said. "I love you too darling," Juliet said in return, as a solitary tear rolled down her cheek. What else could she do?

Chapter 20 –Car, bed, and internet

Yippee, the landline had been connected and they had internet. Juliet's final salary arrived and they bought a car for £545, an old BMW 540. It gave Juliet something to do. It was filthy, and had been kept in a barn and was covered in tar spots so she set about cleaning it up. It was theirs and a means of getting from A to B.

It was a lovely spring day and they had a washing line and bought a curtain pole for the bedroom. Juliet lined the curtains and they were soon hanging in place. Juliet had confessed to Alex that she was having trouble with her hip and he realised that the mattress on the floor that they used as a bed was far from satisfactory so he had won a bid on eBay for a metal framed bed with a barely used, pocket sprung mattress for the bargain sum of £64.00 and it was a king-size. Alex was far too tall to sleep in a double.

It was being delivered that night by a chap named Trafford, who was coming all the way from London. They speculated that he was probably a weed smoking Jamaican with a name like that and wondered whether he would be stopped on the border with Wales, as you never saw anyone exotic in Wales. Even they were viewed with suspicion by the Welsh as they were clearly not from Wales.

The bed arrived at 11pm that night. They had nearly given up on it and the late hour reinforced their hypothetical picture of Trafford. When he arrived, they were quite taken aback as he was very much white and middle class. Indeed he told them he was an "artist" and the name had been given to him because his father had been a staunch supporter of Manchester United.

The logistics of getting the bed up the tiny twisted stairs of the cottage, proved to be something of a challenge. The bed frame had to be completely disassembled, but even so the headpiece, foot piece and the six foot six lengths were tricky to negotiate up the stairs. The very heavy pocket sprung mattress was even more difficult but finally Alex and Trafford had managed to do it. Not without a lot of pushing and pulling. Trafford said his goodbyes and they started to re-assemble the bed frame. It was no easy task as it had sprung slats, but the bed was finally ready at 1am in the morning. It was absolute heaven compared to the little mattress they had been sleeping on before. Too exhausted for sex they both fell fast asleep.

Juliet woke in the morning. It was 10.30am! She hadn't slept that long in years, the combination of the bed and the curtains had worked their magic and she felt refreshed and full of the joys of spring. Well almost full of the joys of spring, there was always Guy haunting her in the background, which marred her total happiness.

She looked over at Alex who was still sleeping. It was usually a joy to wake up with him, but lately, he had been waking up and had immediately started questioning her about Nigel. It was becoming very tiresome and she was getting increasingly worried about what he would be like when he woke.

When he started on the topic of Mr. B, her stomach would lurch and dread would spread through her. It was awful, he was like a dog with a bone and wouldn't let go. "How can I trust you Juliet?" he would say.

Well how could she answer that? There was a certain amount of blind trust when you started a relationship, a presumption of trust that should be there until it was broken and she had done nothing to break the trust with him, but he was pushing her away.

She missed Guy like hell and was worried to death about him with Mark. She went and made Alex a coffee and came back upstairs and opened the curtains. Alex stirred. "Morning darling," she said to him. "The bed was lovely last night," she said, hoping to assuage any thoughts he had of talking about Mr. B.

"Yes, it was," he said, "but we will have to christen it today". Thank god he was in a good mood. They had been too tired to do anything else but sleep last night after they had finally put the bed together. "That sounds wonderful," she said.

It was true, she loved their lovemaking sessions and she was learning to trust him with her body. She had been close to having an orgasm several times but just stopped at the last minute. She knew it was her mind that was preventing her from reaching orgasm and she was determined to beat it.

"I need to phone Faith this morning. I haven't heard anything from her and it has been nearly a month since I gave her the statement for the divorce petition. It shouldn't be taking this long; I don't understand what the holdup is." She picked up the phone and spoke to Faith.

"Hello Faith, this is Juliet, I just wondered how things are going? As time is moving on, and I haven't heard anything yet."

Faith went quiet and then spoke "Juliet, we are still waiting on your legal aid application, I need proof that you are receiving benefits in order to submit your application,"

Juliet was not pleased. Why hadn't she let her know before? "I didn't know you needed one Faith, I haven't heard from you."

"I emailed you a couple of weeks ago Juliet and I left you a voicemail on your phone."

Well that explained it, the stupid woman, why did she email? They didn't have email until a couple of days ago and she knew that. Alex had used his phone to email Faith within the first few days of moving into the cottage. Of course, at that time he had credit on his phone but they had been so skint that he hadn't topped it up, as they had not deemed it necessary. This was further compounded by the fact that Juliet had left her phone in the hire van and had not told Faith her new number. Not that it would have made any difference, as they had no signal at the cottage. And in addition to that Juliet didn't have a computer. She hadn't accessed her emails on Alex's computer as she feared there might be an email from Mr. B. In that event, Alex would be sat next to her when she looked at them, and she certainly didn't want to enrage Alex further over Mr. B. "I will get onto it straight away" said Juliet to Faith.

Juliet looked at Alex and he looked at her. "What was that all about?" he said, so she told him.

"I am annoyed about it," said Juliet "it has just wasted a month and the longer Guy is with him the less my chances are."

187

Alex tried to be positive for her "we have to do it properly Juliet, they should get the legal aid certificate pretty quickly once you have taken in the benefits letter." They got dressed and went into Newtown and handed the letter in.

"I am not very impressed with Faith," Juliet said as they walked away from the office. "I don't think she really cares."Alex said nothing, but he squeezed her hand tighter as they walked to the car.

"I have just got to get something, I won't be long, I will meet you at the car," he said to Juliet, and he turned off into a side street. Juliet went back to the car and waited, wondering what he was up to. It hadn't been five minutes and Alex arrived back at the car and climbed into the passenger seat. "I have a present for you Juliet," he said "but I want you to close your eyes." Ooh thought Juliet, this is mysterious. He reached over and took her hand. What the hell was he going to do? "Keep your eyes closed," he said.

"This is a nice surprise and not a nasty one Alex?" She said. "Well, I hope you think it is nice," he said. "I want you to try and guess what this is?"

She had her gloves on. "Shall I take my glove off?" she asked.

"Not yet," he said. He took her hand over to his lap and placed it around a phallic object.

She laughed but kept her eyes tightly closed. What the hell was it? "Well, I know it is not your erect cock because it is not big enough" she laughed.

"Any ideas?" he said.

"A banana?" she said. It had a slight bend to it so it could be a banana.

"No," he said "let me take your glove off," and he did so.

It was cold to the touch and smooth but Juliet still had no idea what it was. "I have absolutely no idea," she said, "Can I open my eyes?"

"Ok then," he said. She opened her eyes and laughed when she glanced down at his crotch and saw what it was. "Black pudding," she said. "You remembered I like black pudding."

"Well, I know you don't have meat and you are looking a bit peaky lately so I thought you might like a shot of iron in your diet.Now let's go home and have some lunch, I want to take you to bed this afternoon and make you come."

They ate lunch quietly together. Juliet was full of nervous anticipation about the afternoon's lovemaking. "I want you to have a shower and wait for me in bed," Alex said, "I will wash up, have a shower and join you." It really was decadent thought Juliet, all this lovemaking in the daytime, but realistically what else was there to do when you had no TV, no money and no central heating? She felt marginally guilty but then remembered how many years she had endured a shit sex life and had worked all the time. Cut yourself some slack woman, she thought to herself and took herself off to the shower.

She lay in bed naked, luxuriating in the warmth of the electric blanket (birthday present from Alex – not romantic, but a life changer in these circumstances) and the deep, firm pocket sprung mattress. This mattress can definitely withstand a pounding thought Juliet and giggled to herself. They were certainly going to put it through its paces this afternoon.

Alex walked in the bedroom, stark bollock naked, fresh from the shower. What a wonderful sight Juliet thought, you couldn't get more perfect than that. He looked like Michael Angelo's David. The weeks of walking and working in the cottage had honed his body to perfection and his muscles were well defined. He was the perfect embodiment of masculinity and that magnificent cock of his just completed the picture. He was definitely better than Michael Angelo's David in that respect.

He climbed into bed next to Juliet and they started kissing, long, slow and sensually. When Alex kissed her, he transported her to another place. She lost herself in his embrace and his love and fully gave herself to the pleasure of it all. No thoughts entered her head when they were in bed together. All she could focus on was the hedonistic pleasure of his love and the sensations she was experiencing. He caressed her body with care and attention that only a devoted lover would do, taking time and dedication over her pleasure. She was equally careful with his pleasure too and the more she aroused him and his body responded to her touch, the more she was aroused. He adored fellatio and she loved to take his magnificent cock in her hand and in her mouth and feel it grow harder with each touch and lick. He massaged her back and buttocks and kissed and nibbled every part of her body, teasing and making her want him more until finally he put his hands very gently between her legs and found her clitoris.

He knew where to concentrate his finger, just how much pleasure to apply and where to apply it and today she was determined to come. She let him do what she knew would work and today she was going to let go, she was going to let him make her come. When it became too much, she told him to take his finger away from her clit and to circle the inner lips of her vagina gently with his finger then she commanded him to go back to her clit, only this time she commanded him to go faster and to press harder. She was almost overwhelmed with pleasure and when she thought she could take no more, she tried to relax and surrender herself to him.

She was right on the edge, and she knew she must stay fast and let him make her come. "Harder" she rasped "and don't move from there". She could feel his erection pressing into her thigh and he held her in his other arm and he did as she commanded. She was going to explode any time now she thought to herself and let herself love the feeling of being on the edge. Her legs were trembling wildly and he gripped the one next to him with his thigh to keep it still and then suddenly she felt herself rising to the peak It was so intense, she started a long low groan and then finally she burst and exploded with pleasure, shouting loud as she did so.

She gripped him tight and he kissed her hard and then climbed on top of her and thrust himself into her and the pleasure was intense again as he came. He stayed where he was for several seconds and kissed her tenderly, while his erection subsided, enjoying the sensation of being inside her.

"You are a sex god," she said. "You did what no one else has ever done and it was magnificent."

"You were wonderful," he said. "That was just about the sexiest thing I have ever experienced."

They lay together in each other's arms and drifted off to sleep only to be woken by the telephone ringing. Juliet jumped out of bed and ran to answer it. It was her mother.

"Juliet" she said, her voice sounded shaky.

"Oh, hello Mom," she replied.

"Juliet, I have something to tell you, I saw the consultant and he has said that I have stage three aggressive cancer." her mother just blurted it out.

What little was left of Juliet's world fell apart in an instant, she couldn't take it in but she knew what she had heard.

"Oh, no Mom." she said, "does that mean it is terminal?" she didn't dare ask but she knew she had to.

There was a pause and then her Mom said "yes".

A lump formed in Juliet's throat. "Oh Mom that is terrible, have they said how long?"

"They don't know, months, maybe longer with treatment," her mom replied.

"Oh, mom that is terrible," she repeated. "You must try and make the most of the time you have. Go on holiday, and spend time with Dad." Tears were welling up in her eyes, but she fought them back, she mustn't cry, she shouldn't cry, her mother needed her to be strong now.

"I don't want to go on holiday Juliet. I just want to stay at home." Her mother said.

"Well if there is anything I can do, then let me know Mom please?" Juliet said.

"Ok, bye for now then," said her mom.

Juliet just managed to get "Bye, love you," out before she put down the phone and the tears started to stream down her face.

She had sat on the bed when she had taken the phone call and Alex had been watching the drama unfold. "Moms got cancer, and its terminal," was all Juliet could manage to say before she started to sob heavily.

Alex scooped her up in his arms and held her tight, not saying a word, just letting her sob. After a considerable while he said, "do you want to go and see her?"

"No" she replied emphatically "we can't spare the money for petrol and she will need me later. She will be dead before Christmas."

She was distraught and she couldn't risk breaking down in front of her Mom. She needed to be strong before she went to see her. She knew her mother had always feared death by cancer and she would be having a hard time coping. The last thing she needed right now was Juliet blubbing at every turn.

"Let's go and dig the garden together," Juliet said "I need to take my mind off this for now," and they went outside and started to dig but for the rest of the day her thoughts never strayed from her mother and she kept crying. Inside she asked herself why? Why can I not have any happiness in life without it being taken away from me, first Guy and now her Mother? There is no God she thought, only you Juliet and you have to be strong, you are going to have to be very strong.

Chapter 21 –Alex's Birthday

It was April 15th, Alex's birthday. It was a lovely spring day and spring was noticeably a little later this year. Was it the Welsh climate? Or was it that it had been a harsh winter? Juliet wasn't sure which but finally the nights were getting lighter and the weather was getting milder. There were lambs in the fields surrounding the cottage and they bleated at the gate when Alex and Juliet went out to the car or to hang washing on the line and it certainly was a cheery sight. It had been nearly two weeks since Juliet had heard from her mom that she had cancer and she knew from her Aunty Pat that her mother was having treatment but right now she was focusing on her immediate world, her mother would need her later and she would be there for her then. Right now she needed to make Alex's birthday special.

It was a Tuesday and they received their benefits that day. It was always a struggle to make ends meet. Why the DWP thought it was cheaper for two to live than one Juliet didn't understand. Despite careful budgeting and the fact they didn't buy meat, the last few days of the fortnight were bleak and they limped along with whatever food they had left.

Juliet thought that vegetarianism was a stupid idea for a man as big as Alex. He always seemed hungry but Alex did not waiver in his convictions, saying that animal welfare was appalling in the meat industry. Juliet thought that people should learn to treat each other better first before turning their considerations towards animals.

Alex was still asleep and Juliet went into Llani to the cash point and to the spar to get some real coffee for Alex and a bottle of Tiptree's brown sauce. It wasn't cheap but it was the best, and she would make him fresh coffee for when he woke and then a full veggie breakfast. That was another thing she didn't understand, why were veggie sausages more money that real meat sausages? It didn't make sense. Someone somewhere was having a laugh at the expense of vegetarians.

She busied herself in the kitchen and made love tokens for Alex. Home-made chocolate éclairs filled with Chantilly cream and topped with real chocolate. She had laughingly named them love tokens and vowed she would never make them for anyone else. They were quite fiddly to make and time-consuming. She had bought him a book he wanted from Amazon and it had arrived the day before.

She heard the crunch of gravel on the drive behind the kitchen and looked out of the back door. It was Jean, Alex's mother in her little Ka. She was portly and negotiated the little winding path and steps in an ungainly fashion.

"Hello Juliet," said Jean.

"Hello Jean would you like a coffee?" said Juliet. "No thanks, I can't stop; I have just called to say Happy Birthday to Alex. Where is he?" Jean said.

"He is still in bed" replied Juliet.

"What, at this time of the morning?" It was a little after 10am, and Jean shot Juliet a disapproving look. "Well it is his birthday," said Juliet by way of an apology. Who did she think she was?

The old cow thought Juliet. Juliet wasn't going to nag Alex. She had heard stories from Alex about how domineering his mother was and how she had virtually driven the two husbands she had into the arms of other women. Why was it that people whose spouse had left them had not thought to themselves that it was something they had done to cause this behaviour? Why did they insist on blaming the other party for leaving and flying onto the arms of someone else? Happily married people do not commit adultery thought Juliet to herself.

"Why don't you go up Jean," Juliet said, laughing inwardly to herself. Jean would have difficulty climbing the narrow steep staircase and Alex would get the shock of his life when she entered the bedroom. She just hoped for his sake that he wasn't already awake and had his hand around his cock.

It hadn't gone long and she could hear them talking, or rather Jean, demanding to know why he was still in bed. What had it got to do with her? Thought Juliet. Shortly afterwards Jean came back downstairs.

"I need my windscreen washer fluid filling in the car and I wanted Alex to do it," she said.

What was wrong with the woman? Thought Juliet, she can drive so why doesn't she ever look under the bonnet?

"I will do it Jean," said Juliet and skipped up the path to the car with a large jug of water. Jean didn't even say thank you as she climbed into her car.

"That woman is something else," said Juliet under her breath as Jean pulled away.

She took Alex his coffee and kissed him "Happy Birthday Alex," she said. "Sorry about that, there was nothing I could do to stop her, I just hope you didn't have your hand on your cock," she laughed. He laughed too, although he had not seemed pleased about his mother invading his sleep.

"No, I am saving myself for you," he said, "there is something I want for my birthday, I want you." And with that, he took her hand and pulled her towards him and down onto the bed taking her in his arms and kissing her fully on the lips. Since he had learned how to make Juliet come, he had been tireless in his pursuit of her sexual fulfilment and their sex life took on a new dimension. And he could have her virtually when he wanted her because he gave her so much pleasure, she was powerless to resist.

They had applied for jobs and Juliet had been to two interviews, but no job offer so far. It was discouraging to say the least but they didn't give up trying.

Juliet had still not received her legal aid certificate and just thought it was taking a long time. She had phoned Mark several times to speak to Guy but he hadn't let her talk to him, saying it would be upsetting for Guy to hear her voice. She had been so annoyed about this but what could she do? She had a solicitor, although she was as good as useless and Juliet's patience was wearing thin with her.

Alex had suggesting writing Mark a letter telling him why she had left him. He thought this would bring Mark "closure". Juliet had been sceptical but was willing to try anything and she had done as Alex suggested. Since they had moved into the cottage, Alex had received several texts from Mark. He didn't want to leave them alone, he was trying to undermine Alex and Juliet's relationship, and he was doing so in a very clever fashion.

This was fuelling Alex's obsession with Mr. B. Juliet knew that it was largely Marks doing. Mark wanted her back. He didn't care who she had slept with because he didn't love her. All he wanted was someone to look after him and provide for him. But it didn't help Juliet and the spectre of Nigel Baker would rear its ugly head more and more frequently. In moments of lucidness, Alex confessed to Juliet that he knew that he was subconsciously pushing her away. He was afraid of abandonment because of his mother's behaviour when he was young. By pushing Juliet away he was trying to control when she would leave him because he thought that was what she would ultimately do. Juliet felt helpless she could do no more to show him or convince him of the depth of her love, and it was wearing her down.

Alex suggested that it might help him to talk to his friends about Juliet, so Juliet agreed and he phoned a couple of friends. Juliet didn't want to listen in to these conversations, but the cottage was small and the walls were thin and there was no way of avoiding hearing what Alex said.

She was horrified at what she heard. He was actively painting a picture of someone who was a slut and who had no morals. She couldn't believe her ears. Talk about one-sided. Of course, what were his friends going to say about her when he only gave them the bad bits? He said nothing about what she had left behind, the sacrifices she had made and all that she did for him and how much they loved each other.

Well, they did love each other, didn't they? She loved him with all her heart but now, hearing what he said, how could he love her? They hadn't even met her; how could they form an unbiased opinion of her? It was just torture. She was being trashed and there was nothing she could do about it. How were they going to survive all this negative opinion?

He said nothing when he came off the phone. She felt physically sick, empty and hollow. He started to speak but she stopped him. "I heard everything," she said, "and, I can only imagine what they said. Why did you just tell them about the bad bits? What were you expecting them to say? They haven't even met me and you led them to form an opinion of me that was a bad one. Didn't you? You know exactly what you are doing Mr. Ellis, Senior Prosecutor. You must have been really good at your job. I wonder how many innocent people you have put behind bars." Her world was falling apart, why was he actively destroying their love?

"I didn't say anything that wasn't the truth," he said "you have lied and deceived a number of men and how am I to know you are not lying to me? In fact, I think you have lied to me. I can't believe a word you say anymore, Juliet. I think you are lying when you say you love me and I think you are faking when you orgasm"

This was not happening, was he mad? He couldn't possibly believe what he was saying but then he had just had positive reinforcement for his twisted beliefs from third parties. "You're not right in the head" she shouted at him. "I can't believe you are doing this, I gave up everything for you" she continued.

"Well go back to him then," he said. "He will have you back, that is what he wants and all your children will be happy because they clearly aren't now. Oh and you can pick up where you left off with Mr. B." She was utterly and totally horrified by what he was saying. He even seemed convinced by it himself but what could she do. If he didn't love her then there was absolutely no point in this whatsoever.

"Do you really want me to go?" she said quietly. Then he broke, "I don't know," he said, "I am so confused."

This was sheer madness. "You're confused! How do you think I feel? I have given up everything, my home, my job, my children and my mother is dying of cancer. But I know one thing I am not confused about. I know that I love you to the depths of my heart." He was quiet. "Let's go and get a bottle of wine and talk," he said, so they did.

They talked and talked for hours and finally fell asleep. Nothing had been resolved. He didn't seem to be able to control how he felt, and he didn't really understand how he felt. He had talked about all his previous relationships and to be honest, it appeared that he had acted similarly with those women too and in the end had killed his relationships with them. He painted them all as slags, who were going behind his back with other men but Juliet could see that this may not have been the case. In fact, he had confessed that he had been far from loyal in his relationships with them and they were probably driven to extremes in their actions by his behaviour.

She woke up and felt a sinking feeling in her heart as she looked at him lying there sleeping. When would this madness stop? She asked herself. Would he ever accept her love? But times were bad and they would get better and everything would be alright, she told herself. Just keep going.

Then something happened that she could have never predicted. He woke up and it was as if he had been possessed by a demon. His face had the look of pure evil on it." Get out," he shouted and then again. "Get the fuck out of here." He bellowed.

She was absolutely stunned, he was being really scary and she was frightened. She could say nothing.

She got up and started to dress hoping he would come to his senses, but he didn't "hurry up you whore," he shouted at her. Was he sleepwalking? He didn't appear to be. She was so shocked that she could say nothing and she wasn't even crying. She just picked up her bag and threw some stuff into it and all the while he followed her. Now she was really scared and he followed her downstairs. She picked up the keys to the car and he was standing naked in the doorway shouting at her to go as she walked up the path, all the while hoping he would come to his senses and calm down and call her back. George the neighbour had come out of his cottage after hearing the commotion and went up to her. She was opening the car door.

"Is everything okay Juliet?" he asked. His kindness broke the spell and she started to cry.

Alex shouted again, "she is a whore, I want nothing more to do with her, don't listen to her George, she is a lying cow." George looked over to Alex who was standing there naked, he looked ridiculous but terrifying. He was so angry he didn't seem to realise he was naked as the day he was born. Surely he wasn't in his right mind thought Juliet. Juliet turned to George "it's complicated" she said, and got into her car and drove away.

Chapter 22 –Demons

It took Juliet 15 miles before she stopped crying. She went to Tesco to buy a packet of cigarettes and put some petrol in the car. She had nowhere to go but she knew she couldn't go back, not just yet, if ever.

She couldn't go to her Mom's, that was out of the question. Her mother had enough problems of her own, namely dying, to listen to Juliet's woes and Juliet was not going to burden her with that.

As she had to pass Welshpool she decided to go and see if they had her phone at the van hire place. It had been nearly two months since she had used the van but it was on her way, so she might as well. On her way to where? There was only one place she could go, back to Oxford. She needed to see Guy if nothing else. She could think on the way.

They had her phone and she was relieved they didn't mention anything else, like the fact she had glanced a van on her way out of the street all those weeks ago. She drove on and just outside of Shrewsbury she needed a pee, so she stopped in a large lay by with toilets and a mobile café.

When she got back in the car she turned on her old phone. It still had power. She phoned Mark. "I am coming to see Guy," she said.

"What, left him, have you? Thought it wouldn't last," said Mark cynically down the phone.

She said nothing in response to that and just said: "I will be with you in a couple of hours." She desperately needed someone to talk to about Alex but she couldn't trust Mark, he was the enemy. No, she needed someone who understood all of the things that go on inside someone's head, someone who could be impartial. There was only one person she could think of, her old boss Ben. Ben had been a psychiatrist.

She looked at her other phone. Nothing from Alex. No text, no call. She was not surprised. He had been possessed by the devil that morning. How could someone who had been so loving, so caring and so protective, turn into an evil vicious monster like he had that morning? She shuddered at the thought. He was mentally ill that could be the only explanation.

She got to Oxford at midday. The house was a mess, but not as bad as she thought it might be. She had prepared herself for the recriminations she would receive from Mark but she was overjoyed to see Guy. He was distant at first and did not go to her.

Her heart broke in two, but what did she expect? He was only three and he had been left alone with his father. Children are fickle and love is a fragile thing. She engaged his attention by playing with him and talking to him. Alistair was at school.

It was a warm sunny day. It was only late April but it was so much warmer than Wales. She remembered fondly how she had loved the garden of that house in summer.

Mark did the usual moaning about her but in particular he moaned about what she had taken when she had left in March. "I don't have a fridge," he said.

203

"Yes, you do," said Juliet, "you have the one in the cellar that you used for your beer so it is no good moaning to me."

"But I have turned that off because I can't afford the electric," there was nothing you could say to Mark, he had a plaster for every sore. To be honest she was surprised he had not been evicted as she had given notice on the tenancy. He explained that he had gone to the council and although they were going to find him somewhere else to live, in the meantime they had agreed to pay the rent on the house they had lived in.

Well to say he was useless when she was with him, he had got his act together now. "And you took the kitchen table," he said to Juliet, as Guy drove his tractor around the kitchen.

"Well there is a dining table in the dining room you could use, or there is a dismantled one down in the cellar that Charlotte used as a dressing table," she said.

"Oh, I had forgotten about that one," said Mark.

"Let's get it up here then," said Juliet and in no time at all she had assembled the table. It was quite obvious that Mark was itching to know what she was doing there.

"What has gone one between you two?" Mark said, "Have you left him?"

She didn't know what to say and she was struggling to answer his question but before she said anything, he guessed, "He has kicked you out hasn't he?"

Bastard, thought Juliet why did he have to be right? Well Mark had played a game and now he thought he had won. She said nothing. "He has, hasn't he?" he added with a triumphant look on his face.

"Well, you have been playing a nasty little game, haven't you Mark?" she said. She hadn't admitted that Alex had kicked her out but she might as well, as the fact she didn't answer his question told him all he needed to know.

"What on earth do you mean Juliet?" Mark said. "I have done nothing." He really was a nasty little shit, he knew full well what he had done but was trying to play the innocent. "You know he is not right in the head," said Mark about Alex.

Well that was rich coming from him thought Juliet, but even so, at this moment in time, she privately had to agree with his statement. But she could see what he was trying to do. He was trying to get her on his side. She stayed silent and said nothing.

"You can't stay here," said Mark "it will jeopardise my benefits and my house. How long are you going to be here?" he asked.

"I have to see Ben," said Juliet, which was the truth, "and he can't see me until tomorrow as he is in London today. Could I stay here overnight? I would like to see Alistair." Mark looked irritated, he hadn't got her where he wanted her yet and she wasn't giving anything away.

"No, there is nowhere to sleep. You took the spare bed, remember,"

Juliet looked at him "Well, I could sleep on the pads from the sofa in the lounge," she replied.

"I am not letting you do that, you nearly ruined those pads you and that oaf sleeping in there." She blushed as she thought of the lovemaking they had enjoyed on those sofa pads but turned away so he could not see.

"Well, I will sleep on the floor then," she said. The sofa was past its best anyway, he was always an old woman about such things. She would put the pads on the floor when he had gone to bed, he would be none the wiser.

Alistair was pleased to see her and Guy was, when he had realised that she was not going to leave immediately. Mark followed her around continually and watched her like a hawk. He wouldn't leave her alone with Guy and this irritated her no end. What did he think she was going to do? Snatch Guy? And take him where? Alex had kicked her out and she hadn't had a message from him all day. She checked her phone when Mark was not in her presence and there were no messages and no missed calls. She just didn't understand what was going on in his head at all. She hoped Ben would make sense of it all tomorrow.

Things were extremely strained between Juliet and Mark but it was better when Alistair came back from school because at least Juliet didn't have to be alone with Mark and he stopped asking questions. The truth was she didn't know what the hell to do. She was really upset about Alex but there was nothing she could do about it, he had kicked her out, he didn't want her and you can't make someone love you if they don't. She felt so wretched about the whole thing, bruised and beaten. How could he take her love and trash it as he had?

Guy wanted Juliet to sleep next to him and Mark wouldn't let Guy do that. Guy was so distraught that Mark suggested she sleep in bed with them both. Guy was in the middle. What harm can it do thought Juliet? Mark is pissed anyway and Guy will be between us. Mark will be out cold and he won't bother me. So, they all got in bed and soon Mark was snoring his head off and Guy was sound asleep. Juliet had intended to go downstairs but she had stayed up late last night talking with Alex and it had been really draining and then there had been all the upset of this morning not to mention the three-hour drive. She was exhausted and must have dozed off.

She woke up with a start. It was dark and Mark had his hands in her knickers, groping her furiously. She was horrified. "Stop Mark," she said, but he leaned in on her and said, "shut up, don't wake Guy." She was in a bad place and she knew it. She didn't want to make a scene and wake Guy and she was emotionally vulnerable. She tried to push him away but he just forced himself on her.

It was over in seconds and she felt soiled, that was the only way she could describe it, soiled. Yes technically he was still her husband but she hated him and she hated herself for putting herself in a position where that had happened. Tears streamed down her face, as she lay in the dark thinking. It wouldn't have happened if Alex hadn't acted the way he had that morning.

The next morning she got up before everyone else and showered and put her clothes on and went downstairs. She checked her phone, still nothing from Alex. He must have meant what he said. What the hell was she going to do? Whatever happened she wanted a divorce from Mark. Last night was still vivid in her mind. Technically he had raped her, but what the hell could she do about it? There was no point going to the police she was still married to him, they would just laugh at her.

She couldn't stay here and she couldn't go to her mom's given her mom's condition. The council wouldn't house her, she knew that from twelve months earlier, because at that time she had a joint tenancy with Mark and now she had one with Alex.

That was it, the joint tenancy on Gilfach Cottage. She would have to go back to the cottage and she could sleep on the single bed downstairs and she and Alex could just share the house whilst she looked for a job in Oxford. Then when she had a job she could move out and find a room in a shared house. It wouldn't be easy but it was her only option. Secretly at the back of her mind she hoped that if the pressure of what she was going through was taken off Alex, then he might go back to being the Alex she knew, not some possessed monster. Ben would be able to advise, she thought.

She met Ben at 11am in the park. It was a lovely sunny day and very mild for late April. One of those gorgeous days when it feels like summer is not far away. It was so warm that Juliet picked out a linen pair of trousers and a linen blouse. She even put makeup on for the first time in ages. They sat on a bench and Juliet began to tell him all about Alex and their relationship and how he had acted lately.

Ben said that he could not really give an assessment of Alex without actually meeting him but he acknowledged that it did sound as though Alex had been "damaged mentally" at some point in his life, given the difficulties that Juliet was experiencing with him. He also acknowledged that as the relationship was not a straightforward one, Marks meddling games, the separation from Guy and Juliet's mom's illness would also not help with his mental issues.

Juliet walked away feeling as though he hadn't been much help although she had got it off her chest and it felt good to talk to someone about it, someone who was not a close member of the family or a friend who tried to give advice.

Mark was out with Guy when she got back to the house and it was peaceful, so she sat in the back garden. She looked at her phone and there was still nothing from Alex. I will stay here one more night and then go back to the cottage tomorrow, she thought to herself. I don't want to arrive late tonight as I have to explain to Alex what we are going to do, and I will have to get the single bed out of the garage and set it up in the lounge. I will try and get a job back in Oxford and then rent a room here and once I have done that I will leave him. But for today, she didn't want to have to meet his wrath again. It would be better if he had time to calm down and think about things.

It was early evening and Mark had gone to bed with Guy. Juliet was not making the same mistake twice and had gone to the spare room to sleep on the floor. She had told Alistair what had happened the night before and he said if his dad tried to go in the spare room tonight, she was to call for Alistair and he would intervene. She felt much safer. It was light outside and it was only seven o'clock, and suddenly, her phone rang out. It was Alex. Juliet's heart lurched into her mouth. What the hell was he going to say?

"Hello Juliet," he said, "When are you coming home?"

Juliet couldn't quite take it in. He was calm and quiet and talked as though nothing had happened yesterday. He didn't apologise or explain his behaviour the morning before.

"Well, if you remember correctly Alex, you kicked me out yesterday morning," She wasn't going to let him off that easily.

There was a pause "I miss you and this is your home," was all he said.

Her heart immediately melted and she wanted to rush to him, to be with him. "I miss you too," she said, and then added, "I will be home tomorrow."

"Why can't you come home tonight?" he said. Why did he have to do this? But there was no denying she had to ask herself the question.

Why was she waiting until tomorrow? "No reason," she said, "but we need to talk."

He then said, "We can talk tonight. Please come home, I miss you and want to see you."

Chapter 23 – Shit happens

Juliet drove like a bat out of hell. Back towards the cottage and Alex. No matter what demons he possessed she loved him and he quite obviously loved her. The bond between them was too strong to cut, they could only move forward and not go back. Whatever the future held, fate had already written it and she could only follow her heart.

Darkness fell quickly and it was a warm night, but that journey took forever at the best of times. She had set off quickly after they had spoken on the phone and had made good time. She was anxious to get home to Alex and she was driving quicker than she usually did. She was finally nearing her destination and she passed by Welshpool.

There wasn't much traffic on the roads but on the outskirts of Newtown, she was following another car and there was one behind her and she suddenly became aware that the car in the rear-view mirror had flashing blue lights.

Oh shit! She thought to herself, was I going too fast? But the car in front was travelling at the same speed as her. She pulled over when she could and sat in the car. A policeman approached her window, and she sent the window down.

"Turn off your engine," commanded the police officer. "Can I see your driver's licence?" She fumbled in her bag. "This car is coming up as not insured on the police computer, is that correct?"

Shit, shit, shit! Juliet thought to herself. Of course, it wasn't insured, she had completely forgotten to insure it. She had meant to, but then everything was so muddled these days, Guy, Mom, Alex. "I thought it was Officer," she said lying through her teeth, "the direct debit must have bounced," she said.

The police officer just said, "well it is coming up as uninsured and we will have to impound your car unless you can prove otherwise."

This was bad. Another layer of shit. Another thing to make Alex annoyed she thought to herself. "My partner will be really angry with me," Juliet said to the police officer, genuinely meaning it. "Can I phone him?" The police officer said it was ok, and Juliet phoned Alex and explained what was going on.

Alex was surprisingly calm and asked to speak to the police officer. After talking to Alex, the police officer handed the phone back to Juliet and she spoke to Alex. "Juliet, they are being dicks about it, I couldn't change their mind, they will have to impound your car." Juliet stepped out of the car. How the hell was she going to get home? She didn't have the money for a taxi, and there would be no buses running at this time of night.

"How, am I going to get home?" she pleaded to the police officer "I haven't got the money for a taxi," and she explained her situation. The policemen took pity on her and said they would give her a lift. They drove like maniacs along the winding road from Newtown to Llandinam.

Alex was at the back door of the cottage, as the police dropped her off. He was laughing when she came down the path. "Oh, Juliet why didn't you get insurance?"

Juliet was completely taken aback by this attitude. "I thought you would be mad," she said.

"No, I am not mad or angry, I am just glad you are back home. How did you get them to give you a lift?" he said.

"Well I told them I had no money and that you would probably kill me for having no insurance, so I think they wanted to make sure we were ok together," said Juliet.

Alex just laughed even harder but then his mood changed suddenly and he said: "I bet you probably offered to suck them off for a lift."

"No, I did not," said Juliet emphatically.

She was appalled. He really was sick and twisted. What had she come back to? She hated the sudden rages.

"Are you sure Juliet, because you get people to do things for you in return for sex," and then before she could reply he said "Did you fuck Hamilton?" he said.

Her heart lurched into her mouth but she knew he had been banging on about the truth for ages and so she told him. "Yes. But I didn't 'fuck him' as you put it. You sent me off and told me to fuck off and to get out of here. I was so distraught, I didn't know which way to turn," she said to him, and then she told him what had happened.

He didn't appear to be happy to be told the truth. That is the trouble with the truth, thought Juliet. You don't like it when you hear it, do you Alex? And, you were partly to blame for the situation, when you behaved so badly yesterday morning.

But she had not come back to be with him, she knew what she had to do. "I haven't come back to resume a relationship with you Alex. I have come back because I have no choice and I am going to get the single bed out of the garage in the morning and sleep downstairs from now on, tonight I am going to sleep on the sofa. I am going to look for a job and go back to Oxford."

Alex looked at her, he was totally shocked by this, and didn't know what to say, and then, he suddenly changed tack and softened "Do you want some tea?"

Juliet was confused by his sudden change of mood. But what was the harm in accepting his offer of a cup of tea? "Yes please," said Juliet. Alex made tea and softened again, "I can understand, why you did what you did Juliet, it wasn't your fault it was mine. I am sorry for yesterday, I don't know what came over me." Juliet wasn't entirely convinced but she went with Alex upstairs to retrieve some bedding from under the bed. Alex climbed into bed and she reached under the bed for the box containing the spare bedding.

"What are you doing Juliet?" he said and looked her in the eyes.

"I am getting some bedding to sleep on the sofa."She replied.

"Why do that, when you can sleep in a proper bed?"

Juliet was confused. "But why Alex? After what happened last night?"

He looked her in the eye and said "I want you Juliet that is why."

That was all it took. She was like a lamb to the slaughter and climbed into bed with him desperate for his love. Still abused and unable to free herself. Swapping one tyrant for another. But this time it was a different type of abuse. One where she was a slave to her own pleasure and his love. She was powerless, and she desperately wanted a 'fix' of his sex, the kind that utterly blew your mind.

In the morning Alex appeared calmer than the night before and he was back to normal. He examined the situation. "We have to get your car insured, and then get it out of the pound. Did they give you any paperwork last night?" he said. Juliet handed him the sheaf of papers she had been given by the police.

"Right we need around £180 to get your car back. I will get onto Norman, I should be able to get £100 out of him for the partitioning I have done upstairs. You bake some scones, you know he can't resist your scones with fresh cream and look like I have given you a hard time over this when he comes around, and say nothing."

"Ok" said Juliet, not sure what he was up to but she was just dazzled by his display of masterfulness in dealing with all of this.

"But," he added, "if I pull this off, you need to be taken in hand. I am going to fuck you up the arse."

A shiver went up Juliet's spine, she didn't want this. She never had. She had always steadfastly refused anal sex. He was too big in any case, and why? But she had no choice, she was now under his control, "ok," she said meekly.

Norman the landlord came around and he looked at Juliet's scones with a mixture of delight and dread. He loved the scones but knew that Alex and Juliet would be asking for money from him. They had got money for paint and other odds and ends before with scones and cream. Alex had remarked that they were the only tenants who invited their landlord around to ask for money from him, not the other way around. They had both found this rather amusing.

Norman could have been in his mid to late forties, they couldn't be sure, it was hard to tell his age. He had long hair, which he had highlighted and permed. Although it was thinning he wore a baseball cap to disguise the fact. They also suspected he paid regular visits to the sun beds as he was unusually brown for the time of year. When they had first met him Alex had said that he looked as though he had been on the road with Status Quo for the past twenty years. He was in fact a sheep farmer.

The scones and Alex's act worked. Or was it an act? Juliet wasn't sure. He had acted a little scene before Juliet and Norman where he said he was very angry with Juliet. She had responded by sitting shamefaced in the lounge, while Alex ranted to Norman about what a stupid cow she had been. Norman must have felt sorry for Juliet as he coughed up the £100 with no resistance. Juliet was very impressed with Alex's acting abilities but dreaded what was coming.

As soon as Norman had gone, Juliet was overcome with fear. "You had better go have a shower and clean yourself," said Alex.

She was scared out of her wits but knew she had to pay the price and did as he commanded, and climbed into the bed. Alex walked into the room. "What are you doing in bed?" he asked.

"I thought you wanted anal sex?" Juliet said. The fear was in her heart and he seemed angry.

"Get your clothes on, I don't want anal sex, I just thought you needed to be taught a lesson," he said. Juliet breathed a sigh of relief and didn't push it. But she was really, really angry for the cruel joke he had just played on her.

She went downstairs after she had dressed and composed herself, at least he hadn't carried out his threat. But what kind of sick and twisted idea was that? He knew she had never wanted anal sex.

"Well, we have got £100 towards your car, now we just have to find the rest," said Alex.

"I have been thinking," said Juliet. "I got us into this mess, I want to contribute. I have a lot of broken gold jewellery and jewellery that I don't need anymore that I am going to cash in."

"Are you sure?" Alex asked. "I am perfectly sure," she said and fetched her jewellery box. She made a little pile of odds and sods, and then finally added her wedding and engagement ring.

"Are you sure you want to part with those Juliet?" Alex asked. "Absolutely," she said.

They got the car insured, paid the fine and retrieved it from the pound. The weather was getting much warmer and they were at least relieved that it was not bitterly cold anymore. Juliet was concerned that she hadn't heard anything from Faith, but Alex said that as they were unemployed they could file her divorce petition without using Faith. When Alex spoke to Faith on the phone she was only too relieved to get this task off her to do list so they got the petition from Faith and registered it at Welshpool.

Juliet had been receiving texts from Mark, stupid ones referring to the incident the night she went back. They were obviously designed for Alex's benefit but

Juliet was quick and deleted the messages as soon as she received them. But there were times when a text came through and Alex heard it and demanded to see it. Juliet's heart would lurch into her mouth and he would insist that she handed the phone over and read the text first. Alex got so paranoid, that he went back through her phone looking for odd numbers and started to phone them. Juliet was angered by this as she had let Alistair use her phone and there were numbers on there that related to his eBay purchases. This was taking it to another level. She had to do something about it. The world she was in was closing in on her. She had no privacy. But what about his? He could tell people he knew all about the bad things in their relationship and she knew nothing about it. He didn't show her his emails. This was so unfair.

And of course Mark was being clever, forcing himself upon her when she had returned was another one of his little mind games, something he could use over her and he took full advantage of it, in the text messages. He knew that Alex would read them and he was making it appear as if it had been a consensual act. He really was a nasty little shit, he had done that on purpose and it was all designed to split her and Alex up.

Then the one evening when they were sitting outside the phone rang. When Juliet got to the phone it was Mark. He was drunk and ranting to Juliet. He was very clearly not happy that his little plan had not worked and he was being abusive about Alex. Juliet just put the phone down on him.

"What was that all about?" asked Alex.

"It was Mark," said Juliet "He was drunk and ranting on about you and me."

"If he phones again, I will answer it," said Alex, and sure enough, it hadn't gone long and the phone went again. Alex picked up the receiver "Mark, you are drunk in charge of a young child, this is not acceptable," and hung up. "Phone the police Juliet," said Alex.

It took ages to get through to someone on the phone in Oxford and she explained the situation. They said they would pay him a visit and get back to her. It was well over an hour before someone from the police phoned her back. Juliet was frantic with worry about Guy. "Mrs. Hamilton?" The police officer said.

How she hated that name, his name. When she was divorced she would change it by deed poll. "Yes," Juliet replied. "We have visited Mr. Hamilton and he was indeed drunk, so we have called social services, they will be in touch."

"Will Guy be removed from there, by them?" asked Juliet.

"I don't know," said the police officer, "it is for them to make an assessment, but we will stay here until Social Services get here. We will keep you informed."

"He hasn't changed at all," said Juliet to Alex. "He hasn't stopped drinking. He shouldn't be left alone with him. Why is my legal aid certificate taking so long?"

Alex looked concerned. "I thoroughly agree, Juliet, but you really didn't expect him to stop drinking, did you?" "No, I suppose not," she said, "It is Guy I am worried about."

"Well, we will wait and see what social services say," said Alex.

It wasn't until the next morning that Juliet received a phone call from the police. Juliet was anxious to hear what Social Services had said and done. "Well, Mrs.Hamilton," said the police officer. That bloody name again, it really did grate on her when someone called her that. "It took social services some time to arrive last night and when they did Mr. Hamilton had sobered up considerably, so they didn't remove Guy. However, they are going to keep an eye on Mr. Hamilton and Guy from now on."

Was that all? No wonder children died of abuse all the time, Social Services were really useless. "Thank you for letting me know," said Juliet to the police officer.

"I can't believe that," said Juliet to Alex and related what she had just heard. Alex agreed that Social Services were useless but they had done what they could.

"We will get on to Faith today about that legal aid certificate," said Alex. So Juliet phoned Faith. She still hadn't received the legal aid certificate and said it could take six weeks.

Juliet came off the phone and she was not pleased. "I can't believe that Faith is so incompetent, it is as though she doesn't care. She has just told me that the legal aid certificate could take six weeks. Why didn't she say that weeks ago when we took the letter in? That must have been four or five weeks ago. Then she said that she couldn't apply for an interim residency order until I had been to mediation with Mark. She could have told me that weeks ago and I could be doing mediation now, although he won't be co-operative. Is she looking this up as she goes along? Because time does not seem to be an issue with her."

Juliet was really angry, and Alex had to admit he couldn't understand why Faith appeared to be dragging her feet on this. "I am sorry Juliet, I thought she was a good solicitor but she is appearing less and less to be so."

Juliet phoned the mediation services and explained that she lived in Wales. The woman at the mediation centre was not helpful and Juliet had to explain that she could not afford to travel to Oxford just to meet with her obstructive husband, could they do it by telephone or Skype? The woman said that she would have to get back to her.

It was nearing the middle of May now and it had been nearly three months since Juliet had first visited Faith and she had left Mark at the beginning of March. The longer it went on the less chance she would have of obtaining a residency order in her favour. Not a woman who got down easily, Juliet had to admit to herself that she could feel herself sinking into depression. Alex was not himself and was spending more time in bed asleep than before. He wouldn't wake up until 10 or 11 am each day. Juliet had tried to occupy herself with gardening but she was tearful when alone and Alex couldn't see her cry. Everything got to her then.

That evening they were sitting outside talking to George as it was a warm evening. George was an amiable, if not a little inept bloke in his mid-fifties who looked like Friar Tuck and lived in the cottage next door. He was originally from Scotland, divorced several times over and had previously been in the RAF, although he was no pilot; that was clear enough. He was having problems at work and he was asking their advice, as he had just been subject to disciplinary action. It appeared that he and his boss didn't see eye to eye on most things and George was not shy in telling him this.

"I don't think we are really the best people to give you advice George, as we are both presently unemployed," said Alex and he laughed. Alex did have a dark sense of humour but Juliet liked this, as her humour was much the same. George was drowning his sorrows in a bottle of vodka, a little too much vodka. Then all of a sudden two police officers came around the side of the cottage to where they were sitting. Juliet's mind raced and she immediately thought of Guy with fear and dread. "Mrs. Hamilton?" the first police officer said. There it went again, that name.

"Yes" replied Juliet "What is the matter, is it my son?" she asked.

"We have had a complaint from Mr. Hamilton who says that you are being abused by your new boyfriend Alex Ellis. He is worried about you."

Juliet was fuming. The little shit was playing tit for tat. She kept a calm exterior, "Oh dear, my husband is up to his usual games Officer," she said, "do I look like I am abused to you?" and she then went on to explain what had happened. How she had left Mark, what had happened with Guy and social services the evening before and Marks alcoholism. It didn't take long for the police to realise that they had been sent on a wild goose chase and left.

Alex was really annoyed. "This has to stop Juliet. I have never been in trouble with the police in my life and they certainly have never paid me a visit, yet since January, I seem to have become on intimate terms with them." Juliet had to agree it was becoming ridiculous. They argued again that night.

"What happened when you went back there for him to be like this? What have you told him about me?" said Alex.

"Nothing", said Juliet "I have told you all about it. This is just in retaliation for us calling the police the other night when he was drunk and for getting Social Services involved.

Everything was getting to her. " I miss Guy so much," she blurted and started to cry "It was really awful there. The house was a mess. Mark had broken a glass on the garden path and he hadn't cleared it up properly. I am really worried about Guy."

Alex softened when he saw that she was upset. "It is just such a shame Juliet about what has happened. Whilst the law states one thing, it would appear that with residency and children, possession is 9/10ths of the law, as the old saying goes. Not to say that I advocate snatching him."

Juliet stopped crying. "Of course," she said, "I should just snatch him."

Alex looked worried. "You do realise Juliet, that if you do decide to take that course of action, the courts will take a dim view of it and it could go against you" said Alex.

"I realise that" said Juliet, "but I could say that I have done it because I am worried about him, especially after what happened the other night with the police."

"I am just warning you," said Alex.

"I know," she said." But I am quickly running out of options as Faith is doing nothing and I feel powerless."

Alex looked concerned but also caring. "I am only telling you what might be Juliet but I realise you miss him very much and I feel for you."

Juliet sat quietly for a few moments and then said, "He is moving house at the moment and he hasn't got his car insured because it has just expired, he told me when I visited weeks ago. I could offer to help him move and say I want to see Guy. Then, when he is busy and his back is turned, I could bundle Guy into the car. I know it is a long shot but I have not spent any time alone with Guy for months, and he has been obstructive, unhelpful and uncooperative towards any kind of conversations about Guy. And, Faith has done nothing. The longer it goes on, the less my chances get."

Alex lent across to Juliet and cupped his hand around her neck drawing her close to him and kissed her tenderly on the mouth. "I love you Juliet," he said. "I love you too Alex," she replied and they were lost in their powerful physical love for each other.

Chapter 24 – Guy

Juliet got up early and kissed Alex goodbye before she set off for Oxford. "Let me know as soon as you are on your way back," he said. "I shall probably go and see Bill."

It was a beautiful spring day in late May and the scenery was looking spectacular. May is always one of the best months, thought Juliet as she drove along. The greenery is so fresh and young. Well it was, the leaves had only just unfurled on the trees and they were resplendent in their vivid greens and the sun, although it had not been up that long was already shining brightly. It was low in the sky but it would soon climb higher. She listened to the Amy Winehouse CD that Alex had given her for Valentine's Day and thought of him, she was still glad that he had come back into her life, despite all of the problems. He had taken her on a journey of sexual discovery and of love and they were lovers in the real sense of the word.

It was a little after 10am when she arrived in Oxford. She had planned a little rouse for Mark. She knew he would be anxious and watching her although the last time he had been asleep when she had left. She hadn't taken Guy with her then mainly because she didn't have a car seat in the car for him. This time he might be more suspicious of her motives so she had taken an old handbag with nothing much in it that she was going to leave in the house. That way he wouldn't suspect anything when she went outside with Guy.

Mark was surprised to see her but he was grateful for an offer to move some stuff to the new house. That was just typical of Mark, as long as there was something in it for him he was ok. So Juliet put stuff of his in her car and took both him and Guy over to the new house.

"Why did you put the car seat in the back of your car Juliet?" he asked suspiciously. "Well I knew I was going to help you move some stuff and Guy needed to be secure so I just thought it would save time if I put my car seat in ready." Mark seemed happy enough with this answer and said no more. He was more concerned about his new house and the fact that he was waiting for someone to phone him back about arranging a van to move the rest of his stuff. It turned out that Social Services had done nothing but help them. They had bought them a new fridge and Guy was getting a new bed but no mention was made of Mark's drinking. In fact she was quite annoyed that social services had not contacted her to let her know what was going on. She had phoned them the day after the police had been called out to Mark and had made the young woman at Social Services aware of her existence and had asked to be kept informed but she had heard no more from her.

They arrived at the new house which wasn't far from the old one but it was on the other side of the ring road and the wrong side at that, next to a scruffy and notorious council estate. The house itself was ok. Juliet walked around the three-story townhouse built in the early '70s. It was nice enough. How lucky he had been, but then he had Guy and that was why the council was going to such extraordinary lengths to help him. Without the children he would have been out on his ear as a single male.

However she was here for a purpose, and she was getting very nervous. She was also aware that she should bide her time and get it right. One false slip and she could get it wrong and blow her chance completely. So she complimented him on the house. The stupid idiot actually thought she was being nice to him and he responded by talking about what he was going to put where, when they were to move in completely.

He relaxed a little and he was in and out of the house with boxes. The front door was open all of the time. The garage was on the ground floor and the front door opened straight into the hall and the stairs which went up to the first floor where the main living area was.

This is perfect thought Juliet. As Mark was in and out of the garage Guy was naturally drawn to outside as it was a lovely day. I only have to wait for him to go upstairs and then act very, very, quickly. It will take him a while to realise what is going on and by that time I will be away, she thought to herself.

Mark continued going in and out and then Guy followed him downstairs with Juliet trailing behind. Perfect thought Juliet, just be patient. Guy was on his toy tractor on the driveway and Mark tried to call him in when he took some more stuff up the stairs, but Juliet said, "It's ok Mark, I will watch him," she had made sure he saw her leave her bag upstairs in the kitchen. What he didn't realise was that there was nothing of importance in the bag. Juliet waited for him to get to the top of the stairs, and then she seized her chance. She ran to Guy and said quietly: "I want you to come for a ride in the car with mommy, ok." Guy nodded, and said "Ok." Within a matter of seconds she swept Guy up in her arms and had run to the car, opened the passenger door and sat him on the seat. She sped around to the driver's side, started up the car and pulled off the drive.

Her heart was beating wildly in her chest and the adrenalin was pumping. She knew he would call the police as soon as he found her car and Guy missing. Without a residency order they would take a while to react but even so, she would have very little time to get away.

She stopped about ¾ mile down the road and put Guy in his proper car seat. He wasn't disturbed at all but he did not really want to have to be strapped in his car seat when he had just sat in the front. Thankfully he didn't protest too much and she kissed him as she strapped him in. She then drove as fast as she could without speeding, keeping her eyes peeled for police cars, her heart still pounding in her chest.

She didn't take the motorway. No, she had realised that they would be caught very quickly doing that, with all of the cameras. She weaved the country roads and headed towards Cheltenham. There were so many routes that she could take from there, the police would not have the manpower to provide specific police for her they would use ones already out patrolling.

The further they got the safer she felt, especially in areas of the countryside. "I want a cuddle mommy, I want a cuddle," Guy said repeatedly just outside of Cheltenham.

Juliet's heart broke, he had missed her, just like she had missed him. "I want a cuddle too sweetheart, but I am driving at the moment. When we stop mommy will give you a big cuddle." Tears ran down her face but she was steely in her resolve to get him away.

She had turned her phone off when she had arrived at Oxford. If the police had rung it then they would be able to pinpoint her location which would make it a lot easier for them to intercept her. She wondered whether it would be safe to turn it back on again, she wanted to phone Alex and tell him she had made it. She stopped briefly in a lay by after she had bypassed Cheltenham and turned on her phone. There were two messages, one from Mark and one from the police. She was right about what he would do. She replied to Mark and said Guy was safe with her and then she phoned Alex to tell him she had made it. Today at least, they would be a family. Alex sounded happy too. Guy was asleep. She turned her phone off again things would be heating up soon and she had to be careful.

She felt really happy and was making good progress, even though she had gone via Hereford. She was now nearing her destination and had gone through some lovely Welsh scenery, all hills and pine trees and she hadn't seen any police. Then as she went over the brow of the hill and into Pen y Bont there was a police car sitting outside of the garage just before the mini roundabout. Perhaps they won't notice me she thought to herself, but when she passed them they pulled out behind her. When she turned right at the roundabout, they did the same. They are definitely after me, she thought, and sure enough the blue flashing lights came on, so she pulled over.

"Hello," said the police officer.

"I thought you would be after me when I saw you," said Juliet.

"Oh, right" said the policeman, "well it is a good job you didn't try to outrun us in this car because we would have never caught you," and then he laughed. "You are

Mrs. Hamilton I take it?" there was that bloody name again, she had to get rid of it as soon as she could.

"Yes," she replied. "We have had our colleagues from Oxford contact us and say that you have taken Guy without his father's permission," he said.

"Well, that is not strictly correct, Officer," she said. "Neither I, nor my husband have a residency order for Guy at the moment and I am just having him to stay. He is asleep now, but you can see for yourself that he is perfectly ok."

The officer looked in the back of the car and Guy woke up. "He is a handsome little chap," said the police officer.

"Yes, he is," said Juliet. "Are you going to say hello to the policeman Guy?" said Juliet and being a little boy, he gave a big smile and said "hello." I am not surprised he smiled thought Juliet, he has seen a lot of the police in the last few months.

The police officer seemed happy enough with this explanation and didn't want to get involved. "Are you going home?" the policeman asked, "to Gilfach cottage?"

"Yes," replied Juliet. "Well I will let you get on then Mrs. Hamilton, we know where to find you if we need you," he said.

"Thank you,officer," Juliet said and drove off. She turned her phone back on. She would be safe now, at least for the moment.

She knew Alex would be at Bill's so she stopped off there. Guy was glad to get out of the car and clung to his mother and they had a big cuddle as promised. It felt so good to hold him again, he had clearly missed her and they went into Bill's house. Alex had bought Guy a tractor, from a shop in the town and he was very pleased with it. He played with it while they sat and talked and Juliet told Alex and Bill what had happened. It was a lovely sunny day and they went back to the cottage, but stopped off on the way to get some food for dinner and some ice cream for Guy. He seemed content enough, and after dinner soon went to sleep soundly in the big bed.

"He seems happy enough," said Alex. "This was the problem. If we had been able to have Guy from the outset, I don't think I would have spent so much time focussing on other stuff like your past." Juliet knew exactly that this was what Mark had wanted, he wanted to split them up. It hadn't been about Guy, it had been about her. Mark didn't really want to look after Guy, he wanted to get Juliet to return to him, to pick up where she had left off and look after him. He didn't have Guy's best interests at heart because if he had then he wouldn't have deprived Juliet of seeing him. In the beginning Juliet had thought that they could have shared residency, she would have been generous about Guy seeing his father. It was a pity Mark didn't feel the same way but he was playing a game, she knew that, a game which she was determined he was not going to win.

Juliet had not thought what the next move would be but she did not predict what happened next. The next morning which was a Saturday, she got up when Guy awoke and she was downstairs drinking tea while he played with his toys (she had some that were on the van when she had left). It was only 8.30am and a man appeared at the window in the lounge. Juliet knew immediately that this was trouble. He knocked on the window and Juliet went over. "Open the door," he gestured to the front door.

Juliet knew better than to do what he asked. "No" she replied "what do you want?"

She looked at him through the window, still not knowing who he was and why he was there. He showed her some ID through the window and said, "I have come to serve some papers on you regarding Guy Hamilton." Mark had not wasted any time, had he? She thought to herself but she still didn't want to open the door, so she opened the window.

"He is an alcoholic," she said to the man referring to Mark.

"Well, I wouldn't worry love, Moms always get the kids," he said in a cynical tone as he handed her the papers through the window and then left. She could see he had parked a smart car on the grass verge opposite the cottage and she watched him get in and drive off but not before he had taken photos of the cottage.

She looked at the papers in her hand. Mark was applying for an interim residency order and she was ordered to attend court in Oxford on Monday at 10 o'clock. So soon. How could his solicitor manage to pull this off when she had got nowhere after months? She was beginning to feel very angry. The gods were playing with her fate and they were helping Mark yet again. It was all so unfair.

She went and woke Alex and showed him the papers. "They didn't waste any time," said Alex.

"No," replied Juliet.

"I will try and get hold of Faith, but it is the weekend and she will not be in her office," he said.

"This is all just stacked against us and so unfair," said Juliet. It soon became apparent throughout the morning that Faith wasn't going to get her email until Monday morning, although Alex tried her mobile phone repeatedly and left numerous messages. She was going to be no help with this at all. They would have to leave at 6am on Monday to get to Oxford for 10am. They had to go. The papers had said that if Juliet did not attend court, they would send the police to arrest her and she would be charged with contempt of court.

"We are going to have to put a statement together," said Alex. "I need to get some photos of the cottage and of you and Guy together for the court on Monday. I can do a witness statement on your behalf about his alcoholism but that is all we can do I'm afraid Juliet."

Alex worked tirelessly for the rest of the day, compiling the statement and the photos and he produced it professionally drawing on all his experience in court as a prosecutor. He gave it to Juliet to look at. He had done a good job and it was the best they had to work with but when Juliet looked at the photos her heart sank. The cottage looked shabby and she knew objectively that it would not compete with Mark's new house. She was going to lose Guy, she didn't stand a chance. Mark had obviously got a good solicitor who had anticipated Juliet's every possible move and had waited ready to pounce.

She was further saddened when she looked at the photos of herself. She looked gaunt. The only mirror they had in the cottage had been a little face mirror and Juliet had not really noticed how thin she had got. She looked dreadful. She knew she had lost weight but this was something else. However she could not let Alex know that they would lose, he was more upbeat than he had been in months. Just enjoy your time with Guy, Juliet thought to herself. At least you have forced a court case, there is nothing more you can do.

They had a lovely weekend together, walking in the fields and looking at the lambs who were now growing in size but they were still very cute and Guy delighted in them. Even Norman gave them all a ride in his monster truck which Guy just adored, but most of all he loved being with his mom. He had turned three in March but his speech was limited and he was still wearing nappies. So much for Mark's parenting skills thought Juliet. I would have had him potty trained by now.

On Sunday evening they still had not heard back from Faith. No surprise there thought Juliet, she was useless. She has been incompetent from the word go. Alex had got his suit ready and had cleaned his shoes. There was a very sombre mood in the air as they sat together in the late evening talking about the case. Alex was optimistic but Juliet wasn't although she said nothing of this to him, she just knew the clock was ticking and her fate was getting closer as she looked at Guy's angelic sleeping face with sadness and heartache.

Chapter 25 – Oxford County Court

Time moves on and the morning came all too soon. It was 5am when the alarm went off on Alex's phone. Juliet showered and dressed. Trying to look as respectable as she could, wearing trousers and a jacket. Trousers that she had not worn for a long time because they were so small, but they now fit comfortably, that was how thin she had got.

She made a packed lunch and bacon sandwiches for the journey. A flask of coffee, plenty of juice for Guy, fruit and some little custard brioches he was so fond of. Alex looked very handsome and business like in his suit, and they piled into the car at 6am sharp. There was no sun today and the sky was cloudy as they set off through the valley towards Newtown. Juliet had come to know this journey well. Every bend in the road, every cottage, every vista and this morning was no different but there was a dread in her heart which somewhat sullied the pleasure of the beautiful scenery.

They got to Oxford at 9.30 and had used the park and ride. The papers had said to take Guy to the CAFCASS offices but when they arrived, the women there knew nothing of it. What a shambles thought Juliet, so they had no choice but to take him with them to court. They walked into the waiting area. There were many people waiting there and she scanned the room as she stood at the desk giving her name to the clerk.

Then she spotted him. Mark. He was looking as rough as ever with his hair all over the place. It was thin and wispy and he was going very grey. His hair had no style of its own and just flew wildly about, surrounding that ruddy puffed face. He was wearing a tweed jacket and a bow tie. Who the hell did he think he was? Thought Juliet, but then she knew, he thought he was an Oxford Professor. That was the image he liked to portray. Little did people realise that he was just some lazy alcoholic sponging off benefits and taking handouts from anyone who would give them.

He looked angry when he saw Juliet and Alex, and rushed over to Guy, "Oh, my Pup," he said, "come and sit with Daddy."

But Guy didn't budge from his mother's side, and gripped her hand tighter. "He doesn't want to Mark," said Juliet.

"But he is MY PUP," he said, nearly shouting the words. He really was vile, Juliet thought to herself. Selfish, conceited, deluded and nasty and she shuddered at the thought of being in close proximity with him.

They sat down and Mark went over to two people who had just walked in. The one was a fat woman who had straggly greasy hair and looked about thirty-five, although it is difficult to tell someone's age when they are so obese. Juliet guessed that was his legal representative. She wasn't a solicitor as the papers had been drawn up by her and Juliet knew from them that she was a Legal Executive. Obviously a sharp one with no scruples to boot. The other person was a man about forty wearing a dark suit. He had dark, greying hair, a sallow complexion, very crooked teeth and he was obviously gay. Juliet couldn't understand what his role was in all of this, so she turned her attention back to Guy and Alex.

"I am going to go out for a walk," said Alex "I won't be able to come in to the judge's room and there is little I can add at the moment, I can't stand to look at Mark or be in the same room as him and I don't want to be antagonistic." Juliet understood and despite her calm exterior, she was going to pieces inside but she had to agree, there was little he could do at the moment. She sat there with Guy. There was a well-dressed man about 40 who was sat in the corner. He had a kind face and she guessed he was a solicitor as he had a pile of papers that he was working his way through. She had noticed that he had been watching her and Mark and their interactions.

Mark came back over and sat down next to Guy. "Glad you got rid of the oaf," he said to Juliet. He really was deluded. Did he think he was preferable to Alex in her eyes?

"Why is Guy still wearing nappies?" Juliet asked Mark. "I was in the process of potty training him months ago. He seems to have taken a step back." Mark was angered by this and the man in the corner was pretending to work on his papers but he was watching and listening intently..

Mark just ignored her question totally but was clearly irritated by the suggestion that he was failing in his parenting. "Why is Guy here? He was supposed to be at CAFCASS?" Mark said.

"They knew nothing about it," said Juliet "so much for your legal representative, they obviously had not informed CAFCASS." This annoyed Mark and she knew it.

"Where has oaf gone? Ran off already has he?" Juliet just ignored his comment and the man in the corner glanced over to Juliet and gave her a look of sympathy. "Oh Pup, Daddy has missed you, he has been all alone without his Pup to keep him company, naughty mommy took Pup away," Mark said.

Juliet thought the way he had just spoken to Guy was sickening. "Don't talk like that to him Mark, you are a grown man and you are supposed to look after him not the other way around. In any case you have not been alone, you have Alistair with you. I wouldn't have had to take Guy if you had allowed some form of contact or been reasonable." The man in the corner smiled to himself.

The legal executive who was representing Mark came over, "Mark can I have a word please?" and she ushered him off. Obviously he was getting loud, and in danger of making a scene. Despite the crowded nature of the waiting area he had been attracting a lot of attention. He looked and behaved as though he had already had a drink or a 'snifter' as he would call it. He really was a mess. How can anyone think he is more capable of being a custodial parent than me? Thought Juliet to herself, and this gave her heart.

The Clerk called them into the Judge's room. The judge, was a man of about 65, thin and tall and wore glasses. He was not wearing a wig or a robe as it was a family court. "Why is the child here?" The judge asked of everyone who was in the room.

"The papers said that CAFCASS would look after him," said Juliet, "but when we went there this morning, they knew nothing about it."

The judge looked irritated "Go and find Elizabeth Bennett," he said to the Clerk and then looked at Juliet kindly and reassuringly and said, "She is a very nice lady from CAFCASS, she will look after him." The clerk left the room, and soon returned with a very friendly, pleasant grey-haired lady of about 60, who spoke kindly to Guy, and persuaded him to go with her."

The judge looked at Juliet "Do you not have legal representation, Mrs Hamilton?"

Juliet looked back at him. "I do, but the papers were served on me on Saturday morning and I have not been able to contact her."

The Clerk intervened and spoke, "we have a fax from Mrs. Faith Worthington, Mrs. Hamilton's solicitor, it arrived half an hour ago asking for a postponement as she has only just found out about the court appointment."

The judge did not look impressed, indeed Juliet wasn't impressed either. Faith had not tried to phone either her or Alex that morning. Faith could have at least told them what she had intended to do. The judge looked annoyed, "this is most unsatisfactory," he said to himself, "I am not willing to proceed unless Mrs. Hamilton has legal representation."

The man who was part of Mark's entourage spoke up, "we must proceed, it is imperative for the safeguarding of the child, Guy Hamilton. Mrs. Hamilton took Guy from his father without consent and her living conditions are far from satisfactory and we are concerned about the character of her new partner, Mr. Ellis."

What the Fuck, thought Juliet and then it hit her, he must be a Barrister, he had that slimy look about him. How dare they make it sound as though she was living in some hovel with a junkie/criminal. She was fuming inside but she kept calm, this was not fair, she had no one to fight her corner.

The judge reflected a little, and then said "quite, quite," and then he turned to the Clerk "go and find Mr. Selwyn-Jones, he is here, is he not?"

The clerk replied, "yes, he is your honour." and turned and left the room. The judge looked at Mark and then at Juliet "I am going to adjourn this case until this afternoon, to allow time for Mrs. Hamilton to obtain legal representation." And with that, they all got up and left the room.

Five minutes later the Clerk approached Juliet with the man who had been sat in the corner earlier. He stepped forward and proffered a hand to shake "Hello Mrs. Hamilton, my name is William Selwyn-Jones and the judge has asked me to represent you, would you like to come over here where we can talk," he said, gesturing to a quiet corner near a vending machine. He had a kind manner about him and he immediately put Juliet at ease. Juliet told him all about what had happened. About her marriage and leaving Mark and all that had gone on. He was very sympathetic towards Juliet and said that he had witnessed the interaction between Juliet and Mark earlier. She knew it, She knew he had been listening.

"I have to tell you Mrs Hamilton that there is a current fashionable wave going around the family courts, of husbands claiming they are the primary caregiver and being granted residency of the children and awarded maintenance from their more successful wives. I do not hold out much chance of success of you getting a residence order made in your favour."

Juliet's heart sank and then he added, "but if we can prove that he has a problem with alcohol, then we might just be in with a chance. We shall go before the judge this

240

afternoon and I shall ask for an adjournment until Wednesday to allow us some time to prepare."

At least William had done more in a morning than Faith had done in the last few months and at least she had forced the issue. Something was moving forward, for good or for bad. Juliet sat with William and told him all that had happened and he wrote it all down. "There are tests we can perform Juliet," said William "hair strand tests that will prove that your husband has an alcohol problem. The only difficulty is that these are at present voluntary although if we ask and he declines that is as good as proving he has a problem." Juliet was pleased with this. Faith had never explored this with her or mentioned it and Juliet was beginning to think that Faith was out of her depth with her case.

Lunch was nearly over and Juliet sat waiting in the waiting area with all the other sad individuals who were due in court that afternoon. Guy was still with her and Mark came into the room and sat opposite her and pulled out a bus from a shopping bag. "Look what I have bought for my pup," he said to Guy. That was a cheap lousy trick, using a present to lure a small child. It made Juliet's stomach churn and he had been drinking. The deluded idiot had been in the pub. Well, I am glad he has enough money to waste on such fancies thought Juliet. But Mark wasn't finished at that. "No Oaf?" he commented on Alex's absence. "Couldn't take the heat?"

Juliet was enraged by this taunting but said nothing. Elizabeth Bennett was sitting with Juliet and was equally enraged and whispered to Juliet, "don't worry, I can see what he is doing I know what kind of a person he is and I know he is drunkard." Elizabeth really was a lovely woman. She may have been homely and grey-haired but she was shrewd enough to know what Mark was.

241

They were ushered into court. It was a large courtroom but there was no public gallery as this was the family court. It was too large a room really for the purpose but Juliet supposed it was to convey the seriousness of the occasion. Juliet and her solicitor sat on the right and Mark, his fat legal representative and Barrister sat on the left. Juliet then realised that Mark had a barrister because his legal executive did not have rights of audience.

The Judge soon appeared and he was about Marks age and wearing a bow tie. William did a good job of representing Juliet's case and Mark lost his temper and forgot his role when his incompetent Barrister was making a hash of it. The judge commented that if the Barrister didn't tell his client to be quiet, he would hold him in contempt of court. For a moment Juliet thought that she was in a favourable position but then it appeared that the Judge was not looking kindly on Juliet. He took a dim view of the fact that she had snatched Guy and although he adjourned the court until Wednesday to allow more time for the parties to prepare fully. He ordered that Juliet could only keep Guy if they went somewhere neutral.

There was much going back and forth between the legal representatives and William told Juliet that Mark was objecting to her taking Guy back to the cottage alone with Alex. They had to stop with a member of the family. Juliet explained her mother's terminal illness and that she couldn't go there, although the Judge didn't seem to think that this was a reasonable excuse. Why the hell couldn't they go back? Thought Juliet, she needed to get the papers that were evidence of Mark being sacked from his job. This was not going well.

In the end Juliet gave her promise to go to her Aunty Pat's, no one would be the wiser. She had nothing to lose, she needed to go back to the cottage and get evidence, evidence that she felt was vital. How were they going to find out she wasn't there? She would phone her mom and get Pats number to warn her, just in case she asked. William wanted Juliet to go back to the offices with him, to make a statement to one of his trainee solicitors. Mark was allowed to take Guy for a couple of hours on the provision that he bought him to William's offices at 5pm.

As they left the court to walk to William's offices. William turned to Juliet "I do sympathise with you Juliet, I can see what sort of a person he is and I knew he was drunk this afternoon. I personally think that small children are always best placed with their mother and you are obviously a good mother." Juliet was relieved at this, for once someone outside could see the situation for what it was. "He is playing games with Alex and me, he is calculating and manipulative," she said. William sighed, "alcoholics always are, and I knew he drank before you told me, you can tell by the broken veins on his face." He really was kind and he had such a gentlemanly demeanour about him.

Juliet spent all afternoon with the trainee, telling him everything. It was a little rushed and probably not as calculated as Mark's would be, but then he had been preparing for months and she had just been put on the spot.

William came into the room "Your husband is downstairs with Guy," he said. "Are you finished?"

"Nearly," said Juliet "I will be five minutes."

"Come to my office when you are ready, and I will come down with you." God, he really is a gentleman thought Juliet and when she had finished her statement she did as he had asked.

They went into reception together. Mark was clearly now very drunk and Guy rushed to his mother but Mark stayed put and did not move.

Juliet couldn't resist saying "You have been in the pub, haven't you?" Mark looked angry at this accusation.

"No, I have not," he slurred. But he still stayed put, hanging around like a stale fart in the room. Finally, he seemed to realise that he was not going to be left alone with Juliet as William stood firmly by Juliet's side.

"Give Daddy a kiss pup," said Mark, but Guy didn't want to leave Juliet and gripped her hand tightly.

"Don't force him," said Juliet "he is scared."

Mark couldn't contain himself, "you bitch," he spat, "Pup wants to be with me," he added.

"Well clearly he wants to be with his mother at this moment," said William "you had better leave," he said to Mark. Mark screwed his face in anger but knew he could do nothing and left.

Juliet turned to William, "thank you," she said, and she meant it, he was a knight in shining armour to her coming to her aid.

Chapter 26 - Court day two

They drove home to Wales, it had been a long day and they were exhausted, Guy quickly fell asleep in the car. "Will your Aunty Pat put us up?" said Alex.

"We are not going to Pat's," said Juliet "we are going home to the cottage. I need to get that letter from Marks former employer, the one where he is sacked for incompetence. It is the only bit of evidence I have."

"Juliet, you know if the court finds out that you have lied to them, it will blow your credibility out of the water," said Alex.

"I have no choice," said Juliet "I need that letter. I shall phone mom when we get home and get her to warn Pat." But when they got home and Juliet phoned her mom, it was too late. Mark had already phoned Pat and she had told him she knew nothing about it. What had gone on with her family? Thought Juliet, why did it appear that they were on his side? Still there was nothing they could do about it.

The next day they had two problems. First, they needed more money for petrol for the return trip to Oxford tomorrow and secondly, Juliet was determined to get her file from Faith, she had had enough of Faith and her incompetency and William had obtained an interim legal aid certificate to represent her in court on Wednesday.

"I will ask Bill to lend it to us," said Alex referring to the money for petrol.

"You can't do that," said Juliet, "he has already helped us enough and he has very little money himself. I shall just have to sell my gold necklace with the tiny diamonds."

"But, Juliet," said Alex "you love that necklace." It was true, she did love that necklace, but now it seemed to be insignificant against losing her son. After all, it was only an object, it was just a shame that they would melt it down and it would be lost forever. Still she sold it and although the necklace had cost £995 when new years ago it only raised £80 but that would be enough for petrol. Getting the file from Faith was not going to be so easy.

Alex phoned Faith and told her what had happened and he asked for Juliet's file. Juliet could tell from what he was saying that she didn't want to let it out of her possession but Alex had been one of them, a solicitor and he stood firm, "I suggest Faith, that you let Juliet have the file, that is unless you want to be reported to the Solicitors Regulatory Body for incompetency," he said down the phone. Gosh, he really was a force to be reckoned with when he wanted to be. So they went to Faiths offices and collected the file. When they had got back to the cottage, and looked at the file it was apparent that Faith really had not done a lot of work on Juliet's case. Juliet was angry, but there was no point in being angry, there was little she could do about it now.

They sat in bed with Guy asleep in between them in the afternoon and the phone rang, it was William. They exchanged pleasantries and then William said; "you should not have gone back to Wales Juliet. Mark found out and it will go against you."

Juliet sighed, "I know William, Alex said the same thing but I needed to get things from the cottage," she added.

"I understand your motives Juliet, we shall just have to wait and see if it is detrimental to us tomorrow. I have sent you the statement from Mark by email. Have a look at it please and let me know your thoughts."

She put the phone down and opened up her emails on Alex's computer. As she read what Mark had written she felt an iciness spread through her. He was going in for the kill. She was being slaughtered in his statement. He was really clever, he had made no mention of her infidelity and the things he had tortured Alex with were not included in his statement. There was nothing about Mr. B, or James Allen, or Andrew from Uni.

This surprised her. Why had he not included any of that? It didn't make sense, but did it? Of course he was not going to hint at any of this as it would look vindictive and it would be clear that they had a very unhappy marriage and that he wanted residency of Guy to get at Juliet, something the courts would see through at an instant.

No instead he was insidious. He directed his malice in a subtle way. He painted a picture of Alex as someone who was troubled mentally and he spoke about his fictitious treatment of Juliet and the hold he had over her. He suggested that Alex used Cannabis on a regular basis and that Juliet was using it too. He made hints at Alex's character being unsuitable and made it look as though he may not be the best person to be around children. He even hinted that he possibly had sexual tendencies towards children. Juliet was outraged, lies, all lies.

And all of a sudden, like the last piece of a jigsaw, it all clicked into place. Mark had been telling lies about Juliet and Alex to the police, Social Services and even her family. He must have told them that Alex was unhinged, and smoking weed and that Juliet was smoking it also and under his spell. That was why the police had not let her take Guy, why her parents had been cold towards her, why Social Services had been unhelpful, and why Pat had told him she was not staying there. He knew that she would accuse him of being the alcoholic he was and the only way to trump this was to say he thought they were using drugs and that Alex was of dubious sexual persuasions. She sat there numb staring at the words on the screen.

"Juliet," said Alex, "what is wrong, you look like you have just had the death sentence passed on you."

She turned to face him, "I have," she said. "Mark has told lies about us in there, hideous lies. We don't stand a chance tomorrow. It's all over."

Alex looked concerned "It can't be that bad surely?" But her face said everything. "Can I read it?" Alex asked.

Juliet handed him the computer "Be my guest," she said.

Alex started to read the statement and he was fuming, she could tell from his demeanour, as it had dramatically changed. "What have you told him?" he said, "this has all come from you, hasn't it? You have told him stuff about me and he has used it. You stupid girl, you have hung yourself."

She started to cry, why did he have to turn it on her?

"I haven't told him anything Alex, he has been clever, really clever. You sat and talked to him when we lived there. He has joined up the dots. He knew you used to smoke weed from all those years ago. You told him that you were concerned that you weren't getting anywhere with teaching applications because as you were 40 and had no children and had not been married people might think you are a paedophile. He has just used your fears. He has even said in the statement, that he saw empty wine bottles in the recycling bin when we were in Oxford and you know that is not true, we never touched wine whilst we were there, except for that one bottle when he went to visit his mother. It is just a pack of lies."

She could tell Alex was wounded by Mark's statement, deeply wounded. "I should never have got involved in all of this," he said.

That was fucking rich thought Juliet, anger beginning to grow inside her. "Oh, but you did Alex, you did get involved. What the hell did you think was going to happen? Did you think he would just roll over and let me leave? He needs me to survive and he is fighting for his survival right now. It is I who has been a fool, thinking you had the balls to do this. I thought you were a man Alex and I have listened to you and all that "be honest Juliet" shit. I should have listened to myself and been a bitch because now it is too late." They sat in silence and Juliet looked at Guy's sleeping face and her heart broke in two, and hot tears burned her cheeks. They barely passed a word between them that evening.

The next day they set out for Oxford early, like on Monday. This time Juliet had arranged for Guy to go to his nursery so they stopped there first, at least he would be safe there and it was familiar surroundings. Guy didn't want Juliet to leave and clung to her but although she didn't want to, she had to go. She crouched down and took him in her arms and hugged him, kissing his cheeks. Her heart was broken. She knew that she would not be picking him up later that day to take him home, she would not see him again for some time and it was killing her but she stifled back the tears. "Mommy loves you very much Guy," she said "always remember that Guy," and she got up and walked out of the room with cries of "mommy" ringing in her ears.

She was dreading the court appearance but she had to do it, she had to go through with it, whatever the outcome, however horrible it was going to be she just had to. Alex was quiet, he clearly didn't want to do this either. When they got to the court Juliet was dismayed to find that William wasn't there, just the trainee. He is a senior partner so I suppose he is just too expensive for legal aid thought Juliet but her heart sank further.

"We need to go and have a chat with your Barrister," said the trainee and Juliet went to follow him but Alex stood where he was. "You need to come too," the trainee said to Alex, and he followed albeit reluctantly.

They went into a small meeting room and sat down around the table. The Barrister was a pretty young woman who looked far too sweet to do this kind of thing, she couldn't have been any more than 30 at the most. "We need to clarify some things in Mr. Hamilton's statement," said the trainee to them both.

"It is all lies," said Juliet. "He has made it all up." referring to Mark.

"Yes, well I am sure a lot of it is," said the trainee.

The young female barrister took over "Alex," she said, looking at him "Do you smoke cannabis?"

Alex looked at her, he obviously thought she was attractive. Juliet could tell by the arrogant cocky look on his face. "Yes, I have smoked cannabis, it is better for you than alcohol, you must have smoked it?" Juliet couldn't believe what she had just heard. Why the fuck did he just admit that thought Juliet, was he a fool? And why did he have to justify it?

The young woman looked at him "What I have done is not at question here, it is you who are. But Cannabis is an illegal substance and the court will take a dim view of it I'm afraid."Alex was oblivious to what damage he was doing "I would never smoke it in front of a child," he added, as though it made it alright.

Was he mad? Thought Juliet, so she spoke, "I have never smoked cannabis and my husband knows that, he is just making up malicious stories to harm my character," said Juliet "but I can tell you that my husband has smoked it with some old university friends. When they visited us, they always smoked weed and my husband has smoked it with them."

The barrister did not seem bothered by what Juliet had said but that was not surprising, after what Alex had just admitted. He was clearly not going to be a good witness for her and he was her only witness. She was in the shit and she knew it. They touched on the rest of the statement but it was clear that what Alex had said about using Cannabis had left them in a very weak and vulnerable state. He could not be relied upon as a witness and Juliet got the sense of that. She was done for.

The trainee and the Barrister said nothing more to Juliet as they waited to go into court. They all sat there, the four of them waiting for doom and then they were called into court. Alex stayed in the waiting room as he was not allowed in.

It was as before, but this time, Juliet was at a disadvantage. William, the seasoned professional wasn't there and instead of Marks' greasy grey- haired incompetent Barrister, there was now a female Barrister. A woman in her early fifties, blonde and groomed, and she had the no-nonsense look of a mean bitch about her.

They all rose when the judge walked into the room behind his elevated position on the 'bench'. He was the same man as before and he wore a bow tie like Mark. He was about the same age, if not slightly older and like Mark he was a small wizened man. He did not look in a happy mood. Mark's Barrister went first as he was making the application. She went straight in for the kill and said that Juliet was unfit and that Alex was of dubious character. Juliet just sat there, dumbfounded. She wanted to shout out but she couldn't, she wasn't allowed. She was mortified at the character assassination that was playing out before her eyes. Her barrister, the young lovely was not even contesting any of this. Juliet was struck with horror and fear.

Then they produced the evidence of the process server, he was the man who had served papers on Juliet on Saturday. He was apparently a surveyor and his statement detailed the dilapidation of the cottage but he didn't represent the truth, he slated the cottage and basically portrayed a hovel. Juliet was horrified. He had obviously been paid to say these things. The nasty bastard. Why had he said to her; "Don't worry moms always get the kids." She could still remember the supercilious smile on his face as he handed her the papers. Juliet tugged at her Barrister's arm and whispered to her "the cottage is not like that, why don't you do something?" but her barrister said nothing and did not interject. She is not experienced enough, thought Juliet. And how come Mark had a change of Barrister?

Mark's barrister continued. "Mrs. Hamilton has displayed a lack of concern for her son and has only displayed concern for herself. Her sexual desires have been her paramount concern, and she has forsaken her son for them. "

Juliet wanted to scream she was so distraught. How could they portray her like this? Finally her barrister intervened. "Mrs. Hamilton had nowhere to turn, she was in an abusive marriage and she had no one else but Mr. Ellis. It had been an unhappy marriage. She had been trying to leave her husband for years but he had been mentally abusive to her. Mr. Ellis was her only way of getting out. My client is inconsolable at the loss of her son."

Finally, thought Juliet. But the judge had a different view. "Miss Parry, it is clear that your client, Mrs. Hamilton, has found solace in Powys and she has had a flagrant disregard for the law by snatching her son. As you know the courts have a dim view of this behaviour. And I do not believe that Mrs. Hamilton had no other choice but to bring her lover into the marital home. Why did she not employ the services of a solicitor to bring her marriage to an end? That would be what most people would do."

Juliet wanted to scream – 'I tried that but I was told it was not going to be easy and I didn't have the money to do so,' but she had to stay quiet. It was so frustrating. Why didn't her barrister say anything? It was clear she had been brought in at the eleventh hour and had not really understood her case. Juliet's barrister tried to intervene "but your honour, Mrs Hamilton was desperate and Mr. Hamilton was being uncooperative. He has his son sleep with him in bed." It was all going wrong; the judge had made his mind up.

He spoke, "Miss Parry, I see nothing wrong in a small child sharing a bed with his father especially given the fact his mother has left home with her younger lover. The child is clearly upset,"

To right he is upset, thought Juliet, he is upset at the loss of his mother, denied by his father. And what happened to the paedophile accusations against Alex? Doesn't the same rule apply to his father? It was all too much but Mark's barrister continued the onslaught. "I have statements here from other witnesses in support of my client's application, if your honour would permit me to approach the bench."

The judge looked interested all of a sudden. He must have wanted to wrap this up quickly. "Yes, yes, Ms. Greystone, bring them here," he replied.

The judge sat there studying them for a moment. Juliet wondered who the hell they were from. She had been able to get no one to support her. Her neighbour from Oxford who knew her husband was an alcoholic and had once pledged her support, had declined when Juliet had asked her but then Mark must have corrupted her too with the vicious lies about drugs and Alex. "I see," said the Judge "have you seen these statements Miss Parry?" he asked Juliet's barrister.

"No, your honour" she replied.

"Well, you may approach the bench and take them to discuss with your client. We will break for lunch now and the court will reconvene at 2pm."

Juliet looked across at Mark. He had a smug look on that red puffy face of his. He really was vile. After all she had done for him over the years. All that crap he used to say about her being a Goddess was just that, crap. He had never loved her, if he had he wouldn't have tolerated her affair all those years ago, he would have divorced her. No, he had just used her that was all. Used for twelve years. Robbed her of her youth, her money and her dignity and now he was going to take her child and spoil the only thing that was bringing her pleasure, her relationship with Alex. Juliet turned and left the courtroom.

In the waiting area, Alex was nowhere to be seen, where the hell was he? thought Juliet. How could he let her down at a time like this? She needed him to support her now, more than ever before and he was not there. It had not gone unnoticed by her legal team "It looks like Mr. Ellis has left," said the trainee. Did they believe the lies Mark had told in his statement? thought Juliet. Obviously they did but then Alex had not dissuaded them from that belief, indeed he had confirmed it. Juliet took her phone out of her bag turned it on and rang him. "Where are you Alex?" she asked. "I am in Christ Church meadow, I needed a cigarette," he said.

"I am coming to join you," said Juliet "stay where you are". She left the court, glad to be outside away from the torture. It was a lovely day but Juliet didn't notice it, she was so upset, so distraught. She was being dragged through the mire in that courtroom and she could do nothing about it.

"That was horrible, just horrible," said Juliet to Alex when she found him in Christ Church meadow sitting on a bench. "They are slaughtering me in there. Mark has some super bitch for a barrister and she made mincemeat of my young lovely. I just want to run away and when I came out and you weren't there, I didn't know what to think. I need your support right now Alex, I really need it."Alex just took another drag on his cigarette, and blew smoke and looked at her

"Well you shouldn't have gone back to him and fucked him and told him loads of shit about me, should you?" he said finally.

Why was he doing this? Juliet just stood there looking at him. "You fucking shit," Juliet spat venomously, "That was your fault. You admitted so yourself, and I said nothing to him about you. You are more concerned about your own fucking character than me losing Guy. You conceited arsehole. And why the fuck did you have to go and confirm you have smoked weed? They were not going to find out. You haven't smoked any while you have been with me." Juliet was really angry but she said no more. She sat on the bench next to him, and lit her cigarette and puffed hard on it saying nothing but all the while her mind was racing.

He was a coward, nothing but a bloody coward. He hadn't wanted to be called as a witness for her that is why he had admitted to smoking weed. He had known what he was doing. He was frightened, just like her. They had come this far and at the last hurdle, he had bailed out. The fight drained out of her with this realisation. Mark had achieved what he had wanted, he was ruining their relationship.

She sat there a while longer saying nothing. She was now aware of the sun on her face and she closed her eyes letting the sun warm her soul. She had to go back to court in half an hour and she was not looking forward to the prospect one little bit and she needed some more cigarettes. She stood up and turned to leave.

"I am not coming back to court," said Alex "I can't face it."

Juliet looked at him with contempt. What a coward she thought to herself. "I didn't think you would," she said, and walked away.

She turned out of the meadow and walked briskly up 'The High' towards Cornmarket, weaving her way through the crowds of people. She was in a world of her own when suddenly Mark was upon her. He was walking back towards the court.

"It is not too late Juliet," he said. What was he talking about? She just looked at him as he continued "ditch oaf and come back to me? We can all play happy families again. Alistair misses you."

So she had been right all along, he needed her, he needed her to go out to work, to buy his beer, to cook and clean for him, to iron his shirts and to do the laundry, the gardening and the DIY. In short he needed his slave back. She stood and said nothing for a moment and then laughed, "Why the hell would I want to do that Mark? You can assassinate my character in there, you can take my son away from me, and ruin my relationship with Alex but I will never, ever, come back to you, I would rather die first."

His face changed instantly, and he was clearly angry "Bitch," he said and walked off.

Fifteen minutes later, Juliet was back in the waiting area and Miss Parry came up to her. "Juliet, we need to discuss the statements, can we go into a meeting room?" Juliet didn't want to come back this afternoon but she knew she had to. She had to see it through to the bitter end for Guy, even if it was going to be in vain.

The statements were from a worker at the nursery and the neighbour who had refused to give Juliet a statement. People are so fickle, thought Juliet, Mark had obviously gone around town telling his sorry tale of woe to everyone and he must have virtually bullied them into giving him a statement. She cast her eyes over them. They were full of the same old stuff, saying how good Mark was with Guy but these people didn't really know him. Were they aware of the damage they were causing by making these statements? Of course the neighbour didn't have any kids of her own so what did she know? And there was of course envy, the kind of envy you attract when you are happily in love. For some reason, it seems to get right up other people's noses, especially people who are not happy with their own lives but too afraid to take the plunge and do anything about it.

"Mr. Hamilton's barrister said that you were fined for having no motor vehicle insurance a little while ago Juliet, is that true?" They have been digging haven't they, thought Juliet. At first she couldn't quite make out why this was relevant to the residency of Guy but then it was just more dirt that made her look like she was irresponsible, so she could see why it fitted.

"Yes, it is true," said Juliet.

They went back into court and the judge returned from his lunch. He looked at Juliet, but Juliet knew that it was not a look of sympathy he was giving her. Then he spoke, "Is there any more evidence in this case?"

Marks barrister, Ms. Greystone spoke, "Yes Your Honour. It has come to light that Mrs. Hamilton was stopped by the police a couple of months ago for having no motor vehicle insurance. Subsequently her car was impounded and she has been fined and she has received penalty points on her licence. This is further evidence of her irresponsibility.

Furthermore I have here a statement from Alistair Hamilton an older child from the marriage," and she handed the judge a piece of paper. Juliet was pole axed, she hadn't seen that one coming. How could Alistair do this to her? How could he turn against his own mother? She was trying hard to stifle back the tears but she knew that she couldn't contain them for long. The judge looked at the paper "very good," he said, "very good. It would appear, Mrs Hamilton that your elder son has said that he thinks it is in the best interests of Guy if he remains with his father." Juliet wanted to die and the tears ran down her face uncontrollably.

Both of the barristers summed up. Ms. Greystone went first and she went in for the kill. She portrayed Juliet as an irresponsible harlot, who was only interested in her own sexual gratification and Mark as a devoted father. No mention was made of Alex. Juliet noticed how the Judge was smiling at Ms. Greystone. He probably has a sweet spot for her thought Juliet. Perhaps he is knocking her off?

And then Miss Parry, Juliet's young lovely went. She was poor in comparison to Ms. Greystone, thought Juliet. But then Miss Parry had probably been shagging her boyfriend last night instead of reading the case brief. She was so poor that Juliet just wished she would stop, she wasn't even getting some of the facts right. It was painful to hear.

And then the judge spoke. "This case, as with all cases concerning residency that come to court is shrouded in accusations. Both parties are clearly bitter but it is my responsibility to act in the best interests of the child. As

259

there have been serious allegations made here by both parties, I am setting a date for the interim order to be reviewed after a thorough review by CAFCASS. I want medical reports for Mr. Hamilton, Mrs. Hamilton and Mr. Ellis, from their respective GP's, full enhanced criminal disclosure, police records of telephone conversations and a full report from Social Services on the living conditions of both parties." He said.

And then he delivered the coup de grace, "In this instance, I am making an Interim order in favour of Mr. Hamilton as Guy has been in his care since Mrs. Hamilton left the matrimonial home in March." Juliet felt as though someone had just ripped out her heart, she couldn't bear it any longer, she wanted to run, she couldn't control herself anymore and she began to sob uncontrollably.

The trainee solicitor handed Juliet a tissue but everyone else just ignored her sobbing at the back of the court. Mark turned to look at her but there was no evidence of compassion there, he just stared at her coldly while she sobbed.

The judge asked both parties to arrange access between themselves. Was he mad? thought Juliet. How the hell was she going to get to Oxford to see Guy? And she said so but she suggested that Mark visit his mothers in Oswestry and that Juliet could visit him there. But Mark was having none of this. He said he wasn't planning on visiting Oswestry and he wouldn't let Guy go with Juliet unattended because he didn't want Alex to be alone with Guy.

God that really was low, thought Juliet. Mark knew Alex was no paedophile, he just wanted to get back at him for taking Juliet. Mark did suggest that Juliet could visit Oxford and when she said that she couldn't afford to and had no one to stay with, he suggested that she could stay at his house. He didn't give up, did he? Thankfully even the judge said this was not a suitable suggestion. In the end no decision was reached but the judge said Mrs. Hamilton should get a job. Over my dead body am I paying that bastard maintenance, thought Juliet? And with tears still streaming down her face and still unable to control the sobbing Juliet left the court.

The trainee and Miss Parry, sat a while with Juliet, offering her sympathy and support. Sympathy and support that Alex should have given her, but he was not there. She eventually got her sobbing under control and dried her tears. She couldn't blame them. They had done their best under the circumstances. "I want to thank you both," said Juliet, "you did your best but the judge had clearly made up his mind before he went into court. And Miss Parry, please don't lose your loveliness and become like that shrivelled cold bitch Ms. Greystone. No job is worth doing that for." And she left the court to find Alex and to go back home to Gilfach Cottage.

Chapter 27 - Despair

Juliet was heartbroken, destroyed. She felt empty and numb. She just couldn't believe what had happened. How could anyone in their right mind look at Mark and give him residency of a three-year-old child? Mark had clearly been drunk when he had appeared in court on Monday afternoon. And he had shown no mercy when she sobbed at the back of the courtroom.

The lies. How could he tell those lies? And they had swallowed them. Not to mention his Rottweiler bitch of a Barrister, she was awful but clearly very good at her job, and had made mincemeat of Juliet's young inexperienced barrister.

There was no 'In the best interests of the child' in today's outcome, the Judge had made up his mind before he had stepped into the courtroom. It was not fair, just not fair. No one had asked her to speak or had cross examined her. She hadn't even been able to defend herself.

And he wouldn't budge over access rights. No access with Alex. He had made Alex look as though he was a paedophile. Mark had been very calculating and devious. She felt cold and betrayed. You live with someone for 16 years and you think you know them, but she clearly didn't know Mark. She could feel the tears well up in her eyes again. No she shouldn't cry she was driving. Just get home she thought to herself, just get home.

There was nothing to be done about it now. She just had to accept that although the judge had made an interim order, the fact that he had set the next date in late July meant that so much time would have passed since she had left, that they wouldn't want to move Guy. She didn't have a hope in hell.

And that statement by Alistair, that was quite simply betrayal. How could he? She had let him choose, there was no need for him to twist the knife and it just wasn't like him. No, it wasn't like him at all she knew that. Of course, he had been put up to it by Mark. She could just hear him now; "Alistair, your mom won't stay away without Guy. Just do a statement for the court saying that you think Guy is better off here with me and then once I have residency of Guy, she will soon come back and we will all be happy again. She will look after us all."

It made her feel sick. She really was on her own. No one had supported her. None of her family, in fact they had helped him. And then Alex, he had bailed out as soon as the first missile had been hurled at him. Alone, she was really alone but whatever she was going to do, she was not going back to Mark, she would rather die first than do that.

Alex was quiet in the car, he knew she was devastated and there was now a chink in his armour, he had been wounded in the battle and the doubts were growing more and more in his mind, he felt betrayed too. He thought Juliet had told Mark things about him. But he said nothing as he knew how upset Juliet was and now was not the time to voice his opinions.

They got back to the cottage after stopping at Tesco, and Juliet cooked up some pasta. It seemed quiet without Guy. How she would have dearly loved to get very, very, drunk, but they had no money. The two round trips to Oxford had cost them £120 and they couldn't afford a bottle of wine. So she just sank into bed after dinner and went to sleep exhausted.

The next morning, the full horror of yesterday consumed her. How could they give him custody? That is all that kept going around and around in her mind. How could they? What was to be done now? She lay in bed all day, too numb to cry, to numb to be angry, there was nothing she could do. There was no point in going through the charade that the court had ordered. A social worker would never pass the cottage as suitable for a small child compared to the new house Mark had just got, and then there was the question of Alistair, that was the real clincher. Without Alistair living with them the court would not split up the children and put Guy with Juliet. They would also demand medical records for them both. What a mess, she thought to herself. She didn't have a hope in hell of winning the next court case.

Alex knew all was lost and no matter how he tried to console her there was nothing that he could say or do to make Juliet feel better. When they went to the job centre on their fortnightly visit, Juliet broke down in front of the woman at the desk in the unemployment office and told her what had happened through tears.

"Look," said the woman, "you are in no fit state to look for a job, and I am going to transfer you to employment support allowance. You will need to go and get a sick note from the doctor. The money will be the same, you just won't have to look for work. It will give you time to have a break and get over this traumatic event," Juliet nodded, the tears streaming down her face. It wasn't like her, she was usually so composed. But her world had caved in.

It didn't help that they had both been damaged by the experience of the court. Juliet had been made to look like a bad mother and she felt ashamed. They had twisted the facts and made it look like she was self-centred, sex-crazed and cared little for her children. It was so wrong.

And she had not even been given the opportunity to defend herself. It had left her on the edge of a nervous breakdown. It had been her battle and although Alex had been with her, Mark had been playing his games again, and it had wounded Alex.

Mark had fired some pretty nasty missiles at him, mentioning the cannabis from his past and hinting at his character being unsuitable. It was all too much for Alex and it had been calculated to undermine them and it had worked. Alex had rounded on her and said that she had told Mark all sorts of things about him. He was talking absolute nonsense, Mark had drawn on his knowledge of Alex years ago and he had talked to him when Alex had come to live with them in Oxford. Nonetheless, it was another little episode that had sowed the seeds of doubt in Alex's mind, seeds that would not easily be uprooted. However much Juliet denied it, Alex refused to believe her. And now losing Guy was undermining their relationship further, Juliet was desperately trying to cling on to it. She just lay in bed all day and cried. She was inconsolable.

The days went by and Juliet knew that she couldn't go on feeling depressed, it was getting Alex down and it was causing tension between them and she had to accept the fact that she would not get custody of Guy. Ultimately life had to go on, no matter how bleak it felt, she had to snap out of it and they had to move forward. She had lost Guy, she didn't want to risk losing Alex as well. She had come too far and given up too much to do that. It was early June and it was warm and sunny, even in Wales. The orchard was in full leaf, the blossom was everywhere and the nights were light until late.

Alex must have felt the same as one morning when they awoke, he said, "let's make some elderflower champagne, the elderflowers are in bloom, and it will do you good to do something other than sit and mope all day." Juliet had to agree with him there was nothing that could be done, so late that morning she went into the surrounding fields with him.

The lambs had been taken up into the meadow on the top of the hill and the fields were empty, the grass had been left to recover. It really was a beautiful late spring day, everything was so fresh and the greens were so vivid, not like the tired brown hues that pervaded the countryside in late summer. The sun was shining down the valley and the clouds were billowing across the bright blue sky like sails on an old-fashioned galleon, sailing over the line of hills that stretched in the distance. The daffodils had gone and had been replaced with cow parsley waiving in the breeze. Overhead elderflower blossom with its white lacy heads complimented the cow parsley standing at thigh height amongst the tall grass. The sun warmed their backs and Juliet knew that she loved Alex very much. She looked at him. He was so handsome, so sexy and masculine, his blond hair shining in the sunlight. He was all she had left. They picked what seemed like mountains of flower heads. The strange smell of elderflower in the warm afternoon was everywhere and they walked back to the cottage. It was good to do something distracting, she thought as they made the champagne.

"Why don't we go camping for a few days?" said Juliet. "I have a tent, and a cooker and we can go to a no-frills campsite for next to nothing? What do you think? Alex looked at her as though she was mad. "Come on, it will be fun," she said. "We need a holiday, a change of scene."

Alex looked doubtful "I haven't been camping since I went with Janet twenty years ago," he said.

"Well you haven't been camping like this," said Juliet. "I have a huge tent, one you can stand up in. I think we can just about fit it all into the car. We may have to pee in a bucket though," she said.

Alex laughed "you make it sound very appealing," he said sarcastically, "but ok you're on, we will go camping."

They decided on St David's and found a campsite on the Camping Clubs website. Alex emailed the farmer, and they soon had a response and would set off the next day for three days. Alex perked up at the idea of going away and said that they should take his inflatable kayak that he had purchased the year before and never used. He had threatened to take Juliet on the river a couple of times but Juliet had declined as it seemed a bit pointless, and she didn't fancy being capsized into freezing cold water.

Juliet was up early and loaded up the car. She loved this time of year, the light early mornings and the warm weather. Late spring was magical and she was going to enjoy this trip, she had to move forward if only to preserve her sanity and she needed to be active. She carefully packed the camping cooker and some kitchen utensils and saucepans. She was annoyed when she thought of the boxes of camping stuff she had left behind.

She had received a letter from her previous landlord and it had said, that there were many things left behind, abandoned by Mark, and did she want them? Hell yes, she did, but realistically it was impossible for her to get them. They had no money and she couldn't afford to hire a van or pay for the petrol to go and get the stuff. Her piano, the dining table, a wardrobe, Christmas decorations, a steam wallpaper stripper and the camping equipment plus boxes of books had all been left behind. Years of stuff that she had paid for. Mark didn't care, he hadn't worked to pay for them, she had. She stopped herself dwelling on the past. It was no good getting angry about it, there was nothing that could be done now. You have to move forward she told herself.

Alex had made a playlist for them on his computer, and had burnt it onto a CD so that they could listen to it in the car. It was a beautiful morning as they set off for St David's and for the first time in a month, life seemed sunnier than it had been although there was still the fact that Juliet's mother was dying of cancer in the background and the loss of Guy still haunted her.

It had been hard for them to put the court case behind them and they had still not been entirely successful. Alex questioned everything they had done and had blamed himself and her at times when he was down. He could not let go of Nigel and kept dragging it up now and again. Juliet wished he would leave it alone but he couldn't seem to let go of it. Alex had fought against his inner demons and he knew that psychologically he was pushing her away from him. He said that by doing this he was saving himself the pain of abandonment when Juliet would eventually leave him. Juliet tried to reassure Alex that she loved him deeply and would not leave him, but she knew that if he continued to push her away it would be a self-fulfilling prophecy. It was hard and with all her other problems it was taking its toll on Juliet.

She was on edge most of the time and woke up never knowing what kind of a mood Alex would be in. Alex had started to talk about going abroad to work and at first Juliet thought that she would go with him but then she knew deep down that she had responsibilities and she had to face them.

They got to St David's and found that they were the only ones in the field camping. It was a really pretty location on the cliff top overlooking the sea and they set up the tent and went for a walk down to the old harbour. There were a few people milling around and it really was very charming. Parents were holding hands with small children and it made Juliet think of Guy when she looked at them. It was very painful for Juliet.

They went back to the tent and Juliet cooked dinner, they nearly had an argument again, silly stuff really but it was always there, a tension in the background. "We have to get jobs Juliet," said Alex.

"I know," said Juliet, "but we have tried and got nowhere and in any case, I have been on the verge of a nervous breakdown."

"I am thinking of going abroad to work as we can't get anything around here." Juliet felt hurt.

"And what am I going to do here without you?" she said.

"You can stay on at the cottage," said Alex.

Juliet felt sad. There was no use in her staying at the cottage. It was miles from family and miles from Oxford. She couldn't see Guy if she stayed in Wales and it would be lonely without Alex. He was the only reason she was here although she knew that he needed something to do, he needed a job. Life was absolutely bleak without any money and they weren't getting very far with finding a job in Wales. Juliet understood that the Welsh would obviously give jobs to Welsh people first as unemployment was quite high in Wales but it didn't help their situation in obtaining employment. They said no more about the subject but lay quietly in the darkness next to each other. Their sex life did not have the same fevered excitement and frequency that it once had but nonetheless they still made love with a passion and an intensity that other lovers would find difficult to comprehend.

The next morning they went into St David's to find a supermarket. They purchased a couple of Danish pastries and some food for lunch. They had made a flask of coffee and they set off in search of a little secluded cove where they could spend the day. They hadn't gone far when they found one a small way out of St David's with a car park on the cliff top.

The sun was shining brightly overhead as they stepped out of the car and admired the view. This really was a tonic. The sea was blue and the sun was dancing on the waves playing with the light and sparkling as they started to make their way down the winding footpath to the cove below. It was a lovely little cove and the tide was in as they laid out the picnic rug and sat down to drink their coffee and eat the Danish pastries they had bought. They didn't need to say much to each other to be happy in each other's company and it had been a good idea to come away to have a change of scene. Juliet had decided to let Alex have his way and take her out in the kayak and he was as excited as a small child about using it for the first time.

It was a little shaky in the kayak. There was not really enough room for them both and Juliet had to rest her legs on top of Alex's but once settled in there it was quite steady, although it was breezy out on the water. Alex had rowed for Oxford in his youth so Juliet had no worries about his capabilities and they were soon enjoying themselves.

"I have a bird's eye view from here," laughed Alex gesturing to Juliet's open legs and her bikini bottoms.

"You just concentrate on your rowing," laughed Juliet. But soon he took her out too far and Juliet was getting scared, they were nearing the mouth of the cove and the open sea lay beyond stretching into the distance. The waves were getting rougher and the little kayak was getting tossed about "take me back to the shore please Alex, I don't feel safe," said Juliet.

Alex just laughed "you are ok with me, you are quite safe," but Juliet no longer trusted him completely and she protested further. Finally, Alex finally turned the kayak around and headed back to the shore.

Chapter 28 – Depression

The little camping trip was soon over and they were back to reality. The weeks slipped by and things got steadily worse. July came and went and the court case was scheduled. Juliet did not attend, she knew it was futile and she couldn't face it, not after last time. They also couldn't afford the petrol to get there. Juliet had sent a statement to her solicitor asking for him to read it out in court, but she doubted if he would. It read:

"Statement to the Court by Juliet Hamilton

I am unable to attend court today due to my financial circumstances. I am currently in receipt of Employment Support Allowance of £51.37 per week. I have sold all of my jewellery to fund previous visits to Oxford to see Guy and attend court. I am actively seeking employment but have been unsuccessful due to the economic climate and the lack of availability of jobs in this area. My family is unwilling to support me.

Following my last court appearance, it has become apparent to me that I have very little hope of gaining residence of Guy. The fact that the next date for a court hearing regarding residence could not be set until October, means that in all probability, Guy will be deemed to be settled with his father and the final order will reflect this.

During the time since the last court hearing I have not been kept informed as to Guy's welfare. I have not been contacted by Social Services and the whole process seems completely one-sided. In the previous months I have sent small gifts and notes to Guy when I have been able to afford them. It appears that no one gives any regard to the loss of a mother.

I will never accept the court's opinion that it is in the best interests of Guy to remain with his father, a man, who regardless of his other shortcomings as a parent, will be 70 when Guy is 16.

Whilst Guy was with me for three days, he slept happily in his own bed and started to wear pants and use the potty. These things seemed beyond the capabilities of his father. I hope that with the help of Social Services these things have been instigated.

Guy was distraught at being parted from me. During the time he was with me he asked for "cuddles" frequently, said "I missed you mommy" and "don't go mommy". Following the decision of the court at the last hearing I have been bereft, distraught and suicidal. Previously, a child who enjoyed his food, when cooked by me, was now thin and I could see his ribs. I wish to state that should Guy suffer neglect at the hands of his father, who, during our many years of marriage was unable to adequately look after himself let alone a young child, I will hold Social Services and the court responsible.

Failure on the part of my first solicitor, Tompsons, to act swiftly on my part regarding a residence application, and my experience at court, where I was not even allowed the opportunity to defend myself, the adversarial process, which seemed to depend on which party had the more skilful advocate, and finally a judge who seemed far from equitable, has led me to be completely disillusioned with the legal process.

In consequence of this, and giving regard to the future for Guy and what is now in his best interests following the decision of the court to make an interim residence order in favour or Mark Hamilton, and also the failure of the court to make any order for contact. I feel that any kind of non- staying contact would only cause him distress. Judge Kempston stated at the last hearing that Mark Hamilton and I should agree on contact. Whilst this seems perfectly sensible to the reasonable man, I know that it will not be possible or practical to do so in this instance.

With all of the above in mind, and much sadness, I request that the court make an order for contact. I know that it is the motive of Mark Hamilton to undermine my relationship with my partner. This was exemplified by his malicious and false accusations made against myself and my partner, in his statement to the court at the last hearing. His sole intention being, that I return to him, something I will never do.

My eldest son supported my husband's claim with a statement. I have no doubt that he was under duress to do so and I also know from my husband, that Alistair (aged 15) is now drinking beer and smoking with his father, and has had a tattoo. I do not think this is appropriate parental guidance.

In view of the above facts, I see little point in wasting any more public funds on another unnecessary court hearing to determine the interim residence order.

Later the next day an email came through from Juliet's solicitor confirming that an order had been made in Marks favour for residency, no order had been made for contact. She had been expecting it but it was still like an icy stab in the heart when she read the words on the page.

274

Neither Juliet nor Alex had jobs and the lack of money was getting critical. The tenancy on the cottage would end on the 9th September and they would have been there for six months. It had not turned out how Juliet had hoped and her heart was growing increasingly sad and heavy.

The summer was growing old and the nights were getting darker but what was more worrying for Juliet was Alex's mood, he was dipping deeper and deeper into depression and spent most of the day in bed. He had little enthusiasm for going out or for doing anything and what was worse he didn't touch Juliet, they hadn't had sex for two weeks and it showed no sign of getting any better, he didn't even cuddle her at night, he was withdrawing from her emotionally and she knew it.

Juliet woke before Alex did these days and she was back in her old regime of waking early. She felt alone waiting for him to wake up although he was not much company when he was awake. It was all going wrong. They were in a downward spiral and Juliet didn't think she would be able to reverse the process. She was at a loss to know what to do about it.

One of the worrying things about this was that Alex had developed a small spot on his face a couple of weeks earlier and he had repeatedly picked at it. Juliet noticed that when they talked about their problems Alex became anxious and he would start picking at the spot. Juliet had asked him to stop picking at it but he had said nothing, and he soon went back to pick at it and it was getting larger and larger. In fact, he wasn't communicating as he used to and he couldn't give Juliet an answer when she asked why he didn't touch her anymore. Nothing she said or did could get him out of this depressive state and it was bringing Juliet down too.

As she lay there in the early morning light, she had to admit to herself that this was not a satisfactory state of affairs. It hurt her deeply to think that Alex no longer loved her but everything was pointing to that conclusion. He felt responsible for her circumstances as she had given up so much for him, and she had nowhere else to go. He wasn't going to turn around and tell her that it was over between them. She had offered to move out but all he had said was "this is your home, your name is on the lease," but actions speak louder than words and it was becoming increasingly plain to Juliet that she was the cause of Alex's depression. There was no point in staying if he didn't love her. That was just unbearable.

Juliet made up her mind to leave him. It was time to go back to reality and face the music. Her mother needed her and she needed to see Guy although it would not be easy to face. Juliet knew what she had to do and there was nothing to keep her here, not now Alex's love had gone.

But how was she going to achieve this? She didn't want a scene with Alex as he would feel guilty and talk her out of leaving. He had before and he would again, his answer was to go abroad but Juliet knew this was as good as saying it was over. She had to leave early one morning when he was asleep.

She decided to go the next time the opportunity presented itself. She looked over to where he was asleep and studied his sleeping face. She made a mental image of him, to remind herself. I want to conjure up the image of his face in the future when I no longer have him and a tear rolled down her cheek. She could smell him and how she loved his smell, how it comforted her but it was no good staying if he didn't love her. It was better to leave now and not to let it get ugly.

It was three awful weeks of watching Alex's' depression get steadily worse before the opportunity presented itself, and she left before 8.30 in the morning. It was a sunny morning in early September and she had loaded what was necessary in the car (she could fetch the rest later, for now she didn't even know where she was going to stay). Alex was still asleep and had not stirred when she had left a little note on his bedside table. It said:

"My Darling Alex

Words cannot express how much I love you, and how you have brought me so much joy and love but I know now, that you are suffering greatly and you no longer love me. I also know that you feel wholly responsible for me losing Guy but you are drifting away from me and have been for some time. I sincerely wish that things had turned out better for us but they did not. At least we tried. Be kind to yourself and look after yourself and know that I truly love you. I have to try and put right some of the wrongs.

All my love for eternity

Juliet XXXXX"

She was sad but knew it was for the best and travelled along the winding road in the valley at the foot of the hills towards Newtown for the very last time.

The further away she got from the cottage the more she relaxed and felt stronger. She had to put right what was wrong in her life and build a new one for herself alone. First she had to go and see her mom.

Her mom was at home and wearing a scarf on her head. She had been having chemotherapy and her hair had dropped out. Why is she bothering? Thought Juliet, chemo is such an invasive treatment and it is not going to stop the cancer as it is aggressive stage three and terminal.

Her mom could read her mind "it is your Dad, Juliet, he is taking this all rather badly, and thinks I can be cured," she said.

"Oh mom," said Juliet. She felt like crying but she knew she had to be strong for her mom. "How are you coping with it all?" Juliet said.

"I am in remission at the moment," said her mom "but the chemotherapy is awful, I can't taste anything. I can't even enjoy a whisky." Juliet took a little heart at the news that her mom was in remission and that she was complaining, she couldn't be feeling that bad if she was complaining.

"Anyway Juliet, it is lovely to see you but I sense there is something not quite right, what is the matter?" said her Mom.

"I have left Alex," said Juliet.

Her mother just sat for a while, and thought and then she said: "I don't worry about you Juliet, you are a survivor." Juliet was grateful that her mom was not going to worry about her. "Where are you going to stay Juliet?" her mother asked. "Well Mom I don't know yet but I know I have to go and see Guy," Juliet replied.

"You know Mark will have you back," her Mom said.

Juliet was right all along this had been his little game plan. She knew that he had been phoning her mom regularly and playing the victim but Juliet said nothing about this to her mom. "I will never go back to Mark," said Juliet. "It took me too long to get away from him and I will get my decree nisi at the end of the month."

However she thought to herself that she could stay at his house and look for a room to rent. It would be a temporary solution, and not very good but it was somewhere to stay.

"I understand that Juliet, I wish I could say you could stay here but your father is very angry with you." Juliet was angered by this but didn't let it show. Her Dad was angry with her? How dare he. But then she realised that he must be having a hard time coping with her mother's cancer and ultimate future death. He had needed Juliet and she hadn't been there because she had been otherwise occupied. It was all such a mess, why did this have to happen now, she thought to herself.

"I am sorry about that Mom," Juliet said, "but things will be different now but I have to get myself sorted out first."

Her mom looked at her sympathetically and went to her handbag. "Here is £200 Juliet, to tide you over until you get sorted out."

Juliet was truly grateful. "Thank you so much mom, it will be a big help," she said. And it was true it was a big help. She didn't have any money at all and she had to separate her claim from Alex's, and whenever you made any changes to your benefits, there was always a hiatus where you had no money. At least she could eat and put petrol in her car. She kissed her Mom goodbye and set off to Oxford.

She hadn't eaten a thing and she felt sick, really quite sick which was unlike her. She had become accustomed to eating very little in the cottage because they were so poor. She had even gone without meals so that Alex could eat. He was a big man and vegetarianism didn't sit well with him and of late she had hankered for meat. Well at least now she could eat meat but as she drove, the sickness feeling didn't go away and then she realised that her period was well over a week late. With all the upset she hadn't given it a second thought. Oh my god, she thought to herself, I could be pregnant. The feeling of sickness was all too familiar and she knew that there was a real chance she was pregnant. I must get myself a pregnancy test tomorrow if this keeps up, she thought to herself as she drove.

She got to Oxford and Mark was not at home, so she went and bought herself a sandwich and immediately the sickness went. Perhaps I was just hungry, Juliet thought to herself but she couldn't deny that her period was very overdue. With all of the trauma her periods had got a little irregular but she put the thought to the back of her mind. She sat in the car on the drive waiting and it wasn't long before Mark and Guy came down the road. How she had missed Guy and he was overjoyed to see her. Mark was not happy.

"What are you doing here?" he said, "You are not trying to snatch Guy again are you? Because you will end up in prison."

He really was a nasty shit, thought Juliet to herself. "No, Mark, I have left Alex and Mom said you would put me up."

Mark looked angrier, "You can't stay here, you will jeopardise my benefits," he said.

"It is only temporary," pleaded Juliet, "and anyway, no one will know. Let me come in anyway, I want to see Guy and Alistair when he is back from school." She hoped Alistair would side with her against Mark.

Juliet stayed overnight after a lot of ministrations from Alistair and Mark acquiesced. She slept on the floor in the lounge and she felt sick when she woke. She had to go to the job centre and sort out her claim. She hadn't heard anything from Alex and thought about him but he had no credit on his phone and the landline had been cut off at the end of July. They couldn't afford to pay the bill. Then she went and bought a pregnancy test, she had to know for sure, one way or the other.

She waited until Alistair was home and went for a shower and did the pregnancy test waiting with bated breath the five minutes for the result. Before the five minutes was up she could clearly see that it was going to be positive. The wheel of fortune was really fucking things up. This was something else being thrown into the mix. She went out for a walk in the park to think.

After she had got over the initial shock, she realised that this was a positive. She might have lost Alex and Guy but she had a life and it wasn't impossible for her to have a child. It would be good for Guy to have a younger sibling, one nearer his age than Alistair. As for bringing up a child alone well that was no problem to her, she had virtually raised all of her older children single-handed. Mark had been no help whatsoever. She then laughed to herself as she thought of another positive. Mark would not be able to claim maintenance from her if she had another child. After all she was buggered if she was going to pay him maintenance to piss up the wall. She would buy Guy things and make sure he was ok but give money to that bastard to do what he liked with, never, she thought to herself.

She passed the library in the park, and it was still open and she went in, she still had a library card. "Can I use the computer please?" Juliet asked the lady on the desk, and soon she was logging onto her emails. She wanted to contact Valerie her midwife friend who she had known for years. As she opened up her emails there was one from Alex.

"Where are you?" it said, *"I am worried sick about you."*

She closed it down. She wasn't going to reply to him yet, no matter how much she wanted to. There was no point in telling him about the pregnancy he was in a bad place mentally and she didn't want him to feel obligated to her, or think that it was something she had done to keep hold of him. Besides, there was no "Love Alex xxxx," at the end of the email. If he truly didn't love her, he wouldn't want her to have his child. She had a life to build and she had better start building it fast. She emailed Valerie and told her what had happened and she put her telephone number in the email.

As she was walking out of the park her phone rang and it was Val. "Juliet, I am so sorry about what has happened. Do you want to meet up for a drink this evening? I am on call, but I don't have anyone about to go into labour and I should be alright. It would be good to see you". Juliet was pleased, "yes Val, that would be great."

She went back to Marks house and told him she was going out. She bathed Guy and read him a story. He was still wearing nappies although he was now 3 and a half. Mark was a useless parent. Guy's speech was coming on a little and it was lovely seeing him again. He hadn't forgotten her and it made her happy.

When she met up with Val they hugged and started chatting. After a while Val said, "Juliet, I have to say that you look terrible. You are so thin. It doesn't suit you at all. You need to put on some weight especially if you want to keep this baby."

"I know Val but I feel so sick at the moment, I am not sure what I am going to do but let's say I am moving more and more to the conclusion that I am keeping the baby."

Val wasn't the sort of judgmental hippy midwife, and she had been a good friend over the years. "Let me know when you are 100% sure and I will book you in. You do realise Juliet, that the council will house you if you are pregnant. It will be temporary accommodation and be prepared it won't be wonderful but it would be better than staying with Mark. I know what he is like."

As she left Val and walked back to Mark's house she thought about her situation. She was going to keep the baby and that was final. She would phone Val in the morning and go from there.

A couple of days later it had been sorted out and she was being given temporary accommodation. The council had moved really quickly and she was meeting a lady on the Iffley Road at a house full of bedsits to get the keys to her new place.

She didn't have to wait long and the woman soon appeared. She was nice and when she opened the door to the bedsit, Juliet was pleasantly surprised. It was a large downstairs room in a grand old Victorian house on the ground floor with two large windows and high ceilings. It had a double bed, a fridge, and its own small galley kitchen and bathroom. It was much nicer than any of the rooms to let she had looked at a few days ago in shared houses.

It was a start, the beginning of something new. The woman from the council explained that it was temporary, and they would be finding her a flat that was a more permanent solution but it could take a few months. But this was fine and as Juliet closed the door on her new home she relaxed and felt safe. Yes it was nice, and it could be made nicer once she had some more of her things. She would be happy here, it was within walking distance of town and there were a few shops across the road. But she would need some of her things from the cottage.

Chapter 29- Mom

Juliet was rebuilding her life, slowly, very slowly, but it was getting better and she had something to look forward to, a baby, something to give her hope.

She phoned her mother twice a week and they chatted on the phone for hours. Her mother was bearing up well given her circumstances but she said that her quality of life was shit and that made Juliet sad.

Juliet didn't tell her mom about her pregnancy, she knew that her mother was dying and that was final. Her mom didn't need to have anything to worry about so Juliet did her best to cheer her mom up and make her laugh.

Katie and Charlotte visited Juliet on the weekends and stayed over on an airbed. Alistair came every night mainly to be fed, as his father's cooking left little to be desired and Juliet was grateful for the company.

Juliet made frequent trips into town and to the library where she logged onto her emails. She had messaged Alex and told him that she was ok and in temporary accommodation but she made no mention of her pregnancy. He was clearly hurt but she had made the right decision, he didn't need the shit she had on her plate. Things had to be put right and she had to do that on her own.

She hadn't heard from him for weeks but then she received an email from him. He had got a job and would be going abroad although he didn't say where. He also said that he was keeping the cottage on and he had put all of her belongings into the outhouse. Juliet was disappointed he was so cold but she knew that she could expect little more.

Juliet visited Guy twice a week. It was stilted and hard with Mark present. He steadfastly refused to let her take Guy out alone with her. This was totally unsatisfactory and just another element of control. He had been really angry when she had told him she was having a baby and he told her to have an abortion. But he would be angry wouldn't he? It was final, there was no chance of them getting back together and he knew it.

Juliet contacted the solicitor about gaining access rights to Guy but he had told her that first she had to go through mediation with Mark. Her heart sank, as she knew Mark would not be co-operative with this but she had to do it, so she set it in motion. And she was right, he was obstructive and uncooperative at the meetings, even the women conducting the mediation knew this and told her so. He was clearly very, very bitter.

It was late October now and the leaves were lining the pavements like a multi-coloured carpet although the weather was still mild and the sun shone frequently. She wasn't entirely happy to be back in Oxford but walking about the town with the Autumn sun on the limestone buildings she was reminded of how picturesque it was.

Juliet was in the library doing research. She went there regularly and took out psychology books. She needed to find an answer to Alex's behaviour. She knew he was damaged emotionally by his childhood and his mother's behaviour towards him and she wanted to understand it. She needed resolution, she needed closure. She couldn't let him go from her mind and she doubted that she ever would, but still she searched for an answer.

She was getting stronger emotionally and mentally, and was healing from the horrendous marriage,and the traumatic events of the last few months. Val had told her, that she had been domestically abused by Mark. Not the usual violent domestic abuse, but the mental kind, and Juliet began to feel better about herself and what had gone on. She finally stopped blaming herself for what had happened, both with Guy and the court case and with Alex. They hadn't stood a chance with their relationship especially with Marks psychological warfare and Alex's emotional damage. Then there were the other problems, the lack of jobs, the isolation from her family, her mother's cancer. It was surprising they had lasted as long as they had but then they had that wonderful intimacy, that was until depression took hold of Alex.

Juliet's phone rang. It was her brother Lee. "Juliet, I don't want you to get worried, but it is Mom. She has been taken into hospital. Dad was taking her to the hospital for a regular visit, and she fell when she got out of the car and they have kept her in. The cancer has spread to her brain." Juliet stifled back the tears. "Thanks, Lee for phoning, Dad is still angry with me then?" she asked. "She is your mom Juliet, and you have a right to know," said Lee. "Yes," said Juliet "thanks again for letting me know. Keep me informed, will you?"

"Yes, of course," said Lee.

Juliet came off the phone. She had to go and see her mother. The end was coming and she knew it. She had just enough money to make the trip and she would sign on tomorrow, she had to do that but then she would go and see her Mom and tackle her Dad.

She arrived at the private hospital at 2pm the next day and sat in the car preparing herself for the worst, she had to be strong and she couldn't cry. Her mom needed her to be a rock and that was what she was going to be. The mother daughter role had reversed and Juliet had to be there for her mom at this awful time. Thankfully her pregnancy could still be hidden with baggy clothes and despite her thinness, the outside observer couldn't tell that she was pregnant.

She went into the private room where her mother was. She was asleep in bed. Thank goodness Dad has the money for a private hospital, thought Juliet. It was a large room and it was peaceful and sunny there. She looked at her mother lying in the bed. Her hair was growing back after the treatment and it was a short, cropped style like Judi Dench, and it was a lovely silvery grey. Her mother had always dyed her hair and had a perm, she had kept it short, but it was passé and old-fashioned. The new cropped look suited her. She had olive skin and brown eyes, unlike Juliet who had blue eyes and a golden complexion.

Her mom opened her eyes, aware that there was someone in the room with her. "Hello Juliet," she said.

"Hello Mom," said Juliet. "What have you been doing to yourself? You didn't have to go to such extremes as falling out of the car to have some peace from Dad," Juliet laughed. Her mom laughed too. Juliet helped her to sit up, and got her mom a cup of tea from the nurse. You wouldn't get this on the NHS thought Juliet. The nurse had even asked Juliet if she had wanted a cup but Juliet was still suffering from morning sickness, well, all the time sickness and couldn't stand to drink her usual favourite brew.

Her mother didn't look ill but she was taking a lot of drugs. The nurse had bought pills for her mother to take and Juliet noticed she was not taking them. "Mom, you have to take your meds, it is to help you with the pain."

Juliet's mom looked sheepish at being chided by her daughter. "I know Juliet, but I hate taking pills, they are so hard to swallow. Your Dad and I usually take our meds with yoghurt."

Juliet looked at her, "well mom, I will get some yoghurt for you. Is there anything else I can get for you?" Juliet asked.

"I would like some Ribena," said Juliet's mom, and could you bring my pashmina for me out of the caravan?"

"Yes, of course, mom" replied Juliet.

"Are you going to stay long?" asked Juliet's mom. "I would like to," said Juliet, "but I have to see whether Dad will let me. I know he is still angry with me. It was Lee who phoned me and told me that you were in hospital."

"Go and see him," said Juliet's mom, "he will be ok, you know what he is like, his bark is worse than his bite."

They sat for a while chatting and then Juliet could see her mom was tired. "I will go now mom and let you have some rest, but I will come back tomorrow," said Juliet. "Bye Juliet," said Juliet's mom and Juliet kissed her on the cheek and whispered, "I love you mom," to her.

As she walked out of the hospital, and towards the car, her mask slipped and the tears streamed down her face. Tears of sorrow for her dying mother.

She sat in the car and composed herself and grew strong, ready to tackle her Dad. When she arrived at her parent's house her dad's car was on the drive. She rang the doorbell, and her Dad soon appeared "Hello Dad, can I come in?"

Surprisingly her Dad put up no resistance and said "yes". They went into the kitchen and they sat down at the kitchen table. "Have you been to see your mom?"

"Yes, I have just come from there," replied Juliet. The conversation was stilted at first but then her Dad became relaxed and it was as if he had never been angry with her.

Juliet knew he needed her support now, now it was nearing the end. "Could I stay here for a few days Dad?" said Juliet. "I said I would get a few things for mom and visit her every day. I have to go back after the weekend as I have a hospital appointment but I will come up again soon if that is ok?"

"Yes, sure," said her Dad "I visit her every morning early before work, and then go again after dinner". Juliet breathed a sigh of relief. It wouldn't be easy but she had to do it. At least her Dad didn't ask her what her hospital appointment was for. He was too wrapped up in his own problems to notice what she had said.

Juliet visited her mother over the next few days and her mother was glad for the company, it was sad for Juliet to see her mother so ill, and either the cancer in her brain, the treatment, or the drugs were messing with her mother's mind. The one time when she visited, Juliet said the traffic was bad and her mother said it was probably the bank holiday, despite the fact it was November and a Thursday. When Juliet signed in the visitor's book at the hospital, she noticed how few visitors her mother had. All the family of hers that were once so glad for her largesse, had now deserted her. Now it was too painful to witness.

But Juliet kept things jolly for her mother, and took her the yoghurts she needed to take her meds, Juliet also took her some little pots of raspberry jelly with cream and sponge from Marks and Spencer's that she knew her mother adored.

Katie and Charlotte worked but lived with her Dad, and they confessed to Juliet that they had been too scared to visit their Nan in the hospital so Juliet agreed to take them on Saturday. Juliet warned the girls to be strong and not to cry, no matter how distressing they found it and that if they felt they couldn't do this, they were to make an excuse and go and wait in the car.

When they arrived, they were relieved to see their Nan didn't outwardly look as ill as they feared. Juliet's mom Dorothy was pleased to see them but she needed to visit the bathroom. She was on laxatives to counteract the constipation caused by the drugs but as she shuffled towards the private bathroom, Juliet realised she hadn't got there in time. "Do you want me to call the nurse?" said Juliet to her mom.

"No, Juliet," said her mom "will you help me?"So, Juliet dutifully followed her mom to the bathroom to clean her up. Juliet did so with caring and empathy.

Her mother would have been mortified at this before her illness. She was such a proud, clean woman and this made Juliet feel sad, although her mother didn't seem to care now. "Thank you, Juliet," she said, "you would make a good nurse."

Juliet felt pleased but laughed and said, "No I wouldn't, the twelve-hour shifts would see me off." Thankfully her once astute mother was so out of it on drugs that she didn't suspect that Juliet was pregnant.

When Juliet and her daughters returned to the car, the girls were full of admiration for Juliet. "Mom, you were so good in there," said Katie, "we wouldn't have known how to respond to Nan soiling herself," and Charlotte agreed. "You were so cheerful and knew what to say and kept chatting about normal things, we wouldn't have been able to do that."

Juliet sighed, "I know, she said," it upsets me to see your Nan like that but she doesn't want people being miserable and sad around her at a time like this. I wouldn't if I was dying, she knows that and she must feel miserable enough without everyone else mentioning it."

There was silence from the girls and then Charlotte spoke "Dying?" she said, with a wavering voice.

Juliet was taken aback by this, didn't they know? "Yes," said Juliet "she isn't going to get better, it is terminal stage three. I thought you both knew this."

"We did," said Katie, "but the Macmillan nurse said......"

Juliet could feel herself getting angry. "What on earth did the stupid woman say? You need to prepare yourself girls because your Nan is going to die and I personally don't think it will be long now, not now it has spread to her brain." The girls started to cry. "Cry your tears now," said Juliet "and get them over with, because I don't want you crying in front of your Grandad. It is hard enough for him to see her like this without you two going to pieces."

"How are you managing to cope with this Mom?" Said Katie shakily, "you are being so strong, and you have such a lot of other problems at the moment." Juliet sighed, "I have no choice, and I did my crying when your Nan was diagnosed now both your Nan and Grandad need me to be there for them, to be strong. I don't have a choice."

Thankfully her Dad seemed to have forgotten his anger with Juliet, although she knew he had no choice. He wouldn't forget his anger. He had just put it aside. She helped him by cleaning the house. It had fallen into a shabby state since her mother had been diagnosed and she knew it was not up to her mother's usual standards, so she did her best to clean it. She was appalled when she saw her Dad's bedclothes, they looked like they hadn't been changed for weeks, so she washed them for him and she cooked his dinner. Soon Tuesday came and she had to go back to Oxford, she needed to go and have a scan but she vowed she would come back soon.

At the hospital, Juliet sat in the waiting room and looked at all the other mothers waiting for their appointments. They were all younger than her. Although she looked good for her age and the pregnancy was suiting her. Her complexion was marvelous. She was still thin but the sickness was getting less now and her appetite had improved. She was doing an awful lot of walking and this was not helping her put on weight. However the pregnancy was progressing well, and Juliet was grateful for that.

"Your baby is doing fine," said the radiographer. "But I think your pregnancy is more advanced than your notes suggest, so I am going to give you a due date of April 15th". Juliet's heart lurched, that was Alex's birthday, how fitting. She still thought about him often but she hadn't heard from him since he told her he was going abroad. How she wanted to tell him about the baby but then she thought about the consequences of what would happen if she did. He might take it badly and ask her to terminate and she couldn't do that so she decided against it. It was better this way she thought to herself, she was better by herself at the moment. She was strong enough and didn't need to have to worry about his emotional state. She had enough to contend with her mother, her father, her older children and Guy. She gently stroked her stomach and spoke to her unborn child "you and I will be fine alone together," she said softly.

Chapter 30- Death

The weather had turned really cold and despite it only being November, there had been flurries of snow and the temperatures had dipped into the minus figures regularly at night.

Juliet's little bedsit was cosy and she had furnished it with a few things that her mother had given her. The girls loved it when they came to stay. Juliet had no television, but she had her CD player and she listened to the radio.

Her finances weren't as bad as they had been in the cottage with Alex. Whoever worked out the benefits was cruel to the extreme thinking that two people living together needed less each to live than one on their own, but it was all designed to put the squeeze on couples. It was madness. Juliet and Alex had wanted to work but there was nothing available in Wales. Once January came Juliet would no longer have to look for work and would claim income support as she was pregnant.

She kept in contact with Giles at the council offices but there was no news on a flat yet. There was no urgency for Juliet to move and she liked it on the Iffley Road, although it was a little bit of a dodgy area at night. She always made Alistair catch the 9pm bus to go back. She stood on the sofa looking out of the window to make sure he got onto the bus safely.

She regularly walked into the centre of Oxford, it was about a mile and although pregnant Juliet was quite fit, all the sex and walking in the cottage had made sure of that.

She thought about Alex often and missed him like hell, but it was no use if he didn't love her, it was just one of those things she had to put down to experience and despite all of the trauma, she had no regrets. If she hadn't have gone to Paris with Alex she would have regretted it for the rest of her life. She had already spent many years wondering 'what if?' and now, she didn't wonder anymore. They had tried it and done it and it didn't work, although her heart was heavy and sad about that.

She had money again on Thursday and told Alistair she was going back to the Midlands to see her mom and asked him if he would like to go. It would mean bunking off school but she knew that it was getting near the end, and it may be the last time he would have a chance to see his Nan. She told him this and he was happy to go with her.

They made the journey up to the Midlands and the first point of call was the hospital. Juliet was dismayed to find that they had changed her mother's room and the new one she was in was not nearly as nice as the previous, which had a sunny aspect to it. This one was on the other side of the building and it never saw the sun. When they walked into the room, her mother was sitting in a chair looking out of the window. She had just come back from more radiotherapy and was wearing her jacket over her nightdress. Juliet had told Alistair to prepare for the worst, just as she had done with the girls.

"Hello Mom," said Juliet, as she entered the room and walked over and kissed her mother on the cheek. "Hello darling," said her mother. She seemed distant and obviously not well from the recent treatment. A nurse bought in a cup of tea for her mom and set it down on the table in front of the chair. Juliet could sense a vacancy in her mother but she made small talk with her.

"I have bought Dad a piece of halibut from the covered market for his tea," Juliet said.

"That's nice," said her mom "he will like that." And then she paused and went quiet for a while and then said,"You know he thinks the world of you all."

Juliet had to choke back the tears, it was so unlike her mother to make such statements and it took her by surprise. "Yes," replied Juliet "and we think the world of you Mom," she said to her mother.

Her Mother's hand was holding the teacup and she started to shake uncontrollably. Juliet gently took the cup from her Mother's hand and said "Mom, you must be tired after your treatment, I shall buzz for a nurse and you should get into bed." Her mother made no comment, nor did she put up any kind of resistance to this request and soon a nurse appeared and helped her get into bed. Juliet kissed her mother on the cheek, "We will leave you to get some rest Mom. I love you."

Alistair said, "Bye Nan," and they left the room.

"I had no idea she was in such a bad way," said Alistair once they were back in the car.

"She is worse than the last time I saw her," said Juliet, "but it may have been because she had just had treatment," trying to make it sound not so bad but she knew it was bad.

"I am glad I came," said Alistair.

"I am proud of you Alistair," said Juliet "you were very grown up in there and it is not easy to do that, the girls found it difficult when they saw her."

Her Dad was delighted with his halibut and so he should be thought Juliet, it was more expensive than steak and he went off to see Juliet's mom after he had eaten. The girls sat talking with Juliet and Alistair after dinner, and they watched TV together. It was good to all be together again without Mark, who had always been an "aura of stress" as Charlotte had once put it.

They had all gone to bed including Juliet's dad and Juliet was just drifting off to sleep when the doorbell rang. It woke her into a fully conscious state and she knew that Alistair had opened the front door and she could hear her brother's voice.

She immediately got up and went into the hall, to find Lee standing there "Mom has had a stroke" he said, and then her father came out of the bedroom. Lee was going to take him to the hospital. Juliet knew that this was the end for her mother.

The girls came out of their room. "What's happening?" said Katie.

"Your Nan has had a stroke," said Juliet.

"What does that mean?" said Charlotte.

Juliet explained what had happened, and said "I don't think it will be good. You have to prepare yourselves, your Nan is probably going to die tonight. It must be serious if Lee came to get Dad at this time of night. The hospital has clearly rung him and they wouldn't do that if the situation wasn't grave. We need to go to bed and keep out of Dad's way when he comes back".

The girls looked mortified but Juliet knew what she had to do. She felt so sad they hadn't asked her to go but her children needed her so she could understand why. She went to bed, but thoughts were running through her brain. Was that a mini-stroke her mother had experienced this afternoon when her hand was shaking? Why didn't Juliet tell the nurse? But then Juliet realised that there was no point in all of this, whatever she had done,or failed to do, there was nothing but nothing that could prevent her mother's death.

The one thing that did haunt her though was that her mother was going to die in the hospital and she knew that her mother had really wanted to die at home. That was all her Dad's doing. Her Dad who she had thought of as strong had in the end, turned out to be very weak. She realised he was afraid of her mother dying.

About 11.30pm, she heard the front door open and she heard Lee's voice again. She went out into the hall and saw her Dad disappearing into the bedroom. Her brother stood in the hall. "We just made it to the hospital in time, and Mom had another massive stroke, Dad was by her side when she died," said Lee.

"I see," said Juliet. "I thought it was serious, thank you Lee," she said and saw him out of the door and went and told the girls, they were all very quiet and went to bed.

A little while later Juliet could hear her father crying in the next room. She had never known her father to cry before, and she felt very sad, that now for the first time in over fifty years, he was truly on his own.

Juliet stayed at her Dad's house for a week and for the funeral. It was a sombre affair and the girls cried all the way through it. The day after Juliet was relieved to return to her little bedsit. As soon as she had shut the door she sat on the bed and cried her heart out. Her mother had died on the 25th of November, just days before her 73rd birthday. "Oh Mom," Juliet wailed as she sobbed into the pillow on the bed.

Chapter 31 – New Home

The snow was falling quite thickly now. Juliet was in town doing some shopping early one Saturday morning. It was mid December and she had been so engrossed in the shopping centre, she hadn't realised how much it had been snowing. It had only been an hour but there were people everywhere talking about the buses. It appeared that the snow was causing disruption. Juliet decided not to wait and to walk back to her flat even though she was loaded down with shopping bags.

At least the snow was fresh which made walking in it relatively danger-free but it still made for hard going, and her bags were heavy. Just one bus had passed her by, but it had been packed with people and it was clearly so full it was not stopping at any stops.

She was relieved to get back to the flat, and hung up her wet clothes to dry, and sat on the bed watching the snow fall outside. At least I have plenty of food to eat, she thought to herself. She had books to read from the library and had prepared a stew to go in the oven. It was economical, nutritious one-pot cooking and would last her for three meals. She opened the envelope that had come for her in the post that morning, it was her decree absolute and she was finally divorced. No longer did she have to be called Mrs. Hamilton, she would change her name back to her maiden name of Grosvenor.

It is strange how snow makes everything so quiet. It muffles sounds and everything seems to stop.

It was early afternoon when the snow stopped falling, and the sun came out. There must have been at least ten inches of snow and people were in the street with children and sleds, but Juliet had no desire to venture out into it. There was no point. She was warm, and she snuggled down into the bed for an afternoon nap and put her hand on her abdomen, feeling her baby move inside her and drifted off to sleep.

She woke and it was late afternoon. The light was fading and she thought of Alex and what had happened. She shouldn't think about it, she knew but it was hard not to. She was carrying his child and he didn't know. In an ideal world, she would tell him about it and everything would be wonderful, but life was not like that and she knew it. She couldn't bear the thought of him being horrified at the pregnancy. That, would prove he had no love for her and she couldn't live with that.

She missed him like hell and longed for him to hold her in his arms and make love to her but it was never to be. He was damaged and he couldn't handle all that had gone on but it didn't stop her missing him and his love. I will always have my memories she thought to herself, no one can take those away from you.

It had been an eventful year to say the least but it was nearly over. She only had to get through Christmas with Dad without him noticing her pregnant state. It would not be easy, as she was showing quite a lot now but it was something she had to face and if he guessed, there was nothing she could do about it.

Christmas passed by and her father didn't notice her bump. At least, if he had, he didn't say. Juliet was glad to get Christmas out of the way. It wasn't filled with joy following so shortly after her mothers death. Everyone was just going through the motions.

She welcomed January and as a treat with her meagre grant, she bought herself a small TV. She hadn't had a TV for almost a year and as she was alone it was a joy to sit and play with the remote. She had never been master of the remote with Mark. So much in fact that she had once remarked that if he had somehow magically disappeared, she wouldn't know how to work the TV. Now she was about to remedy that and soon found herself a fan of all the trashy TV programmes she had once been denied.

Her pregnancy was progressing well and she was eager to get a flat so she phoned the council once a week to remind them that she was there and waiting. She wanted to get settled in before the baby came and she wanted to get all of her furniture from Wales. The weather was improving slowly and the days were growing longer and she thought about how a year ago she had been looking forward to going to Paris. She wondered if Alex was thinking about that too.

Val her midwife and friend had agreed to a home birth whether or not she was in her own flat or the temporary accommodation she was in now. Juliet bought a second-hand pram from eBay and was ready for the birth but the lack of a real home was worrying her. It was ok if she had the baby in temporary accommodation and was then given a flat but she knew that with a baby to look after, it would be hard to hire a van and get her stuff from Wales and even harder to give the flat a good clean, or re-decorate.

Finally at the end of February, she was given a much promised flat. It was near Mark and Guy. Just down the road from where they lived, about 200 yards. She got the keys from the council offices and took the bus to have a look. She had been forced to scrap her car when it had failed its MOT.

The flat was at the end of a little Cul de Sac, in a little development of two storey flats. Juliet's was at the end of the block overlooking the car park and it was a ground floor. To her delight the flat had a small garden. She was overjoyed, she couldn't have wished for something so wonderful. It was owned by a private landlord who had an arrangement with the council. She opened the door and went inside. Giles had said that if she had waited the council would re-decorate and clean the flat but Juliet couldn't wait and said she wanted to take it immediately.

There was furniture left in there that she didn't want, and the carpets were not clean. The kitchen was absolutely filthy. There were two bedrooms, but they were both painted in garish colours, bright blue and purple, but that didn't deter Juliet. She could soon get some white emulsion to cover that and Alistair would help her. The garden was overgrown but again, it was only late February, she would soon have that sorted out after the baby was born and the weather got better.

She told Alistair all about it that night when he visited. Juliet was hiring a man with a van the day next day to move all of her stuff as she was going to spend the night at the new place on the airbed.

The next night after she had moved in to her new flat, Alistair came down, and they sat watching TV together. "Something smells funky in here," said Juliet.

Alistair had to agree with her, "I don't know where it is coming from," he said.

"Neither do I," said Juliet. "Everything needs a good clean, I shall make a start tomorrow. The kitchen is the first thing that needs doing, and all this horrid old furniture needs to go out into the garden and I will get the council to collect it. I will hire a van for Thursday and we can go to Wales and get my stuff from the cottage, can you get Miles to come as I can't help you move furniture?" Miles was Juliet's eldest child and he lived alone.

She knew from an email she had received from Norman the landlord at Gilfach that Alex had gone abroad in November but he had kept on the cottage and put all her stuff in the outhouse. She just hoped it hadn't got ruined.

It didn't take long to transform the flat. Juliet hired a van and made the 260-mile round trip to Llandinam to get her stuff from the cottage and they stopped off at IKEA for a few things on the way back.

It had been strange to go to the cottage after all that time but thankfully Alex wasn't there and the cottage was shut up. Another time she would have been sad but she was excited to be reunited with her belongings and eager to make a home out of her new little flat. She cleaned and cleaned and they painted and soon the flat looked completely different. Alistair moved in with her and Juliet was glad for the company and his help. She even cleaned all the carpets and bought a metal bed frame from eBay and a brand-new mattress. Val was absolutely amazed at the transformation when she visited for the second time (she had visited the day after Juliet had moved in).

By the end of March Juliet was ready to have the baby, she had just had her 45th birthday and she was now eager to greet her new child. Juliet had not wanted to know what the sex was, she never had. She always liked to keep that as a surprise. She was physically and mentally prepared for the birth.

Juliet visited Val on the 9th of April for an antenatal appointment. "I have had a show Val," said Juliet. That usually means that I will go into labour in a few days,"

Val looked at Juliet "Well that is just typical Juliet. Michael is away on business over the weekend and I have no one to look after Rebecca so you can bet it is sod's law you will go into labour."

Juliet laughed. Val had wanted to attend the birth. "Well, I can't be sure that will happen," said Juliet, but she had a good idea that it would given that she was a week away from her due date.

The next day Juliet made sure that there was enough food in the fridge just in case. She settled down to enjoy a peaceful weekend. Everything was ready if the baby came, she had no worries and she really felt safe and at home in her new flat.

On Sunday evening Juliet became aware that she was having mild contractions. She was settling down to watch an old episode of Morse on the TV and after an hour, she was certain she was in the early stages of labour. "Alistair," Juliet said, "I think I am in labour, so, it may be best if you stay at your Dad's tonight."

Alistair looked concerned, but they had discussed this and he knew what he was to do. "Are you sure you will be ok mom?" he said. "Don't worry about your mother, I shall be fine," said Juliet. Juliet sipped a glass of wine. The contractions were not progressing much yet and she needed some sleep. I will go to bed in a minute and try and sleep. I need to be refreshed she thought to herself.

Juliet did manage to sleep lightly, but awoke at 3am, and decided that the contractions were getting stronger, and she was leaking amniotic fluid, not a lot but she definitely was leaking. She messaged Val but received no response. She didn't really expect a response as it was 3am so she phoned the community midwife and at 3.45am there was a knock on the door. Juliet let them in, she didn't know Nicky the midwife who had turned up but she had met the student midwife as she had agreed for her to attend the birth, as she had never attended one before.

Of course, the contractions slowed, as they always do when you are a little anxious. But Juliet started chatting to the midwives and soon started to feel safe and more relaxed. She paced the room, and soon the contractions resumed. Her labour was progressing well, and she felt in complete control.

This is going to be a lovely birth thought Juliet to herself. She thought of Alex and how she would have loved him to be there with her but she quickly dismissed this thought. She had thought it through months ago and had made her decision and she knew it was the right decision to make. She was in a strong place mentally and she didn't need to be fucked up at this time. She had to do this for herself.

"You are a really strong woman," said the student midwife. This gave Juliet immense determination.

She had been to hell and back over the past year and it had made her stronger, and she wasn't going to fail at this. The contractions were getting really intense and she was using the gas and air. She was still feeling in control and she knew she must be really quite dilated. She was going in on herself, retreating into her own little world, and was oblivious to everything happening outside of her and she knew that she was transitioning.

Suddenly she wanted to drop to her knees so she fetched a pillow from the bedroom and knelt on it, with her arms and upper body resting on a dining chair, and the unmistakable urge to push washed over her. The older midwife knew what was happening "go for it," she said to Juliet "push if you want to". Juliet threw herself into each contraction with a vigour, and a strength that came from deep within her.

After fifteen minutes, Nicky said, "pant, the head is crowning," so, Juliet did as she was told and the burning sensation soon passed and the head was out. "Just one more push and the shoulders will be out," said Nicky, and with the next wave of contractions Juliet's baby was born. The midwives quickly placed the baby in a towel and passed the newborn to Juliet.

"Hello you," said Juliet softly to the beautiful little bundle in her arms. She peeled back the towel to discover it was a little girl, a beautiful, perfectly formed little girl. "Al-hamduli-llah," said Juliet to herself. And indeed, it was praise to God for giving her this gift. Juliet was overjoyed and filled with love for the tiny little babe that represented her love for Alex.

At that moment, Val walked through the door "I came as quick as I could," she said.

Nicky laughed, "you missed it," she said.

The midwives were fantastic. They ran a bath for Juliet once they had delivered the placenta and checked her and the baby over and they soon tucked Juliet up in her bed. The sun was shining outside and it was spring.

Nothing could have been more perfect, thought Juliet as she gazed lovingly at her new baby daughter.

Val had been to Waitrose and fetched them all pastries from and a sandwich for Juliets lunch.. They all tidied the lounge until it was as though nothing had happened. They said their goodbyes and Juliet was left alone with her new child. She sent her daughters a text message to say that she had given birth and both she and baby were fine. She sent a message to Alistair and then she drifted off into the most contented sleep she had known for a while.

Chapter 32 Joy

Juliet was up and about the next day. She was quite fit and well and radiated the wonderful glow of a new mother. Although she was forty-five at this moment she felt twenty-eight. She had named the baby Clara and she took her out for a walk in the pram.

As she got to the top of the road she saw Mark and Guy coming towards her. "Hello Guy, Mark," she said. "Do you want to see the baby Guy?" Guy looked excited,

"Yes," he said, and Juliet picked him up to peer into the pram."She is beautiful," he said, and Juliet was filled with love for him and Clara. She had made the right decision, Guy would love his step sister and she would be a friend for him.

"Are you ok?" said Mark.

"Yes thanks," said Juliet. Things had got slightly better between them. A lot of the wounds were still raw but at least they could now talk to each other without getting angry and Mark had accepted that she would never be with him again. That was finished for good. "Why don't you two come for tea tomorrow?" said Juliet. It was a way she could be with Guy and she knew he would have something decent to eat even if she did have to put up with Mark.

"If you are sure you are up to it?" said Mark. "Yes, I am sure," said Juliet, and they parted.

Juliet knew however that Mark had softened his attitude towards her because Alex was no longer in her life. She still had to take Mark to court to get proper access rights to Guy without Mark being present but she knew that she had to get stronger before she could face going into the court again. She had been deeply scarred by the whole court case and it was as raw and fresh as if it was yesterday. But at least for now, she was having regular contact with Guy.

It was Monday when Juliet had given birth and now it was Friday and both Juliet and Clara were doing well. The girls were coming to visit when work finished and they were going to stay for the weekend.

They arrived just after 6pm and Juliet was pleased to see them. They hugged each other and the girls rushed in to see the baby. "Oh, Mom," said Charlotte, "she is absolutely adorable.

"Katie was equally smitten with her new baby sister. "Fancy doing this all on your own," she said "I thought you were going to call us when you went into labour?"

Juliet laughed, "well I did say I would but after you two went green when you watched that birth DVD I thought it was better not to. Anyway, I managed fine by myself and the midwives were lovely."

After they had all eaten and they were sitting in the lounge sipping their wine, Katie looked at Juliet, "Have you told Alex?" she said.

Juliet froze. "Oh, Katie," she said, "I have been over this with you before, you know why I haven't told him."

"But Mom," said Charlotte "I think he has a right to know." Neither Charlotte, nor Katie would give this up, and Juliet softened, perhaps they were right. After all, today was Alex's birthday. "Ok, ok," said Juliet picking up the computer, "I will email him". So, she did.

Hello Alex

I hope you are well. I know it has been a long time, but I just thought you should know that I gave birth to a baby girl on Monday. She is your daughter. I found out I was pregnant shortly after I left you in September. I didn't want to tell you then as we had been through so much, and I thought you wouldn't have wanted me to have the baby. But I decided to go through with it, because I wanted something good to come out of all the badness. I hope you forgive me, and I entirely understand if you don't want anything to do with us. She is fit and well. Happy Birthday.

Juliet.

She pressed send. There was no way of taking back what she had just done and she left the computer open. Within half an hour, she received a reply. She didn't want to open it but she knew she had to.

Hello Juliet

It is lovely to hear from you. I have thought about you often and have missed you. I cannot quite take in what you have just told me, but I can say that it is the best Birthday present I have ever received. I hope you are well, and I feel sad that you had to go through this alone. I felt sure you had gone back to Mark.

I am working in Iraq, and am saving hard to buy a place in France, but I want to give you some money. I don't have a bank account here and have to send money to Mom via Western Union Transfer. I left her some blank cheques before I left, so if you could give me your address, I will get her to send you a cheque. Please email me. Have you given her a name? I want to hear all about her and you. Can you send me a photo?

Alex

Well, that was a better response than Juliet had expected. The girls were smug with themselves.

"You know you still love him Mom, don't deny it," they said giggling.

God, they really are irritating, thought Juliet, interfering with their mother's love life but she saw the funny side of this, and started laughing too.

"Ok, you two, pack it in," said Juliet.

"We saw the look on your face when you read his response, and there was a tear in your eye," said Katie.

"Don't be silly you two, it is just the baby blues. I would weep at anything right now." The girls knew better than to push it with Juliet and Juliet knew they were right, there had been a tear in her eye and it wasn't baby blues.

Alex and Juliet started to exchange emails on a daily basis again, they had a lot to catch up on and they made up for lost time. True to his word five days after the initial email a cheque arrived for Juliet for £500. It was a little boost for Juliet. She had been struggling on benefits and had set up home using the £3k her father had given her from the sale of her mother's car, but it had nearly all gone and she had less than £300 left from that.

Juliet grew in strength over the next few weeks. She had not put on any extra weight during this pregnancy unlike previously. Although she was not gaunt and too thin like she had been in the cottage, she was healthy and happy. Daily walking to the shops helped and the weather was really good, she adored the spring and May was the best month of the year.

It was good to have Alistair's company and he was nearly finished at school, he had a collection of friends that popped around on a daily basis and he was in and out with them all of the time, as they lived nearby. It really was in a pleasant location her little flat and she considered herself to be truly blessed.

One afternoon she was sitting on the bed breastfeeding Clara when there was a knock on the door. It is probably one of Alistair's friends thought Juliet, how bloody irritating just when I have got my tits out. She took Clara off her breast and put her into the pram and covered herself up and went to the door.

She opened the door, and received the shock of her life. There before her stood Alex, resplendent in his 6'3" blonde sexiness. "Hello," he said in that deep sexy voice of his. Juliet was so shocked, she stood there for a moment open-mouthed.

Alex smiled "Can I come in please?" he said.

All Juliet could manage to utter was "yes."

He walked through the door and threw his bags on the floor. He swept Juliet up in his big strong arms and kissed her fully on the lips in a passionate embrace. Juliet didn't resist, she didn't struggle. She surrendered herself fully to his kiss.

When they had finished he released her from his embrace and he looked at her, "I have wanted to do that for a long time," he said. Juliet looked at him, she had wanted it for a long time too. How she had missed him

"Where is Clara? Can I see her, I think I can hear her crying." Juliet led him into the bedroom and to the pram where Clara was lying, annoyed at having her feed time interrupted. She was wailing away. "I was just feeding her," said Juliet "that is why she is crying."

"Well, don't let me stop you," said Alex so Juliet picked up Clara, sat on the bed and put her to her breast. Alex looked on in admiration. "She is beautiful Juliet so beautiful, just like you. I am so sorry about all that went on."

Juliet looked at him, she had tears in her eyes and she raised her hand, and shook her head as if to say, 'it doesn't matter let's not talk about it.' But Alex was not going to be stopped.

"Juliet, I have to say it. I have to say sorry for my behaviour in the past. I know it was wrong but everything was such a mess. I am sorry I ever doubted you. I love you. I have never been more certain of that in my life and I want to put things right. Will you marry me?" he said.

But would Juliet say yes?

If you are a victim of emotional abuse there are many organisations around the world that can help, including.

www.refuge.org.uk in the UK

www.stoprelationshipabuse.org in the USA

www.womensaid.ie in Ireland

So did Juliet say 'yes' to Alex? Find out in Book Two

'Juliet'

JOANNE HOMER

The sequel to "The Woman Who Ran Away"

"Even better than book one - I could not put it down"

**Alex and Juliet Series
Book Two**

About the Author

Joanne is a woman of a 'certain age' as the French say. Slightly eccentric and often stressed, she is a self confessed Francophile and loves all things French, especially the food, wine and the men; she just can't resist that sexy accent. Joanne has a collection of berets that embarrass her youngest child, but that are so useful in the winter when she is out walking the dog.

When she is not writing, Joanne has six children and four grandchildren to keep her busy. Thankfully cooking is one of her hobbies. She also likes to 'have a go' at painting.

Why don't you join her on social media? She would love to hear from you.

If you enjoyed this book then please leave a review it would mean so much to me, or get in touch through social media.

And don't forget to subscribe to www.joannehomer.com to claim your free EBook.

Thank you for reading.

.

Other Books in By Joanne

<u>Alex and Juliet Series</u>:

'Juliet' Book Two in the series – Join Juliet as she embarks on a journey to become her own person. Full of twists and turns and adventures for the heroine. But will they be with Alex?

'Paris Revisited' Book Three in the series – Juliet's journey continues with more surprising events. The star crossed lovers visit Paris again, but will it be as memorable as their first visit years before?

<u>French Dynasty Series</u>

'Rinse and Repeat' – The prequel – A light hearted steamy romance.

'Sleepless Nights at the Chateau – Book One in the Series – It would be perfectly natural to assume that being married to a gorgeous Frenchman and living in a Chateau would guarantee your happiness but trouble comes from more than one source in this delightful story. Will they live happily ever after?

Printed in Great Britain
by Amazon